Perception

by

Katja Desjarlais

The Haunt Vault, Book 2

Perception

Cover Art by *Diana Carlile*

The Wild Rose Press, Inc.
PO Box 708
Adams Basin, NY 14410-0708
Visit us at www.thewildrosepress.com

Publishing History
First Black Rose Edition, 2020
Print ISBN 978-1-5092-3156-0
Digital ISBN 978-1-5092-3157-7

The Haunt Vault, Book 2
Published in the United States of America

With dusk on the horizon, she squatted beside Mickey, anxious to read Jagger's condition through him. The intense stillness of vampires when they rested was disconcerting, their chests not rising and falling, their eyelids motionless, their muscles void of movement. It was like staring at wax statues. Beautifully crafted wax statues with toned arms and hardened abs.

Mickey's inactivity boded well for Jagger's current status, his mind no longer siphoning Jagg's lows or highs. She moved slightly closer, watching the darkened lashes for any sign of distress.

"Hey," Mick's voice whispered into the silence.

Blue eyes snapped open, destabilizing her gracelessly until a long arm gripped her waist. She blinked slowly, locking her gaze as she scrutinized Mick for any sign of agitation.

"That's pretty unnerving," he whispered.

"No more than you not blinking," she hushed back with a smile. "How are you feeling?"

Mickey stood, flexing his shoulders while running a hand through his mop of hair. He motioned toward the hall, smiling briefly when she led him out.

"I'm good," he said quietly, his eyes darting back toward the room where his hauntmates slept. "Jagger's resting. He's muted right now. Probably a good thing."

Dedication

To my amazing children,
who will be allowed to read this when they turn 40

Chapter One

The mop of crimson hair lay motionless on the cold hardwood, its owner immobile with frustration while Mickey used his booted toe to push at a clenched fist.

"Stop that," came Louis's muffled demand as he drew his arms closer to his lithe frame and curled into a tighter ball.

Undeterred, he snaked his foot under Louis's ribs and with a swift kick, flipped him onto his back.

He stood over his friend, grinning. "Get up, you pathetic bastard. We'll try again tomorrow."

"Whatever," Louis grumbled as he accepted the proffered hand. "Did Nichol get the common room sound system tweaked?"

"That's what Dom texted. Everyone's heading there now. Lace up and let's go."

As Louis attended to his combat boots, Mick slouched against the bunk's wall and slowly pulled some of Louis's frustration into himself until his companion's emotions returned to their familiar flat affect. Louis glanced up, shaking his head.

"I don't know who benefits more from that little trick, me or you," he said as he moved toward the door. "How can you handle it, though? That link with Molly has left all sorts of crazy in my head. I swear on my grave, that woman does not sleep. She's like one of those tiny flies swarming around you that you can't

1

quite swat away. The ones that crawl up your nose and destroy your fucking soul. Dominic better take her over again. Soon."

He grinned and followed Louis into the hall.

His friend had created a mental link to Molly a few months earlier during her botched rescue attempt from a psychotic vampire named Dovidas. Although Louis managed to save her life by feeding her his blood, Molly's connected partner Dominic still struggled with the knowledge someone else had the inside scoop on her emotions.

But as much as it chafed Dominic, Louis was far more inconvenienced by the link, so Mickey did his best to help drain Molly's highs and lows from his friend's mind as much as possible. For both Louis and himself.

Sheltering himself within the monotonous expanse of Louis's emotions had become a guilty pleasure in which he greedily indulged. The sporadic spikes of frustration Louis experienced while practicing his hypnosis skills were easily funneled and discharged, providing a much needed sanctuary for Mickey.

The duo approached the common room, halting in the doorway to assess the seating arrangements. Nichol sat cross-legged in front of the bureau, auburn brows furrowed as he adjusted various settings on the amp. Two of the haunt's resident Tenders, Dahlia and Justine, were perched on one end of the large chesterfield, Jagger at their feet. Amy sat deep on the other side, motioning for him and Louis to join her.

Ever obliging of his favorite Tender, he led Louis across the room, passing Dominic, the youngest member of the haunt. He was sprawled across the love seat with Molly curled up under his arm. Dominic's connection to Molly, an intense attachment usually occurring in vampires several centuries old, had caught the whole haunt off-guard. Seeing them snuggling up and whispering together made the events of Molly's imprisonment and escape from Kaspars Dovidas four months ago feel almost surreal.

He glanced over at Audra, her body positioned toward her charge as her cat-like brown eyes appraised Molly and Dominic's interactions from the old black recliner in the corner of the room. She caught his eye briefly and acknowledged him with a nod before returning her attention to Molly, notebook and pen secured on her lap.

Amy stood, allowing him and Louis to sit before she squeezed herself between them with a bright smile. Mickey leaned into her, closing his eyes and scenting her O-negative blood as she instinctively offered her neck, her Tender training ingrained in her every movement.

"Is he going to sit there all night?" she inquired with a chin tilt toward Nichol.

"Probably," he grinned. "The slightest imbalance in the sound system and it'll ruin the whole movie for him. Is Rhys coming by tonight?"

"He said he'll be up after he finishes cataloguing the latest delivery."

The third and final shipment of bloodslaves from California had arrived the night before to replenish the Kaius haunt numbers. Boy and Rhys had spent the past week processing the humans, typing their blood and assessing them for maladies. He suspected Rhys was also sizing up the female bloodslaves for potential

Tender material.

"Speak of the devil," Louis muttered as he repositioned himself closer to Dahlia.

Rhys sauntered into the common room, his eyes scanning the area for a place to sit before he settled on planting himself in front of the old black recliner. Audra's nose wrinkled slightly as Rhys's tattooed arms stretched over the seat and draped over her crossed knees.

The dynamic between Rhys, the haunt's Tender trainer, and Audra, Molly's psychologist and a former bloodslave, provided much entertainment for him. Her role of psychological reparation for Molly placed her within Rhys's realm, yet Audra stood firmly outside the established lines of the Rhys-trained Tenders.

And Rhys had no idea how to interact with a woman who served a prominent position outside of blood or sex.

Observing the subtle arch of Audra's perfectly sculpted brows as she inched her legs out from under Rhys's heavy limbs, he noted a sly smirk gracing his older hauntmate's face. Rhys had been trying, unsuccessfully, to get under her skin for weeks, to make Audra as flustered as he was in her presence. Mick found it fascinating to watch the poised, restrained woman deflect Rhys's innuendo and overtures with little more than a cocked brow or pursed lips, a deliberate withholding of her attention or emotion.

It drove Rhys insane.

Amy settled in against his chest as Nichol fired up the movie and resumed fiddling with the sound system. With his Tender comfortable, he stretched out his senses.

Nichol was predictably frustrated, short bursts of anger tempered with strips of satisfaction.

The static contentment tinged with sorrow was Jagg, his soft baritone humming little more than white noise to the haunt's residents. Justine sat quietly behind him, her hand resting on his broad shoulder.

Dominic's hunger was broadcasting loudly, overshadowing his pleasure over Molly's proximity. Mickey carefully drew in the craving and pulled out his phone to send a reminder to Boy to get Dom fed before dawn.

Passing through the stoic Louis, he turned his attention to the myriad of emotions emanating from Rhys.

Annoyance.

Anger.

Curiosity.

And Rhys's base state, horniness.

He caught Rhys's eye and grinned as Rhys arched and stretched his long arms back, brushing Audra's thigh before folding his hands behind his head.

"She's going to put that pen through your eye," he murmured, his voice too low for human ears to pick up.

"If it gets me a few days off from reading her lists, I'll take it," Rhys responded.

Turning his attention to the sweet-scented woman beside him, he absentmindedly stroked her chestnut hair and continued to monitor his brethren.

****

As the closing credits rolled, the sound of Audra tearing a page from her notebook sent a wave of exasperation through Rhys. He held up his hand to receive the offending paper, refusing to turn and acknowledge the woman in any other way. He didn't have to look over to know Audra had filled the lines with her perfect scrawl, noting every nuance her perceptive eyes picked up between Molly and Dominic.

Between Molly and Rhys.

Between Molly and everyone she came in contact with.

Audra's notes were frequently peppered with comments regarding Molly's interactions with the Tenders and hauntmates. She had taken it upon herself to actively assist Molly in 'defining a role within the confines of her community' in order to provide Molly with 'a necessary sense of contribution and acceptance among her peers'.

"She has a role waiting for her," he had responded the first time Audra had mentioned it during what she deemed a 'case conference'. "Once you fix her, she'll fulfill the role of Dominic's connected female."

The only response was a slow blink of Audra's cat eyes coupled with a deep, centering breath.

Since that night, her meticulous notes had included numerous suggestions he could implement for Molly and, in turn, the Tenders and hauntmates within the compound.

Suggestions.

Demands.

The haunt-wide movie night had been brought up three weeks earlier.

"An activity open to all members of the community would foster an inclusive environment through a shared experience," Audra had stated. "It will also assist in shrinking the divide between humans and vampires within these walls."

He had stared blankly. "I don't wanna."

A clear, concise reply.

And once again, Audra had blinked, breathed deep, and handed him her notes from the night.

It had been his own frustrated venting on Jagger during a sparring session that had brought the movie night to fruition.

"It's fucking bullshit," he snarled, dodging Jagg's blade with ease and ensuring Jagger could see his lips at all times. "I know my fucking role. You know your fucking role. Justine knows her fucking role. We all know our place around here and it's been working just fucking fine for hundreds of years. We don't need a…watch the neck, man…a fucking group hug."

Jagger halted his assault and adjusted Rhys's grip on the new blade. "A few hours a week of forced relaxation and social interaction wouldn't be a terrible thing," he mused softly. "The pressure is high right now, and our tension is trickling down to the Tenders. They're on edge as of late, as you've surely noticed."

He examined the angle of the blade. "Sure, but that's what they're here for, right? A safe outlet?"

"But what's their safe outlet?"

Jagger resumed his attack with his soft humming reverberating off the steel walls, leaving him to deflect the knife's advances and focus his mind away from Audra and her inane request.

An inane request Jagger had communicated to Justine during pillow talk.

Which found its way to Amy.

Who put the idea in Mick's head.

Who passed it by Louis.

Who mentioned to Nichol that a tweaked sound

system in the common room would get some use.

Which left Rhys sitting on the floor, in the common room, clenching a paper in his fist as Audra carefully unfolded her long legs over his shoulder and followed Molly and Dom out.

Chapter Two

"Bedtime."

Audra smiled as her command snapped Dominic from his lust-filled haze, brokering no room for argument. Molly grinned against his lips and peeked over his shoulder at her, effectively dampening the mood.

"The warden has spoken," Molly laughed, disentangling herself from Dominic's arms.

He sagged against the hall, thumping his head against the plaster. "Heard you loud and clear, Audra," he called out, shoving his hands into his pockets while her heels clicked across the floor. As she stepped up alongside Molly, he leaned over and gave his connected female a quick kiss on the cheek. "I'll be by tomorrow after sparring," he promised as he snuck past them and made his way out of the Tender area.

Motioning toward Molly's bedroom, Audra left her charge and broke into a jog to catch up to Dominic.

She knew he simultaneously despised and adored her. She had taken on her responsibility as Molly's psychologist with fervor, interjecting herself into all aspects of Molly's life and, by association, most aspects of his.

"We've seen some more improvement in Molly's assertiveness," she stated as she caught up to him. "She mentioned last night that she feels as though she's rediscovering herself, like she's fifteen again."

"I'm currently feeling fifteen as well," Dominic muttered, skulking down the hallway in an obvious state of hunger and sexual frustration. "You walking me to my room again?"

Smirking, she stopped outside the common room and crossed her arms. "Do I need to again?"

He rolled his eyes and smiled. "I'll behave. Just going to grab a few albums from in here to listen to in my bunk."

As she turned to walk away, Rhys's voice hushed through the silent haunt. "You get sent home?"

"You hiding out here until Audra's in bed?" Dominic countered and she stayed in spot, listening in.

"Damn right I am."

Dominic's footsteps echoed on the hardwood, the squeak of leather punctuating his flop onto the sofa. "How much longer is she going to do this?" he growled. "It's been months."

"She'll ease up soon enough," Rhys muttered. "Because I'm going to drain her. I'm going to drain her dry and put her body in a freezer so I can open it every once in a while and scream at her. Scream therapy."

"Big talk for a scary vamp hiding behind a sofa in the commons," Dom laughed and Audra covered her mouth, biting the inside of her cheek. "Seriously, though, I'm dying here. I've jumped through every hoop and Audra's still chaperoning us like teenagers."

"She's scarier than Kaius," Rhys grumbled and she cocked a brow. "Female vamp kind of scary. Holy fuck, Mini. No one can ever bring her over. Ever. She would organize us all. The lists…the notes…"

"The lack of sex…" Dom lamented.

"How're you holding up with that?"

"Since my hand is the only thing doing any holding, I'd say fan-fucking-tastic."

Scrunching her nose, she resisted the urge to reveal her presence, to stop the intimate conversation she wasn't intended to overhead.

But her feet were apparently as nosy as her mind in the moment, the rare glimpse of the Kaius males giving her more insight than she gained when they knew she was nearby.

"Why don't you get one of the Tenders to come by? Might tide you over until Molly's ready," Rhys offered and her hackles rose.

"No way would I cheat. It's so weird, Rhys. The few cleanup runs I've done? Nothing. Not a single female looks even remotely attractive anymore. So it's me, my hand, and Audra's voice reminding me my abstinence is for the greater good."

Good boy.

Rhys merely snorted in response. "Good luck with that. I'm going to hunt down Justine or Dahlia. I think Amy went off with Mick tonight."

"Justine's with Jagger. Dahlia left with Louis."

"Fuck."

"Not tonight, you aren't."

She slipped her heels off and tiptoed down the hall, ducking into the wing where the vampire bunks were. As Rhys disappeared toward the Tender compound, Dominic wandered down the corridor to his bunk, his turquoise eyes narrowing when he saw her standing against the far wall, heels in hand.

"Boy just went into your room," she offered up. "We discussed your need to remain on top of your feeding schedule."

Dominic looked chastised and nodded, opening his door to reveal Boy standing there, his empty blue eyes unseeing and two bags of blood in his hand. Without hesitation, Dominic reached for the bags.

"Thanks, Boy. I'll eat in a bit."

Boy's gaze moved to Audra and she shook her head, pleased when Boy stood in the doorway and crossed his arms. Taking the hint, Dominic sliced into the first bag.

"I suppose you're both staying until I'm done?" Dom grumbled, leaning against the wall as he sloshed the first bag around. "Yeah. I figured as much."

She waited silently with Boy while Dominic downed his meal. With a quick show of the two empty blood bags, he watched Boy slip from the room and turned to her, bracing the door frame. "Satisfied?"

"For now," she smiled, striding off as his door slammed shut.

****

Mick lay silent in his bed, Amy's brown locks tickling his arm as she vented on him.

"It's not that I dislike her. Or what she's doing. But she's so, I don't know, impersonal. Cold. I thought psychologists were supposed to be friendly, but she never really smiles. Or laughs. And she's making Rhys more insufferable than Molly ever did. He's hardly around anymore, and when he is, he pretty much ignores the rest of us. And he's always going out of his way to get her mad, but she just ignores him. It's not right, Mick. Don't you agree?"

He hummed on cue.

"I know. Rhys is our boss, but she talks to him like

she's in charge. And he just lets her! Half the things he's having us do during the day now are coming from her instructions. I just know it. Like the museum. When has Rhys ever made us go? Never. Suddenly we're on these…these field trips. And this new rule about no clothes shopping online? It's just silly. There is no way Rhys came up with it. She shouldn't be coming in and changing everything."

An intense craving shot through him, disappearing as quick as it came. He sifted through the hauntmates' web before chalking it up under Dominic. "Maybe Audra's trying to bond with everyone."

Amy huffed. "She doesn't even come with us. Rhys won't let her leave the haunt. So it's Molly, Justine, Dahlia, and me driving all over hell's creation to do what? Buy a shirt and look at a painting? And she gets to stay back all day and sleep. Or read. Or whatever she does. I think Rhys needs to put his foot down. Don't you?"

He hummed on cue again, refusing to criticize the way Rhys ran his domain. The male had been dealing with Tenders for centuries longer than Mickey had been around, and he had no desire to gossip about his older brother with a Tender. Even if that Tender was Amy.

Happy under the misguided belief he was in agreement, Amy snuggled deeper into his arms.

"You're staying a bit?" he asked as his body acknowledged the rise of the sun.

"I don't want to go on the grocery store outing today. She won't come looking for me here."

He closed his eyes and stretched out his mind, touching each of his hauntmates quickly.

Frustration.

Relaxation.
Annoyance.
Hostility.
Contentment.
Sorrow.

****

Audra perched on Molly's bed, reviewing the evening's events. It had become a routine for the women, meeting at dusk to discuss how Molly would spend her night, then reconvening as dawn broke.

"He lets go immediately now," Molly shared. "If he feels me get tense, he backs off right away. That's helped a lot."

She scratched a quick comment in her notebook. The previous week, Molly had mentioned to her that sometimes she felt trapped, caged, when Dominic put his arm around her or held her hand. Simple gestures of fondness, but Molly still struggled with the memories of her captivity under Dovidas, the vampire she called Dove, and she instinctively shied away from restraint of any form.

Audra had stopped by Dominic's bunk quickly to discuss it and was secretly thrilled when Dominic responded with compassion and understanding, promising to be more aware of his physical presence around Molly.

Molly was lucky Dominic was the one with the unexplained connection to her, and not one of the other less flexible males.

Maintaining communication with Dominic had been a key element in Molly's recovery as his ability to read her cues without guidance was sorely lacking. Audra liked the dark-haired, scruffy male with the

14

sarcastic wit and mischievous eyes. His eagerness to participate in Molly's therapy had been instrumental to Molly's improvement, the mysterious connection he had to her ensuring he placed her needs above his own.

Monitoring the pair had been more entertaining than she had anticipated, as neither censored their thoughts and both were rather impetuous. Observing their capers throughout what was referred to as 'the haunt' sometimes proved exhausting, as the duo frequently went out of their way to harass anyone they felt they could get a reaction from. Being the youngest member of the haunt, Dominic was brushed off as a pesky younger sibling. By association, Molly was also granted the same latitude.

Nichol was the exception.

She learned quickly Nichol had little patience for Molly and the Tenders. Audra, however, had not yet had an issue with the growling, unpleasant male.

Thankfully.

She moved to leave Molly's quarters, hoping to corner Rhys for a quick conference before bed.

"I think maybe I'm ready to have some unsupervised time with Dom," Molly called out as the door swung shut.

She stopped in her tracks.

"I mean," Molly continued, her voice muffled, "We fit. And he's a good guy. And…I'm just ready."

With a deep, centering breath, she replied. "Provide me with a written petition, and I'll make an assessment from there."

Chapter Three

Mickey watched as Nichol ran his hands through his hair, sending it shooting in all directions. "Half. Maybe half of the American haunts have responded. Unless I go on foot, half the vamps in the country are unreachable."

Jagger frowned in concern. "What percentage have young vampires?"

"Of the unreachable ones? At least half. Maybe more."

The vampire registration and tattooing law was expected to go into effect in three days. Congressmen and Senators had unanimously supported the legislation in a bid for public support, using media to vilify the small groups of vocal detractors.

Mick's attempts to sway support through bribery had been unsuccessful, his contacts within the government moving further underground to avoid discovery. Nichol had been on a mission to notify every American vampire of the Kaius haunt position on the matter: Do. Not. Register.

More than a record of names, more than a permanent marking, vampire registration required a verified address. Verified by a specially trained human militia. Despite Kaius' absence, the hauntmates attached his name to their decree, confident the head of the haunt would support their decision.

The roadblock they hadn't initially anticipated was that almost half of the known haunts had yet to move into the electronic age. Hidden in some of the most inhospitable territories of the country, many haunts were run by senior vampires unwilling to adapt to modern human technology. A few had been reachable by land lines, but many had rejected any contemporary form of communication.

"It's too goddamn risky to send the message by mail," Mick growled. "Why the hell didn't we push for an email address for all haunts a decade ago?"

Jagger pondered the dilemma. "Perhaps those haunts are the least likely to trust the government's claim that the tattoo is solely for identification reasons. I would be more concerned about some of the young haunts. There are many haunts in the cities being led by males less than two hundred."

"True," Nichol mused. "However, it's the old bastards we want on our side should the government militarize against us en-masse. So contact is necessary."

"Assemble a list of locations. I'll begin knocking on doors," Jagg stated resolutely as he left the communications room.

Mickey pulled out his phone and fired off a message to Kaius, knowing it would go unanswered. Kaius had been absent from the haunt, unreachable since they'd taken out Dovidas' Deepfryer operation in Memphis, slowing the legalization of the vampire-baking devices even if it hadn't ended it. Setting the phone down, he turned his attention to Nichol's computer screen and began reading the comprehensive list Nic was putting together for Jagg until his ears picked up the sound of high heels in the hall.

All three vamps sat back and faced the door, awaiting Audra's appearance.

She paused in the doorway, silent, until Nichol flicked his wrist, permitting her to speak.

"I'm looking for Rhys."

"Not here."

With a curt nod, she turned on a heel and left, her black and cobalt hair swaying across her back.

"Audra is proving to be the least bothersome woman I've encountered in the haunt," Nichol muttered, brows knotting as Mick leaned over his shoulder to get a better view of the screen. "Her scent doesn't offend. Her speech wastes no time. Her attire is always professional. Unlike others who parade shamelessly through the halls in sleepwear and denim shorts."

Mickey snorted and flopped back in his chair. "I'll let Louis know you're sick of seeing his thighs in his workout gear."

Nichol glared at him. "The blue waves in her hair are odd."

As Nic returned his attention to the computer monitor, Mickey arched his head toward the corner of the room. "You can come out, coward," he snarked, ignoring Rhys's snarl as the male crept out from behind a filing cabinet and headed down the hall toward the bloodslave compound.

****

"That one."

Boy followed Rhys to the cells, opening the locks and pulling his selection from the group. The blue-eyed brunette struggled against Boy's hold to no avail as he assessed his choice.

"She'll do."

With the flailing woman flung over his shoulder, Rhys sauntered down the hall into the Tender area. Dahlia and Justine met him at the entrance, their wide eyes taking in the filthy, barely-clothed female before their teachings kicked in and they moved swiftly into the training room.

"Rhys?" Dahlia ventured. "Do you want us to prep Molly's bathroom or Audra's?"

Fuck.

"Audra's," he huffed. "Gather her things."

"Where should we put them?"

Dropping his head, he momentarily regretted his impulsive decision to select a new trainee this evening. "My bunker."

He didn't miss the shared look of surprise on his Tenders' faces before they rushed into Audra's room and began running the shower while he debated calling for Dominic as his newest acquisition howled and kicked. Dominic's ability to soothe came in handy with unwilling assets, and he was unable to effectively take temporary control of a hysterical mind without Dom's assistance.

But Dominic was on an in-house date with Molly.

Which meant Audra was also occupied.

And few knee hits to the jaw was worth the break from Audra's arched brows.

He forcibly straightened the woman's legs and set her in the warm water. Upon realizing what he was doing, she stopped fighting and turned instinctively to the heat. Brown water pooled at the woman's feet as months of dirt blasted from her skin. Dahlia passed him a bottle of body wash and a cloth before returning to the bedroom to pack Audra's things. He set the items on the shower ledge.

"Take as long as you need," he instructed. "There's a robe behind the door. Once you're ready, I'll be waiting on the sofa."

Unlacing his boots, he reclined on the couch and watched as Dahlia and Justine began removing piles of pencil skirts and camisoles from the smaller Tender bedroom. There would be backlash from his snap decision. But no backlash could compare with the flood of relief he experienced every time he closed his eyes and saw an Audra-less training room.

He could lock the door.

Lock the demon woman out.

Back and forth, Dahlia and Justine emptied all remnants of Audra from the room. As they passed him with the final load, he followed behind through the kitchen, grabbed some fruit off the counter, and returned to work, clicking the lock and relishing the weight that lifted from his shoulders.

Laying back on the sofa, he set the fruit down and monitored the heart rate of his newest acquisition. Slow, steady. Strong. The water turned off and he waited patiently, playing round after round of Solitaire on his phone. Finally, the door opened, and the short brunette appeared, her thin frame drowning in the white bath robe. Her wary blue eyes focused on the table.

"Banana?" he asked, gesturing toward the food.

The woman skirted the walls, placing as much distance between herself and Rhys as she could. Using his foot, he pushed the table across the floor toward her.

"Eat. No strings attached."

Stillness.

"One of us is eating within the next two minutes. Make your choice."

With speed that would rival a vampire, the woman snatched the fruit off the table and returned to the sanctity of the wall, her eyes never leaving him.

"What's your name, sweetheart?"

The woman swallowed her bite of banana. "Simone."

"Well, Simone, I'm going to give you two choices tonight."

****

Droplets of ice water fell from Mick's hair and rolled down his neck, dampening his shirt. Nichol and Jagger had fought him hard in the sparring room, pushing his strength and speed for hours. The frigid hosing down was almost a welcome reprieve from the tingling sensation of healing flesh wounds. Heading to the quiet of his room, he was stopped abruptly by Amy. She grabbed his hand, dragging him toward his bunker and tapping her foot impatiently as he opened the door.

"Are you okay with this?" she demanded.

He looked around in confusion. "Yes?"

"We, you, know almost nothing about her. She could kill you during the day. How are you fine with this?"

"What the hell are you going on about?" he growled, removing his wet shirt and pulling a dry one out of his closet. His patience was frayed from spending the night bombarded by Nichol and Jagg's aggression, which was further compounded by Dominic's lust and a weird echo of determination from Rhys.

"Audra? Moving in here?" Amy huffed.

He glanced around his room.

"Across. The. Hall."

Sitting on his bed, he massaged his temples. "Could you just tell me what's got you so worked up?"

Amy's hands flew to her hips. "Dahlia and Justine just finished moving Audra into Rhys's room. The rule is Tenders live in the Tender area and vampires are in the bunkers."

He could feel his eyes ovaling in hunger. Amy offered her wrist and continued to talk. "She's been here for four months. She's not even a Tender. What if she's a hunter?"

Pausing his feeding, he responded. "She's not a hunter."

"But she could be," Amy argued. "And it's against the rules."

Realizing his meal was going to be tainted with hostility, he pulled away and lay back on the bed. "What's the reason she's been moved?"

"Rhys selected a new trainee from the bloodslave cells."

That explained the determination he felt. He opened his eyes and peered up at the tall brunette before him. "Seems like the only logical solution. So what's your issue with it?"

"It's against the rules!"

He reared up, rising to his full 6'7. "The rules we set. Now lower your damn voice. I'm completely drained right now. Are you going to calm down and stay or…"

Amy crossed her arms in defiance. "If you can't see why this is a problem, I'm leaving."

"Good," he spat. "Tell Dahlia to swing by on your way out."

From the stomp of Amy's feet, he was pretty sure his command was going to be conveniently forgotten. He sat down, slumping over his knees as he stretched his tendrils out in search of Louis. The empty zone's location indicated Louis was down the hall in his own bunk. Snaps of lust and possession pierced the quiet bubble intermittently as he sought a few moments of peace.

She's had too much leeway, he thought to himself. Since Dominic had begun 'courting' Molly, Amy had become more possessive over Mick, her actions reflecting that of a girlfriend and not a trained courtesan. Pinching the bridge of his nose, he fell back on the bed and drowned himself in Louis's barren cocoon until a sharp knock yanked him out of the tranquility.

He opened the door to find Boy standing there. Confused, he poked his head out the doorway as Boy peered in.

Ah, right.

Boy was linked to every Tender who passed through the compound, a way of tracking them during transitions between the Kaius haunt and wherever they ended up. Amy's anger had likely caught the mute male's attention.

"Amy's not here," he stated. "Check the Tender compound. Or Jagg's room."

Boy nodded once and ghosted away.

Back in his bed, he located Louis again before softly draining a little sorrow from Jagger and a hint of possession from Dom. Cycling through his brothers, he eased their most intense emotions as daybreak came. One by one he felt them fall asleep, their affects muted and stable.

Except Rhys.

He didn't need to reach out to feel Rhys. He could hear him loud and clear in the hall.

"…spur of the moment decision," Rhys snarled low.

"Impetuous decisions often have negative consequences. A few hours' notice and I would have had ample time to prepare Molly for this upheaval," Audra countered, finality ringing in her voice.

"Impet…do you have any idea how old I am? I know about fucking consequences."

As Rhys's voice graveled in anger, Mickey moved toward his door, cracking it enough to lay his eyes on the pair.

"If your age is tied to your decision-making, I would expect you to be more conscientious in your choices."

His eyebrows shot up. Ready to intervene should Rhys finally snap, he adjusted his stance and began to pull Rhys's anger into himself. Audra reached the bunk door and turned to a cooling Rhys.

"There's no lock."

"Trust me, you won't need one," Rhys retorted, scanning Audra's form with disgust. "It's not like any of us want to break in and fu…what are you…are you adding that to your notes? Hand it over."

"No."

Audra stared Rhys down, pen and notebook in her hand, until she purposefully ripped the paper from the pad and proceeded to slowly crumple it, dropping it to the floor. Rhys's eyes darkened as they followed the paper to the ground.

A smirk.

Mickey watched his brother take a step forward, his large boot crushing the balled paper as he closed in on Audra, fangs elongating. He opened himself to Rhys's fury, siphoning it too quickly to safely channel as Rhys's hands hit the wall, effectively locking Audra in place.

A feral snarl echoed in the hallway.

The aggression propelling his feet forward was not his own, but he was incapable of halting his attack as he sent Rhys and himself to the ground. Fangs tore at exposed skin, fists connecting with bone. While he had the advantage of size, Rhys's age and strength quickly ended the skirmish, his long, tattooed arms pinning Mickey against the wall.

"The fuck, Mick?" Rhys snarled, his fangs crimson.

He clenched his eyes shut as the congested lines of the haunt's incessant emotional onslaught loosened and drained. "Overdosed. Let me down. I'm good. It's all good."

Rhys hesitated before releasing him.

"Are you two done?"

Audra.

He looked over Rhys's shoulder at the woman. Not a hair out of place.

"Go to bed, Audra," Rhys commanded, his eyes focused on his brother. "A lock will arrive tomorrow."

With a final scrutiny of the males, Audra disappeared through her door.

Rhys backed up. "She really pisses me off."

"No shit," he muttered, shuffling toward his bunk.

He closed his door and slumped to the floor, the

echo of Rhys's guilt pounding in his skull.

Chapter Four

Metal scraping against metal.

Mick's eyes snapped open at the unexpected sound. A shiver traveled down his spine, his body registering that the sun had not yet set. Hoisting himself up from the floor, he stretched his senses. His hauntmates were predictably at rest, projecting little more than a whisper into his mind. Cocking his head, he located the sound.

Hallway.

Grabbing his blades off the coffee table, he flung his door open.

"Morning. Did I wake you?"

He moved into the corridor, glancing toward the closed doors of his brothers' bunks. Audra sat on the floor, her stockinged legs tucked neatly under her skirt as a disassembled doorknob rocked slowly at her knees. Her cat eyes zeroed in on his daggers, a manicured brow lifting.

"Eight hours in this wing and I've already witnessed a bar brawl and a weapons display," Audra declared, setting a screwdriver on the floor and standing swiftly on her stilettos. "Acclimating to the aggression in this part of the compound will take some time."

He slid his knives into his cargo pants. "Sorry," he muttered. "Home renovations aren't common around here during daylight hours. Need any help?"

Searching the floor quickly, she dipped down to retrieve a small leaflet. "Please. The instructions are here."

Waving the paper off, he knelt in front of the door. "I got this."

Audra stood in his peripheral, her nimble fingers unfolding the tiny pamphlet as he assembled the knob in place.

"Your assistance last night was appreciated," she stated. "Unnecessary but appreciated."

"Unnecessary?" he scoffed, tightening a long screw.

"Rhys was self-regulating moments before your well-intentioned interference. I was in no danger."

"Yeah, well, you're welcome for his self-regulation, too," he grumbled as he tested the new knob.

Backwards.

Of course.

Sitting back on his haunches, he began dismantling the lock.

"Fascinating," Audra breathed, lowering herself to the floor and laying the instructions subtly on his thigh. "You were responsible for it. His ability to calm while highly agitated."

Swatting the offending paper from his leg, he ignored Audra's statement and continued to work.

"Does it work on humans? Can you manipulate their emotions as well?"

The door slid closed with ease.

"Is it a conscious effort? Do you replace feelings or dampen them?"

He slid in the lock's key, jiggling it a few times.

"Is it a mental or physiological phenomenon?"

Collecting the remnants of the old lock, he handed the leaflet and key to Audra and returned to his room to shower.

****

The clicking of her heels in the empty corridor was comforting, evoking memories of eons past when she strode among her peers toward her office. Audra slowed her gait as she approached Nichol's communication room.

"How has Jagg gone this long without his own vehicle?" Nichol muttered. "Homebound asshole probably going to fuck mine up."

"Relax," Dominic drawled, "If Rhys hasn't trashed it yet, Jagger sure as hell won't."

Nichol grunted in response before turning toward the door. "What."

She entered the room and scanned the space-age technology cramping the large room. "I would like a word. At your convenience, of course."

"You heading out tonight?" Nichol asked Dominic, ignoring her request as he slid his chair over to the printer.

"Nope. Rhys texted me last night. Said not to bother."

She stood patiently while Nichol pulled sheets of addresses from the printer and read over the list. He slid the papers in a duffle bag packed with disposable cell phones and handed it to Dominic.

"GPS is online, phones are activated. Remind Jagg that 48-hour check-ins are a must."

"Ten-four, captain," Dom replied as he squeezed past her with a nod.

Nichol looked pointedly at a chair, the closest to a welcome she would receive from the cantankerous vampire. She crossed the floor quickly, ever conscious of Nichol's obvious disdain for time-wasting.

"I would like your permission to inhabit Rhys's bunk in your hall," she stated.

With a snort, Nichol resumed typing. "You're already in it."

"Without your permission. I'm asking for it now."

"You're demanding it now," Nichol grumbled.

She leaned forward. "I'm letting you know I understand my presence is breaking protocol and I would like the breach to be addressed before it amplifies, and I end up dead."

Nichol relaxed back in his chair, swiveling back and forth. "Keep it quiet during daylight. No strong scents. Never knock on my door. And don't fucking analyze me."

"Done," she agreed as she rose and began to exit the room.

"If I said no?"

"As you said, I'm already in the room. This was a merely a courtesy call," she called, heels ticking as she marched toward the common room in hopes of circumventing Jagger before he left.

Maneuvering through the halls of the compound was significantly easier than navigating the antiquated males and their rigid, archaic social constructs. Prior to her seizure and subsequent time in the bloodslave quarters, she had been blazing a name for herself in her profession.

Her clients were high-profile, her fees astronomical, and her results unmatched. She specialized in counterfeit interpersonal relationships, her no-bullshit, logistical approach to behavior modification appealing to CEOs, tycoons, and executives.

More specifically, she catered to corporate psychopaths holding those positions.

She had spent the beginnings of a promising career working intimately with strong-willed, obstinate men with patriarchal tendencies. She had a steel spine and a deft tongue.

What she did not have was comprehensive knowledge of the social hierarchy within the vampire system. The hundreds of hours spent with Molly had revealed much about the physical manifestations of vampire-human relationships, but little about the rationale.

Week after week, she had observed the males. She watched them as they conversed in the hall, as they discussed plans and argued about music, and as they joked around with the women designated as 'Tenders'. It was an amicable, finely-tuned community.

And utterly obsolete.

The silent vampire who ran the bloodslave quarters was Boy. He was an impenetrable fortress, his empty eyes unreadable, his actions mechanical. Tall and broad-shouldered with long blond hair, he moved like a stalking lion, a slight feral hunch to his back. She had spent her first few months of captivity scrutinizing him in hopes of finding a chink in his iron facade.

It was no facade.

Through Molly, she had discovered Dominic was the least vampiric of the males. He mirrored human mannerisms with ease, blinking and breathing unnecessarily, fidgeting incessantly. However, despite spending his human life during a time of emerging gender equality, Dominic apparently saw no need to alter the caste system within the haunt. The perplexing connection he had to Molly made him more malleable to Audra's suggestions, but in his mind, those changes were for Molly and Molly alone.

The women referred to as 'Tenders' defended and embraced their roles in the haunt zealously. Under the guise of assisting in Molly's recovery, she had arranged various experiences and day trips into the city and among other humans. She had hoped to gain allies in the women by exposing them to freedom, a taste of independence on par with that the males enjoyed. The women had gone reluctantly, but she sensed it was Rhys's influence and outward support for her methods that drove them, and not her own persuasive arguments.

Arguments.

Rhys.

Had Rhys walked into her office two years prior, she would have taken him on eagerly. He was intelligent. Humorous. Charming. Suave. A perfect candidate for her style.

But Rhys wasn't a client seeking assistance to convincingly masquerade as a compassionate, benevolent boss under media scrutiny.

Rhys's relationship with Molly enthralled her. His primary role within the community was, in her opinion, to brainwash and fuck women into submission before passing them on to others. While she was repulsed at the thought, her extensive time with Molly had brought Rhys tightly into her sphere of observation. The more she watched him, the more intrigued she was with the charismatic vampire.

He knew the Tenders well, was attentive to their light-hearted chatter, and appeared interested in their activities. He was actively involved in their lives, checking in with each woman nightly and entertaining their requests quickly. He had spent her own first few weeks closely monitoring her sessions with Molly, tracking her progress, and providing assistance or information as needed. He had also worked as a liaison between her and Dominic during the crucial introductory period.

What was most curious for her regarding Molly and Rhys's dynamic was they fought frequently, his annoyance evident but without anger or hostility. Fangs were often on display, and the foulness of Molly's language rivaled that of a sailor.

Rhys fought Molly like an older, impatient brother.

But when it came to Audra, Rhys fought like a caged tiger. By her third night, she had realized that although Rhys had likely been questioned and resisted by dozens, possibly hundreds of women, he had securely retained the balance of power. He was the captor. The teacher. The leader. The decision maker.

And her expertise placed Rhys squarely in the classroom beside Molly.

Drawing from her years working alongside some of America's most aggressive corporate manipulators, she applied the same principles to her current circumstances. Everything from her style of dress to her tone of speech was intentional, a deliberate display of strength, knowledge, and authority. Rhys had appeared confused initially, taken aback by her demands and allowing her to station herself closer to the role of associate from the start.

In the early morning hours, when everyone was asleep, she would indulge in her guilty pleasure, replaying those glorious moments when Rhys would stammer out his responses before racing from her presence.

The principles that worked on Rhys were also easily applied to the miserable Nichol. She was quick to ascertain his loathing of females and obsession with flawless structure. Their limited interactions had been relatively smooth, despite the warnings Molly had bestowed about the irritable male. Ensuring her appearance was impeccably professional at all times, she spoke directly to Nichol, every word serving a purpose.

He had yet to bite her, so she figured she was doing something right.

As Jagger and Dominic entered the common room, she stood. Despite her limited exposure to the hearing-impaired vampire, she had immediately favored Jagg. He was quietly observant, his glacial eyes missing nothing. His constant humming was rarely interrupted by speech, but when he did speak, it was insightful, respectful, and perceptive. She aimed to engage the vampire more upon his return from his mission, believing him to be the least antiquated in his views. And the most likely candidate to provide Molly with a productive position within the community.

Jagger nodded in acknowledgement of her presence as Dominic approached her.

"Moll and I are going to be listening to albums in my bunk later," Dominic said. "If you need her, you can find her there."

"In here, you mean," she corrected, unwilling to approve of Molly and Dominic squirreling up behind a closed door.

With an eye roll, he conceded. "Yeah, we'll be listening to albums in here."

Jagger's lips turned up briefly.

With a nod, she addressed Jagg, ensuring she spoke clearly. "Safe travels. I'd like to speak with you upon your return."

His head cocked slightly before he tilted it in assent and she clicked out of the room, determined to find Mickey.

Chapter Five

Mickey didn't often spend time in the bloodslave quarters with Boy, preferring to keep his distance from both the indecipherable vampire and the stench of filth emanating from the cells. However, desperate times called for desperate measures, and he welcomed the odor of rot over another interaction with Audra.

His empathic skill had manifested itself almost instantaneously when Kaius first brought him into the haunt. The initial bombardment had been crippling, leaving him little more than a screaming, snarling mess on the floor. Surges of rage, lust, and irritation had pulsated relentlessly though his skull, fusing with his newly-augmented senses.

Luckily, Kaius had recognized the incident for what it was and had not put him down as one would an id-driven Deviant, a turning gone wrong. With Boy's assistance, Kaius had evacuated him to a remote location in the Germanic forests, spending much of the subsequent years acclimating him to his brothers and guiding his control over his ability.

He didn't like to talk about it.

Over the next two centuries, he had experienced a multitude of what he now described as overdoses, moments when his own emotions were enveloped by another's, driving his thoughts and actions. Vampires, he learned quickly, were a violent, hostile species despite their restrained exteriors.

Tempers flared unexpectedly, ire rose without warning, and he spent his nights in a constant state of preparedness to accept and dilute the onslaught. Last night's episode had been an unfortunate combination of physical exertion, mental exhaustion, Rhys's excessive rage, and Amy.

Amy.

He moved a crate of bagged blood into a freezer, double tapping the door to ensure it was closed tight.

Amy had been a Tender in the compound for three years. Rhys rarely kept compound Tenders for longer than two before transitioning them into other haunts, yet he had kept Amy.

Mick had long surmised he was the reason.

During his low periods, Amy was the Tender he turned to. She understood silence. Comprehended his need for companionable isolation.

And the blood and sex were damn good.

Following Boy down the blood-letting aisle, he collected the filled bags as Boy disconnected the humans and returned them to their cells with food and vitamins.

It was difficult for him to reconcile the impeccably dressed, immaculately manicured Audra with the grimy, powerless humans cowering in their cells. Shaking it off, he continued the mindless bag collection, resolving to distance himself from Amy to halt the attachment she was developing.

It would never be reciprocated.

The Tender, while exceptional at her job, was just that. On Rhys's whim, she would be sold, and another would take her place. His affinity for Amy didn't extend past friendship.

A friendship with benefits.

A cool roommate.

Crossing the line from Tender to lover was a reportable offense for Amy. Rhys ran a tight ship, the women residing within the compound adhering to strict guidelines outlining their interactions with the haunt's males. An unspoken preference for one vampire or another held little concern, but Rhys was draconian in his insistence that all Tenders be available to serve up their veins to all males at all times. The last Tender to latch on to one of the brothers in an attempt at exclusivity had been quickly reassigned overseas.

Nichol had been grateful for Rhys's swift negotiations.

He packed the last of the blood into the freezer and waved at Boy as he left the bloodslave compound. Dawn was fast approaching, and he was anxious to hide out in his bunk for the day. With his ears attuned to the potential sound of stilettos, he moved silently through the halls, relaxing only when his bunker door was shut behind him.

"Where've you been all night?"

His eyes narrowed. "Around. Why are you here?"

Amy crossed her legs, her bathrobe riding up high on her thighs. "None of the others were with you last night or tonight. I figured you'd be hungry."

Dropping his head momentarily, he moved toward the sofa. "Yeah. I guess."

As he descended on the offered jugular, he tuned out his brethren, a muted echo of guilt, and the soft click of a key.

****

Kaius drove quietly through the night, his eyes scanning the darkness for his exit. Without the luxury of Nichol's advanced GPS systems in his SUV, he was left to his infallible memory and a crumpled gas station map. A smile formed briefly on his thin lips as he probed Dominic. His volatile young vampire was blissful and expectant, hunger reigned tightly. Locating his eldest, he assessed Nichol. Hostile. Determined. Satisfied.

Exiting onto the secondary highway, he tapped Rhys and pulled back. Lust. Pure, animalistic need. An improvement from the incessant frustration and spikes of fury from the previous few months, culminating in a rather accentuated jolt a week earlier.

He ran a hand through his hair, mentally preparing himself for a new Tender in the compound, another female to side-step in the halls, and he prodded for Jagger.

Distant.

He frowned. Jagger was a good thirteen hundred miles away from the haunt. East coast. Placid. Melancholy. Resting.

One hour to go.

He reached for Mick.

Damn it.

He accelerated, pushing his old SUV to its limits.

****

Mick's brow furrowed in concentration, his blue eyes narrow and focused on the empty wall. Plaintive mewling. Pleas for more. Praises to a deity he didn't acknowledge. He sank back on his haunches and pulled Amy's spine flush with his chest. As her head turned toward him, he brought a hand to her lips, grateful when she took the hint and began nibbling gently on his finger. Satisfied with the silence, he lowered his head and nuzzled her neck before piercing the soft skin.

An incoherent moan.

Shifting his hips slightly and fixating on the task at hand, he increased his rhythm and zeroed in on the sound of wet skin.

So close.

Amy's hand reached back, weaving through his long blond hair as she'd done hundreds of times before. He unlatched from her ideal O-negative jugular with a snarl.

"What's...your...problem?" Amy panted, dropping her arms to the bed and arching forward.

His tempo sped up, his determination to find release greater than his annoyance with his partner's constant vocalizations. As he rose up on his knees, the flawlessly trained Tender lifted her hips with him, whimpering as her walls gripped him.

Tight.

Wet.

He lost himself in the sensation as Amy cried out, drawing his own forceful orgasm out with a howl. Lowering the brunette to the bed, he untangled himself from her and stormed to the shower.

Eight nights.

He hadn't left his bunker in eight long, sex-filled nights. For the first four, he'd alternated between Justine and Dahlia, ignoring their unsatisfying blood types in favor of their aesthetically pleasing bodies. By night five, he'd acquiesced and texted Rhys.

Send Amy.

She'll be up in 5. All good?

Fine. Thanks.

Amy had arrived at his door quickly, her chestnut hair brushing over her sheer negligee. He had reclined on his sofa as the long-legged beauty undressed for him, a practiced sway to her slim hips, a perfected pout on her lips. She'd traced her graceful neck with her fingers, a reminder of the sweetness of her blood.

Enticing.

The heat of the shower water sliced across his back. He leaned back and scrubbed his hair, careful to keep the water out of his ears as he listened for the telltale sound of Amy exiting his bunk. With the final click of the doorknob, he rinsed the shampoo out and wrapped a towel around his hips.

Adhering to his recent routine, he slowly pulled the sheets off his bed, balling them in the comforter and tossing them into the corner. He ran his hand through his damp hair as he scented the air.

Sex.

He lay back on his naked bed, assessing his brethren and monitoring the sounds of the hallway until dawn broke and the day's monotonous hum took over. Gathering the sheets and blanket, he cracked the door to his bunker and shoved them into the corridor.

Chapter Six

Rhys's booted feet thumped languidly through the hall toward the communication room. He had been reluctant to leave the Tender training room, his newest recruit an absolute gem of a find. He was back in his zone and it felt incredible.

Simone was everything Molly and Audra were not. Her scathing blue eyes absorbed every lesson in decorum. Her mind ran numbers faster than any of Nichol's computers. Her nimble fingers danced, albeit rustily, across the piano keys. She rarely fucking spoke. And she'd come on to him hard and strong within days of training.

Bless the human professional escort business.

The glaring differences between his past year and his past week made him almost giddy. Cloistered in the training room, he'd had little contact with Molly as she raced from her bedroom every night at dusk with no more than a wave over her shoulder. Audra had been noticeably absent in the days following her unannounced arrival during his tabletop speed sex session.

The infinitesimal rise of both sculpted brows when she had opened the door had been glorious.

His hauntmates had maintained contact via text, keeping him abreast of Jagger's travels and summarizing important intel.

And requesting Tenders.

Mickey's first request had come in nine nights earlier, naming Justine as his choice for the evening. He hadn't been surprised, given Amy's foul mood the previous night. Justine had returned to her room at dawn, her legs shaky and blonde hair a tangled mess.

Dahlia had returned at dawn the next night in much the same condition.

By night three, he had fired off a text to Dominic.

Seen Mick?

Hiding out in his bunk again.

Texting off a quick warning of Mick's condition to Nichol, he had returned his attention to the stunning Tender that would soon replace Amy.

When Mickey sank into a low, his MO had long been to hide in his room, cycling savagely through the compound's Tenders in a desperate search for something to feel right.

It never worked.

He rounded the corner into the communication room and paused in his tracks. "You're fucking kidding me."

Kaius grinned at him from across the room, his fangs on full display. "You're doing well," he chuckled. "Very well."

He pulled up a chair and straddled it. "I have 5'5" of leggy perfection awaiting me after this meeting, how could I not be? When did you arrive?"

"Shortly before dawn last night," Kai replied. "Nichol has spent the day filling me in on everything I've missed. Dom will be joining us shortly. He and his connected were stealing a moment in the common room."

"Audra won't like that," he grumbled, plunking his long legs onto the table.

"Audra? New Tender?"

Tossing his head back, he groaned. "Long story short, no, I'm sorry, and you'll meet her soon enough, I'm sure. If you hear a click, click, click coming, my advice is to run and hide."

Kaius glanced at Nichol. "That bad?"

Nichol shrugged. "I've met worse around here."

Rhys bared his fangs at Nichol, who promptly ignored the gesture as Boy silently entered the room, followed by a smirking Dominic.

"Kai!" Dom exclaimed. "When did your old ass get here?"

Kaius cocked a brow. "Few hours ago. You are well."

"Hell yes."

Rhys scented the air and slammed his hand against the seat of his chair. "You lucky little bastard. How did you get past the warden?"

Kaius eyed the males with confusion as Dominic sat. "We submitted a written petition. It was approved."

"Tell me you're kidding."

Dominic snickered. "Nope."

With a quick head shake, Kai muttered under his breath. "I have to meet this warden." He assessed the room. "Louis will be arriving in a moment. He's gone to collect Mick since his phone appears to be off. Once they arrive, we'll get started.

****

Mickey lay back on his bed, his arm thrown over his eyes. "Yeah, yeah. I'll be there in five," he called out to Louis through the door. Five, ten. Probably closer to ten. He stood reluctantly and pulled a pair of boxers over his hips, debating if he should track down Amy to wait for him. Whatever the guys had to discuss couldn't take too long.

He could be back here plowing the ideal Tender in under an hour.

Decision made, he tossed on a black shirt and his cargo pants, securing his blades and lacing his boots as he tried to block the strange echo of guilt and wrongness that had been plaguing him for a week. His hand reached for the door, hesitating momentarily when it gripped the knob. Females voices were rising in the hall.

"Some of us have more responsibility in the evenings than others. Ever consider that we don't want to spend our days fulfilling your escapist fantasies because you can't?"

Amy.

"I just want to remind you that there's a bigger world out there. One where our accomplishments aren't tied to the spreading of our legs."

Audra.

"Have you even bothered to look at what we do around here?" His eyebrows shot up as the usually soft-spoken Tender yelled. "While you walk around here judging us, we're doing the laundry. Scrubbing the floors. Feeding the guys. Running their errands. Keeping them company. Providing an outlet for them when they need to unwind. Making their beds…"

"They can make their own damn beds!" Audra retorted, her ire evident. He glanced over at his naked mattress. "You're prisoners here! How does this not infuriate you?"

"Because this is better than the lives some of us were living. Here, we have value. We have an important role. We're safe. We're clean. We have a roof over our heads and a full fridge. Not everyone has the luxury of a degree, Audra," Amy snarled.

"I worked my ass off for my education," Audra growled back. "Now I'm being held prisoner among glorified call girls whose thighs pop open when the big, bad vampire calls."

At the sound of a hand making contact with skin, he launched into the hall. Audra and Amy both froze, a red handprint forming on Audra's cheek. "Get in here," he barked at Amy. When her feet remained anchored to the floor, he bridged the distance between them and linked his arm in hers, leading her toward his bunker with Audra hot on his heels.

"Let her go," Audra demanded.

"Assault is grounds for immediate sale," he stated, forcing his voice to soften as he caught sight of the realization on Amy's face. "Don't move," he instructed the Tender before he strode out of his room.

He didn't need to be dealing with this shit.

Audra stormed up beside him, her heels echoing in the corridor as they approached the communication room. "This doesn't have to go through Rhys."

"Yes, it does."

"I was more at fault than Amy. I pushed her reaction."

"You're good at that."

Audra's hand latched onto his forearm. "If you do this, Rhys will send her away. Amy's good for you. She cares for you. Don't use my actions as an excuse to run from that."

He halted and growled low in his throat. "Amy is one of hundreds. Just like Dahlia. Just like Justine. Just like the new screamer in the training room. The sooner you accept their positions around here, the easier life will be on everyone. Now let me the fuck go."

Yanking his arm from her grip, he turned into the com room and came eye to eye with Kaius. Kai arched a brow and poked his head out the doorway before returning to his seat.

"Glad you could join us, Mick," he began. "We're all," he stated pointedly, "going to ignore whatever just occurred until later."

He moved toward an empty chair, seething while the others muttered their acknowledgment of Kaius's decree, side-eying him in curiosity.

"We'll do a quick round table then move on to the matter of Jagger and our response plan for the registration act. Agreed?" Kai asked, bringing the focus off Mick and onto the tasks at hand.

"Jagger has checked in as of an hour ago," Nichol began. "He's currently holed up outside Franklin, West Virginia. There is an old haunt in that area he wants to check in to before moving north toward Albany. He expects to complete the East coast within the week."

Dominic leaned forward. "Any luck? What are the haunts saying?"

"So far, they are in agreement. No registration, preparing to hide out or leave as necessary. Kaius, your name has provided a smooth ride on this mission."

Kai bowed his head in acknowledgement.

Rhys flexed his arms and placed them behind his head. "All good on the Tender front. My new one will be in circulation sooner than expected, and I should fetch a high price for Amy. Offers have been coming in en-masse since we've slowed on the rescue mission front. We basically have a bidding war on our hands for anything I churn out."

Mick ground his teeth and stared at the floor, his jaw flexing.

With one eye on him, Kai turned to Boy. "Nichol says Rhys negotiated a large replenishment of the pool. I trust everything is going well down there?"

Boy nodded, his gaze never leaving the door.

"Dominic, you and Louis have taken over Jagger's place in the sparring room, correct?" Kai inquired.

"Unfortunately," Dom grumbled. "I didn't know his job involved so much oil and sharpening. We need one of those electric blade sharpeners."

Nichol's fingers swiped over his keyboard, pulling a variety of machines up on the screen. "I can have one here in four days."

Louis grinned, silently observing the haunt meeting.

With a look of exasperation, Kai waved off the order. "Tonight's assignment is lists. Lists of supplies we have, supplies we need, and bolt holes. I want them on Nichol's desk at dusk tomorrow. Rhys, Mick. Stay behind."

The other males grunted, exiting the room with their assignment.

Kai rose and closed the door as Rhys spun his chair around and hunched over his knees. "What did she do now?"

With a hand instinctively running through his hair, Mick flopped back in his seat. "Cat fight."

"You're fucking with me. Audra?" Rhys frowned.

"How'd she do it? Amy, I mean. How'd she get to Audra?"

Kaius perched on the table, listening intently.

"I dunno," he mumbled. "They were arguing about Audra's little field trip things. Amy got pissed and yelled at Audra for being smart or something, then Audra got pissed and called the Tenders call girls. Amy slapped Audra, and I ended it there. Amy's in my bunk waiting for instruction."

Kai frowned. "That's sweet Amy, right? The nice brunette you favor?"

He groaned, his head beginning to fill with the emotions of his hauntmates. "I'm weak for O-negatives. You know that."

Rhys stood, walking toward the door. "I'll deal with this. Mick give me twenty before you head back to your bunk. I'll send Louis over in a bit."

The door slammed tight, Kaius staring intently at him. "Louis helps you."

"Yeah. He's a lot less intense than our line is."

"Amy will be sold. You are fine with this."

He pursed his lips, his head pounding. "She's attaching herself to me. Getting squirrelly. And I just don't fucking care," he growled. "How is that, Kai? Amy's the perfect Tender. She tastes incredible. She's intelligent. Gentle. Beautiful. Spectacular in the sack. She lives for this life. Some vamp is going to buy her, link with her, and keep her for centuries. And I don't fucking care."

Kaius was motionless, minutes ticking by slowly in the silent room.

"There are thousands upon thousands of women with O-negative blood," Kai finally mused. "Millions who are intelligent and gentle. Hundreds of thousands are beautiful. And wonderful lovers. Perhaps you know this, and don't instinctively feel you must grasp on to the one who happens to be revolving in your immediate sphere."

He snorted. "You kind of make sense, Wise One."

Kai rose and ushered him toward the door. "I'll accompany you to your bunk. I understand this Audra is in the vampire wing, and a proper introduction is required."

Chapter Seven

Audra lay back on her bed, arm thrown over her eyes. She had spoken out of frustration, a momentarily lapse of judgement, and another woman was going to be punished for it. Her stomach churned in disgust. Changing the behaviors and mindsets of people desiring change was difficult, but it was damn near impossible if they didn't desire it themselves.

And Amy didn't desire change.

She desired Mick.

Kicking her high heels off the edge of the mattress, she forced herself to her feet and padded to the shower. As the warm water cascaded down her back, she groaned in frustration. She had been willfully ignoring the signs Amy and the other Tenders were broadcasting. They didn't want to be 'saved'. They didn't crave 'equality enlightenment'. They were completely content living among vampires as professional courtesans.

Content.

Brainwashed.

She took a deep breath, turning the water off and wrapping herself in a towel.

Their future was set. Hers, on the other hand, was ambiguous. On her table sat a paper, a barely legible petition that essentially terminated her usefulness, and it was only a matter of time before Rhys or one of the others decided her contribution to the haunt was null.

And the bloodslave quarters she'd come from were mere steps away.

The arrival of the new vampire, the tall blond with the sobering blue eyes, made her uneasy. Mickey obviously knew the male, if the subtle flicker of gratefulness in Mick's harrowed eyes meant anything.

She wasn't sure she wanted to meet anyone who the frightening, intense Mick felt gratitude toward.

Determined to hide out in her room for the rest of the night, she walked into the closet and perused the clothing Rhys had abandoned in his haste to move her into the vampire wing.

****

"I should knock, yes?" Kai asked Mickey. "Peculiar thing, a female in this hall," he mused quietly.

"There's a lock now, so yeah. Knock," Mick replied, his back against the wall.

Kaius's hand rose before halting. "She's not the haunt's carpenter," he muttered as he examined the newly replaced doorknob. "Perhaps you should have assisted with this."

He glared at his handiwork, each tiny scratch and chip on the door a reminder of Audra's hand extending the instructions.

Fucking knob.

With a swift pound, Kaius made his presence known. A few moments later the door clicked open, and Audra peered out of the opening, her foot holding the door only slightly ajar. With her face makeup-free, the upturn of Audra's cat eyes was more pronounced, accenting the heart shape of her face.

He narrowed his eyes. "Open up."

The lift of a brow.

But she obeyed.

Stepping back, Audra allowed him and Kai to walk unencumbered into Rhys's old bunk. It was as bare and impersonal as it always had been. While he dropped unceremoniously onto the sofa, Kaius extended a large hand toward Audra.

"Good evening," he began slowly, as if simultaneously assessing the woman and choosing his words. "My name is Kaius. Kai, for short. I'm the head of this haunt. You are?"

Mick's eyes locked on Audra. She was skittish, her weight shifting from one foot to another as her hand reached and dropped from her damp onyx and turquoise hair. Fitted pencil skirts had been replaced by gray sweatpants he vaguely recognized. A faded black singlet, far too large for her frame, hung haphazardly on a body always encased by fitted blouses.

"Um, Audra. Audra, sir."

Straightening in his seat, he watched the unflappable woman stammer in the presence of Kai. She had been caught unawares, her armor hanging neatly in the closet and her heels lying haphazardly on the floor.

Audra was shorter than he thought.

And slowly backing her way toward the corner table.

"What's your position here?" Kaius inquired, his voice conversational. "Unfortunately, I haven't been kept abreast of any new haunt members in recent months."

Glancing briefly at Mick, she zeroed in on Kaius and her back stiffened slightly. "I've been working with

Molly, Dominic's connected female. I'm a registered psychologist."

Kai nodded. "You've done good work, then. My youngest is quite pleased right now."

He scoffed, hushing himself with a stern glance from Kaius.

"How are you finding life in my haunt?" Kai continued, returning his attention to Audra. "Is there anything we can do to make you more comfortable?"

While her fingers stroked a paper on the table, Audra's shoulders turned slightly.

Mistrust.

"I'm fine, thank you."

Kaius's unblinking blue eyes scanned the bunker. "This room looks like Rhys's."

"It is Rhys's."

With slow, advancing steps, Kai closed in on Audra. "But it's no longer his. It's yours. What do you require to make it so?"

He bit back a laugh as Audra rose up slightly onto her toes as though attempting to close the height gap between herself and the 6'4" vampire. She remained silent, her calculating eyes narrowing in thought.

"I would like to participate in the group meetings."

Kaius took a quick step back. "Perhaps we could paint the walls a more feminine color."

He leaned forward with interest, wondering how subtly he could pull out his phone to record this.

"I feel it would have a positive impact on the haunt's cohesion if all residing members were involved in some of the decision-making," Audra ventured, her voice gaining back its strength as Kaius cocked his head in confusion. "Dahlia, Justine, Molly, Amy…they possess untapped skills that are being wasted based on their assigned roles. As leader, you could facilitate their involvement in the plans to move against Dovidas."

He rose to his feet guardedly as Kaius stood motionless.

"You are aware of Dovidas," Kai stated with forced calm. "How."

There was no question in his voice.

Audra's fingers subconsciously stroked the paper on the table. "Molly. And Dominic. And Rhys. Being a part of Dovidas's demise would bring closure to Molly and as her psychologist, I fully support her involvement in whatever twisted death you plan for that sick fuck."

Kai turned on his heel, striding from the room. "I'll have Nichol set you up with computer access and an expense account to update your decor and your wardrobe."

Pursing her lips, Audra watched the door close and crossed her arms. "Well," she murmured, "he didn't kill me."

He pushed his hands through his long hair and exhaled a long, unneeded breath as he followed his sire out the door.

****

Rhys's large thumb moved deftly over his phone as Amy leaned dejectedly against the Tender kitchen counter. The availability of an experienced O-negative brunette had started a bidding war among his clientele, a war he was happy to facilitate.

"We're down to four," he muttered to Amy as another text message popped up on the screen.

"What's the price sitting at?" Amy inquired, her curiosity piqued despite her aching heart.

He glanced up, his navy eyes sparkling as his lips curled up. "Just over three."

Amy straightened, craning her neck to see the incoming texts as the group message exploded with bids.

"I'm putting it to a silent final bid," he stated. "This nickel and dime-ing could go on for hours."

Nodding in agreement, Amy resumed her position as he fired off a text to the four remaining bidders, set down his phone, and stared at his commodity. "Care to explain while we wait?"

"Not really."

He moved forward, his hand cupping the chin of what was priming to be his second-highest sale. She truly was a perfect specimen, he mused as Amy's head tilted instinctively. "Any male that wins you, despite the hit to his pocketbook, will be getting the deal of the century. The remaining bidders are all strong matches for you. They are kind masters. Fair. Lonely. Mickey was never meant for you, nor you for him." He paused, observing her soft eyes welling. While he held no love for the women he worked with, he was proud of them, of their accomplishments and transformations. "Erase the mopey bastard from your memory."

Amy nodded again, her tears threatening to spill as his phone chimed with the final bids. "So," she opened as her shoulders squared. "Who won?"

Chapter Eight

Mick emerged from the sanctity of his bunk, his mind refreshed, and mood lifted after three nights of solitude. Thanks to Kaius's siphoning of the hauntmates' thrumming emotions, he was feeling temporarily renewed, ready to filter the onslaught once Kai pulled back. Flicking his phone back on, he strode down the corridor toward the communication room. Louis met him along the way, falling into step.

"All good?" Louis inquired casually as their boots echoed in the hall.

"Fuckin' A," he replied. "Anything I should know heading in there?"

Louis hesitated.

"Aside from Amy being sold off. I already know," he assured his friend.

"Thank god," Louis mumbled. "You cool with it?"

"Yeah," he stated with certainty. "Rhys texted me a couple days ago. I'll swing by the Tender area later to say goodbye before she flies out. She'll do well in another haunt. She's, like, absolutely perfect at her job."

Louis hummed in agreement as they entered Nichol's work room. Mickey swung a chair up beside Kaius. "You can lift the blanket, dad."

As Kai slowly plugged his own drain, he could feel his hauntmates coming online in full force in his head.

Despite the initial intensity, he welcomed the streams as they waxed and waned.

Kaius was muted, calm and serene. A quiet ripple until he went silent.

Rhys was sated.

Louis's bubble of monotony remained steady.

Dom was horny. Very horny. And happy.

Nichol's drumming frustration spiked intermittently with concern and uncertainty.

Adjusting his position, Mick focused his attention on Nichol. The meticulous male was alternating between assessing his various monitors and scanning his phone. He repeated the ritual in sequence until his nostrils flared slightly and he called out into the hallway. "Be done in thirty."

He arched his neck to see around the door frame.

Audra.

He watched her pause before turning and retreating, throwing a questioning look at Nichol.

"I'm getting her set up online after tonight's debriefing," Nichol muttered as he returned his attention to the devices and Kaius brought the meeting to order.

"Jagger's been out of contact for two nights," Kai announced. "Nichol is monitoring the situation, but as of fifty-two hours ago, there's been no response on his end."

"Last location?" Louis asked.

"West Virginia," Nichol grumbled. "After he made contact with the DeChamplain haunt."

Rhys's eyes blackened as Mick sprang into action, siphoning Rhys's anger. "Why weren't we informed last night?"

Nichol's hazel eyes flicked to his phone again. "The 48-hour check-in period expired only four hours ago. DeChamplain has confirmed Jagg left their haunt the night he arrived. They're keeping an ear to the ground regarding his whereabouts."

"DeChamplain is an ally?" Dominic inquired.

"Reclusive but powerful," Kai responded. "He and I sided in Europe over the centuries. He wouldn't harm one of my blood."

Rhys stood, tossing a quick nod of gratitude toward Mickey. "I'll load the SUV and start off toward West Virginia tonight."

"You'll stay until we hear word of Jagger's whereabouts," Kaius stated, his voice brokering little argument. "I sense nothing unnerving from him at this point in time. There've been no spikes to speak of."

Rhys's blackened eyes narrowed. "So we sit on our asses," he spat in frustration over his absentee brother.

"We prepare to move," Kai said calmly. "Nichol and I will monitor the online chatter and man the phones. You'll pack Dominic's car for an extended mission. Louis can prepare my own for movement. Mick, you assist Louis. Dom will run weapons up. Boy, prep a mobile stockpile for two weeks plus enough for three injured."

Boy exited the room as silently as he had entered, his presence barely registering to the others. The clomping of Rhys's boots followed, their heavy falls echoing the helpless anger radiating off Jagger's closest brother. Mick moved to follow Louis as Nichol called after him.

"If you pass Audra, tell her I'm free now."

His advance stuttered as a split-second burst of

longing blasted him.

****

Audra re-adjusted her bun, meticulously placing equally spaced bobby pins around the base. While anxious to meet up with Nichol and begin her virtual foray back into the real world, her hesitation to be within the sphere of the haunt leader kept her far from the communication room until Nichol summoned her.

So she stood, and she waited.

Rhys's boots announced his presence long before she saw him.

"Evening, Rhys," she greeted as she took in his snarling demeanor.

The male grunted as he passed her before stopping. "Why aren't you with the others?"

"It's a Tender affair."

Rhys cocked his head. "And you're not a Tender."

"Correct."

She watched Rhys, anticipating his acknowledgement of her lack of a defined role within the haunt now that the most intense of Molly's recovery was complete. With a quick frown, Rhys turned and continued his march down the corridor.

Smoothing her pencil skirt down, she began her trek back toward the communication room. Louis passed her with a quick salute, and she smiled at the red-haired vampire, saluting back. Despite her limited interaction with the quiet male, she quite enjoyed his quirky mannerisms and watchful silence.

Rounding the corner, she came face to chest with Mick. The blue-eyed vampire had been noticeably absent for a few nights, his door sealed tight since the evening he had brought the haunt leader, Kaius, to her room. And since then, the only visitor she had had was Nichol.

With her laundry collected into a manageable pile, she slipped on her heels to begin her search for the compound's washing machine. A pounding, abrasive knock on her door startled her, testing her precarious balance as she slipped on a second shoe. With the bundle of clothing under her arm, she opened the door to a frowning Nichol. He stood motionless, his eyes jumping from her face to her neatly bundled laundry.

"What can I do for you, Nichol?" she ventured, unsure how to read the male's silence.

Nichol furrowed his brow and arched his neck slightly to take in what he could of her bunk.

"Rhys's scent is all over this place."

"Expected, as it's technically his."

Stepping back further into the hall, Nichol wrinkled his nose slightly, his freckles dancing as he did so. "Kaius would like you to have monitored computer access."

She followed Nichol into the corridor, shutting the door quickly behind her. Rhys's scent in the room, while unnoticeable to her, was apparently affecting Nichol and she was anxious to eliminate anything that could bother the twitchy vampire. "He mentioned I should paint the room and order some clothing. Are you able to set me up?"

Eying the laundry bundle with distaste, Nichol nodded. "I'll have a system ordered in and will assist with the paint order. You may select the color, but the brand will be my choice as paint odor can be extremely invasive."

"Appreciated," she thanked him. "Could you direct

me to the laundry facilities?"

Nichol pursed his lips. She could see the movement of his tongue running across his fangs. "I don't do laundry. It's not your place to do it, either."

She laughed low. "Well, I need it done and am more than capable."

A flash of anger passed through hazel eyes. "You aren't a Tender. Laundry is below your station."

"Self-care isn't."

"You carry Rhys's clothing as well."

She glanced down. "I wear those during the day. I don't have any lounge wear of my own."

Seemingly appeased, Nichol strode past her and toward his own bunk. "That will be remedied in two nights' time."

"Nichol's waiting on you," Mick muttered as he maneuvered his way around her.

"Are you heading to the Tender area to say goodbye to Amy?" she asked quickly as the tall male inched by her.

Mick glared at her and continued on his way.

Entering the communication room, her confidence was thrown upon laying eyes on Kaius. His return to the haunt was unnerving, the age and power emitted from his every calculated movement and word a testament to how lethal vampires could be. His unblinking blue eyes and statuesque stillness was intensified by his unreadable expression. Next to Kaius, the others appeared significantly more human, their small quirks and tics amplified next to stone immobility.

"Welcome, Audra," Kai spoke slowly. "I hope I won't be intruding. A situation has arisen that requires continual monitoring. I will, however, remain out of your way while you and Nichol work."

She pulled a chair up beside Nichol.

Somewhat closer than she would have had Kaius been absent.

Nichol glared at the offending proximity momentarily before scooting his own seat away a fraction. He ran his fingers across a laptop, the screen springing to life. "You may choose any color carried by this brand. The odor is less offensive than that of others, and it's less likely to create uneven patterns throughout the room, regardless of skill."

She began perusing her choices. "This must be the company Molly used for her room in the Tender compound," she mused aloud. "I didn't smell a thing when she redid her walls."

"Of course you didn't," Nichol groused. "We, on the other hand, detected the stench for weeks."

"Really?" she queried in awe. "Your senses are truly that much more developed?"

With a pointed look, Nichol sat back and crossed his arms. "You used an ammonium hydroxide-based cleaner within the past five days. You switched toothpaste brands last week. Your mascara is three months old and should be thrown out. And your hair dye is just under six weeks old."

She felt her jaw fall open, impressed and amazed.

"He is, as Mickey would say, full of it," Kaius interjected quietly. "The cleaner is the only thing outside your nightly hygiene products that he can scent. The rest he likely pulled from memory as Nichol places most of the haunt's online deliveries."

Nichol licked the tip of his fang, a glint of silver

shimmering in the light of the computer screen.

"It's still impressive," she chuckled as she pointed out her selection. "This one, please."

Nichol cocked a brow. "White."

"Chantilly."

"The room is already white."

"And now it will be Chantilly White."

A few quick clicks, and Nichol placed the order. "Anything you select for purchase online will be fed through the haunt's system and will be placed in queue for approval and designation to the appropriate account. A confirmation email will be automatically generated once I approve th…"

"You have to approve my choices?"

"Security is paramount."

"What would be flagged?"

Nichol began unplugging the laptop and wrapping it carefully. "The usual. Weapons, chemicals, electronics…"

"Anything he finds personally offensive," Kaius muttered softly.

She grinned. She was warming to the haunt leader. "Namely?"

Nichol growled. "Country music and cheap perfumes will not be tolerated." He placed the computer roughly into her hands. "Any websites visited will be monitored. Closely."

Nodding her agreement, her heels clicked rhythmically down the hall toward the loneliness of her room.

Chapter Nine

With Dominic's flashy sports car prepared, Rhys made his way into the Tender compound to check in on Amy's farewell party. The excited chatter of the women reverberated through the halls as the Tenders reminisced and light-heartedly teased each other. He stilled, assessing his newest trainee's interactions.

"So what's the difference between being a Tender and what you do?" Simone's Boston accent apparently became more pronounced under the influence of alcohol.

"You'll be fucking them all, I'm fucking one. For, like, ever," Molly's husky voice laughed. "I mean, I could technically be with other guys, but I love him to pieces and none of them would ever touch me out of respect for Dom, and Dom's now hardwired to only want me. So there's no chance of him cheating. Or hurting me…"

His brows furrowed as Molly trailed off. Despite how far she had come with Audra's assistance, those once flitting, carefree eyes had remained hardened and cagey.

"So are the rest of you tied to one vamp or is it just a free-for-all?" Simone inquired.

Amy's soft laugh reached him. "The males develop preferences. We're here for them, not the other way around."

"Well," Simone breathed, "If the others are anywhere near as hot and as skilled as Rhys, I'm prepared to do my part for the vampire minority."

He grinned as his Tenders erupted in giggles and started comparing notes on their training sessions, with Molly periodically interjecting with howls of eeeewwwww and nasty. Having heard enough, he swaggered into the Tender living room.

"Evening, ladies," he called, enjoying the cheerful camaraderie of his women as they bit their cheeks to halt their giggles. "I trust your evening is going well?"

Simone's scathing blue eyes shot toward him, her lower lip catching in her teeth.

"Did you see Audra?" Molly asked him, her words slightly slurred from her indulgence.

"I did," he stated, his gaze focusing on Amy as all humor left her face. "Perhaps you should invite her to join your little soiree."

Molly beamed and rushed from the room, completely oblivious to Amy's souring expression. Dahlia and Justine averted their eyes, well-deserved embarrassment glimmering as he turned his attention to Simone.

"As you can see," he began, "our haunt Tenders are a very close group. I've always prided myself on selecting strong, compassionate women to remain among my brethren." He locked eyes with Amy.

"Unlike your human social standing, your position within the haunt is elevated on the basis of your words and your conduct, not your birthright, education, or financial situation. Your human past is irrelevant. Throughout your existence as a Tender, you'll dine as an equal among whores and doctors, druggies and architects.

"You'll falter, and your fellow Tenders will hold you up. You'll err, and they will correct. What they won't do is ostracize you, treat you as lesser, or judge you unfairly. Largely because I have taught them better and I do not fail."

Simone nodded her acknowledgement of the lesson and he caught sight of Amy's jaw tensing at his words, her gaze on the floor.

"Except Molly," Dahlia piped up. "You failed hardcore with Molly."

He closed his eyes in exasperation. "Except Molly. Thank you for reminding me, Dahlia."

The women fiddled with their drinks while the group awaited the telltale sound of Audra's heels on the hardwood floor. Molly burst into the room first, her heavy footsteps mocking him as Audra appeared in the doorway, her feline eyes surveying the room before she walked quickly to Simone.

"You must be Simone," she smiled. "I'm Audra Verdi."

****

Mick cocked a brow at the overtly hostile stance of his brother.

Tattooed arms crossed.

Leaning against the door frame.

Navy eyes narrowed and blackened.

Fangs peeking out from tight lips.

Rhys was pissed, and he didn't need to tune into his brother's line to figure that out.

"Problems in the hen house?" he asked, taking up a similar position to his hauntmate.

Rhys grunted in response.

He turned his attention to the living area where the women were chattering a mile a minute, their peals of breathless laughter punctuated by howls and gasps for air. Amy's chestnut hair covered her beautiful face as she pitched forward in a fit of giggles. She truly was a stunning woman.

"And then," Molly sputtered, her voice hoarse, "then Audra gets that blank look, yeah you did, and tells Rhys 'It's pronounced meeeeeeem, not mem.' And he stomps out of the room in a full-on snit!"

He allowed his fangs to dig deep into his lower lip and focused on the discomfort of the wound.

"It's been going on for over an hour," Rhys growled.

Not trusting his voice, he stared at the ceiling.

"With so much animosity, you should sleep with him. I bet it would be so hot," an unrecognized, heavily-accented voice snickered.

Rhys shuddered.

Mick stilled.

"I cou…" Audra started, abashed.

"She would never do that," Amy's voice chimed in, sticky in its artificial sweetness. "Our Audra is too cerebral for such tasks. It would be unprofessional, fucking your coworker. No matter how good he would be or how much you sorely need it."

His brows rose at the attitude presented in Amy's usually placating intonation.

"Am not," Audra countered, her words less enunciated than her traditionally impeccable cadence. "It would be unprofessional. And gross because Rhys is…Rhys, right, Molly?"

Rhys's head thumped back against the frame.

"Perhaps you should invite Audra, I said."

"You wouldn't sleep with any of them? At all?" the unknown voice queried. "Why would you deny yourself?"

"Maybe she has a good vibrator," Justine tossed out.

"God no!" Audra gasped. "With Nichol checking everything I ord...no. Just no. Could I please have another glass? Maybe more whiskey than coke this time."

The women dissolved again, Amy's prodding sliding by as they compared embarrassing purchases passed through Nichol. He and Rhys leaned forward imperceptibly. As the discussion turned to sex toys, he adjusted his stance, uncomfortable with listening in but too enthralled to step away.

"I should go," Audra muttered suddenly. "I am far too drunk for this."

An uneven clicking of heels.

"When you tire of your shower head," Dahlia teased after Audra, "I highly recommend taking one of the boys for a ride!"

Audra laughed, her voice nearing the threshold where he and Rhys stood.

"She's just waiting until I leave to jump into Mick's bed," Amy offered with false cheer.

"So well," Rhys murmured. "It was going so well."

Audra froze in place. Then, with the squaring of her shoulders, she called out behind her. "I guess that leaves you with fifteen minutes to get on a plane."

Chapter Ten

Mick's feet moved him away from the doorway before his mind could process the action. As Audra's flushed cheeks came into view, he hunched further, willing his 6'7" frame to disappear into the shadows. Light brown cat eyes caught him instantaneously.

"I have a propo…a favor to ask."

Mick shook his head warily and flattened himself against the wall.

Audra glanced over at Rhys, who stood smirking at Mickey's panic. She sized him up for a minute before shaking her head violently and returning her attention to him.

"Please walk me to my room."

A polite demand.

A deeply ingrained sense of propriety compelled him to comply, to escort the woman safely to her quarters.

The coward in him almost bolted from the hall.

He ran his fingers through his hair and turned toward the exit of the Tender compound, motioning for Audra to follow him and refusing to look back. Breaching the outlet, he pointed to a corner.

"Wait here."

Audra sank into the corner, busying herself with the clasps of her shoes.

He slunk past her and back toward the Tender

living room as Rhys remained in the doorframe, studying him as he went by.

"Amy."

Amy rose quickly from her chair, her chocolate eyes snapping to his. The other women turned their bodies from them, providing the illusion of privacy.

"You came to say goodbye?" she asked, a quiver in her voice.

He nodded.

"I'll miss you," Amy whispered softly, reaching up to stroke his long hair. He remained motionless, allowing the Tender to brush his locks from his face, her gentle fingers tracing his cheekbones, the line of his nose, the curve of his chin. As they skimmed his fangs, his head snapped back.

"Goodbye, Amy. And, uh, thank you."

Amy's eyes darkened, narrowing into slits. "You're in that much of a hurry to get to her?" Amy hissed. "I knew it. I knew you'd defend her over me. Enjoy your subpar lay, Mikhail. You will never have a Tender as good as me again."

He turned on his heel and stormed away from the angry Tender for the last time.

Ambivalence.

He felt nothing more than ambivalence toward Amy and her crafted perfection. He was eager to return Audra to her room and then crash on his own bed to forget the entire evening had even occurred. Pausing to assist Audra to her feet, he continued his trek back to the bunkers, albeit at a significantly slower pace than usual with the tipsy psychologist marching unsteadily on bare feet. Rounding the corridor toward the sleeping quarters, he charged headfirst into Nichol.

The snarky male assessed the duo. "She reeks of liquor."

"We just left Amy's farewell party," he grumbled without a twinge of regret over how the farewell had gone.

Nichol's hazel eyes narrowed as his nose twitched. "She's impaired."

"She," Audra slurred, "is right here."

Ignoring the woman's words, Nichol stared him down. "Where's she going?"

"Her room," he answered.

"His room," Audra corrected.

Nichol's fangs elongated slightly. Audra's eyes widened before emitting a loud guffaw. "Sex toys," the drunk woman snorted as her shoulders heaved with laughter. "You approve vibrators but not country CDs."

A stunned look crossed Nichol's face before he snarled, snatching Audra's arm from Mickey.

"S'funny," Audra mumbled as Nichol threw her limp body over his shoulder and stormed down the hall.

"Key!" Nichol barked, setting Audra on her feet. Mickey lunged forward, stabilizing her as she wobbled.

"Not locked," Audra muttered, swaying slightly in spite of his support.

Nichol flung the door open, grabbed Audra's hand, and pulled her inside. The cocktail of emotions rolling off Nichol propelled Mick into Audra's room and onto the sofa where he could monitor the situation.

"Make her sober," Nichol commanded him as Audra moved gracelessly toward her bed.

He rolled his eyes. "Audra. Be sober."

Audra's wavering steps halted, and she dropped to her knees in front of the dresser. As her hands lazily searched through the drawers, she nattered away cheerfully. "M'not drunk. I've just got a rosy glow right now. I'll just…get this on…and we can work on that proposition."

Nichol growled low in his chest, his limited interactions with humans over the centuries leaving him confused and ill-prepared for dealing with an inebriated female. He stood in the doorway to block Audra's exit from the room, his body crouched slightly as if preparing for battle.

"She's not going to run, Nic," he said quietly. "She can't even stand up without help."

Nichol's fangs lay tight against his lip. "What's this proposition she speaks of?"

"Nothing."

Audra chuckled to herself as she rose to her feet and sat on her bed. "Nothing, nothing nothing!" she sing-songed. "You take a turn! He takes a turn! Everyone takes a turn! Means absolutely NOTHING! Fucking misanthropic chauvinistism. Chauvinistism. Is that a thing?"

"It's not a word!" Nichol barked. "Stop this."

Mick leaned back on the couch and focused on pulling some of Nichol's aggression into himself. The male radiated a combustible combination of annoyance, confusion, anger, and desire.

"Maybe you should take off," he suggested softly. "I'll deal with it from here."

The hazel of Nichol's eyes was barely visible past the blackened irises. "I am sure you would. I am fine right here. You, however, may retire for the day."

The insinuation behind Nichol's words was not lost on him, and his ire was already on the cusp. "What exactly are you implying, brother?" he snarled, rising to his feet in challenge.

Nichol remained rooted to his position, the hint of silver in his fangs shining in the lamp light. "She's not in a sound mind to work on any of your propositions, brother," he spat.

He could feel his own eyes blackening in rage as he stalked toward his elder, stronger hauntmate. "I'm not talking about any fucking propositions tonight," he hissed, his vision narrowing on his prey.

"Awwwwww c'mon! Why not?" Audra mewled, her voice void of any of its standard authority.

He halted his advance on Nichol at the plaintive sound. A look of surprise crossed Nichol's face momentarily before it hardened into an unreadable mask, his emotions frozen and eyes averted toward the ceiling. Mick turned slowly.

Holy fuck.

Audra and impeccable were a cohesive unit.

Professional.

Meticulous.

Clothed.

As his brain registered the situation, he became acutely aware he was staring slack-jawed at the nearly-nude woman. Relegating his eyes to the same spot on the ceiling Nichol was examining, he violently shoved the image of a panty-clad Audra to the recesses of his mind.

"Mickey?" she murmured, her bare feet shuffling toward the frozen males. "Will you?"

"No...I...god, no," he sputtered as Nichol barked, "No, he won't!" behind him.

In his peripheral, he could see Audra's hands raise

to her hips.

The jutting forward of her lace-encased breasts was ignored.

"M'not drunk," she snarled. "Just tipsy."

Shaking his head quickly, he began counting flaws in the plaster.

"Nichol?" Audra ventured.

A grunt of refusal was her only reply. Out the corner of his eye, he could see Nichol's muscles twitch as they tightened. The mosaic of emotions coming from the ancient male swirled and pulsed but remained controlled.

"Well what am I good for here, then?" Audra cried out, turning unsteadily to her bed. The males stayed motionless as she continued her tirade and hastily pulled Rhys's singlet over her head. "I'm good at what I do. No. Not good. Amazing. Phenomenal. Men, powerful men pounding at my door for my skills and now I'm here where my snatch has more use than my brain."

"You're the one reducing your value to your body," he ventured quietly, lowering his gaze to meet hers.

Audra's cat eyes transformed from hazy to a sniper precision as she slithered within inches of him. "I know where women stand around here," she seethed. "I've just come from a party celebrating what happens when they're no longer deemed useful. Sold to the highest bidder? Like cattle? Prize pigs? I survived the two years in the bloodslave quarters, and I intend to survive here much longer. I'll make any deal necessary to save myself from Rhys's auction block, or to keep me from being returned to the bloodslave cells. Any. Deal.

Necessary."

As she spoke, Audra's left hand planted itself squarely on his chest while her right fluttered across Nichol's shoulder and trailed down his forearm. Nichol's statuesque frame vibrated with warring feelings of hunger and disgust too amplified for Mick to safely drain in his own heightened state.

He stretched his mind instinctively for Louis. Kai. Any refuge from the onslaught of lust, desire, and carnality leeching from Rhys, Dom, and Nichol. Logically, he knew his rampant thirst was driven from the unassociated cravings of his brethren. Logically, he knew Audra was not only drunk but also acting out of desperation. Logically, he knew he would regret any advance he made tonight.

Logic, however, was not reaching his dick.

And Audra's calculating eyes caught it.

This was very bad.

Very fucking bad.

"My body and blood on tap in exchange for a contract stating I won't be sold as a Tender," she purred, pressing her soft stomach against the straining fabric of his pants. "Yours to use or not use as you see fit. Exclusively. Contractually bound solely to you. No connection. No emotion. No attachment. Just the knowledge no other will enter my bed. Impersonal utter devotion. I'll do errands, cleaning, any task you require. The offer," Audra turned her attention to Nichol, her fingers skimming his belt, "is open to either of you."

Panting.

Nichol was panting.

No.

He was.

Nichol was snarling.

"Hand. Off," Nic ground out. As Audra ghosted daringly across the hardened bulge in his cargos, Nichol's control snapped.

Disgust, as always, had won.

In the eight seconds it took for everything to unfold, human senses would have picked up little more than a flurry of movement, a door, and a scream.

But he wasn't human.

One.

Audra was tossed to the floor, her head padded only by the vice grip Nichol maintained as he pounced.

Two.

A hint of silver flashed before fangs pierced the taut flesh of Audra's throat.

Three.

A scream of fear swathed in pain.

Four.

Mickey launched onto the broad back of his eldest brother.

Five.

The crackling of a door being shorn from its hinges.

Six.

He hit the dresser, shattering the wood and surrounding his body with thousands of minuscule stakes.

Seven.

Nichol's fangs tore across Audra's throat as he was flung from her body.

Eight.

Kai dropped to his knees, hollering out for Boy.

Chapter Eleven

Kaius kept his back to his hauntmates, secure in their recognition of his unbridled rage. The woman's carotid artery pumped her blood out in waves upon the dark wood floor, puddling at his knees. With the immediate appearance of Boy at his side, he relinquished control of the woman's life to the mute male and stood to his full height as Boy hunched over her.

"Explain."

Silence.

He turned his cold blue gaze across the scene, cataloguing every nuance.

Clothing haphazardly strewn across the orderly room.

Two males pulsing with hunger and aggression.

The permeating odor of alcohol.

A half-naked woman unconscious on the floor, the staunch of blood stemmed by Boy's quick response.

"The woman insulted my honor," Nichol finally snarled, drawing his attention to his eldest.

As Nichol drew to his feet, Kai's shoulders shook, and he emitted a mirthless laugh. "Your honor. The honor which found me pulling my second-in-command off an undressed, drunk human female. That's the honor that found insult?"

"She offered herself to me as a whore," Nichol

hissed in defense. "Presuming to touch me like a common tramp."

He appraised the woman as Boy's blood trickled over her lips and down her throat. "Your intentions?"

"Fear," Nichol growled. "Nothing more."

Tuning in to his eldest's tumultuous center, he motioned toward the shattered doorway. "You're dismissed."

An uneven heartbeat steadied in the quiet of the room and he turned his attention to Mick. "He's over five times your age."

Mickey remained hunched on the floor and Kaius opened his mind to his hauntmates, easing the ocean in Mick's head to allow him time to siphon the overwhelming emotions.

"You've attacked two of your brothers in defense of this woman," Kaius said quietly.

Boy lifted the limp body onto the bed unceremoniously before slipping from the room.

"Yet you have no signs of connection."

Mickey's tired eyes finally flashed to him, his face tinged with relief and streaked with disappointment. "Care to elaborate on what the fuck is wrong with me, then?" he muttered, carefully standing to avoid the multitudes of wood shards.

He watched as his empathic son made his way toward the bunk's bathroom. The splash of rushing water against porcelain echoed before Mick returned, a damp towel in his hand. "I don't know why I'm doing this," Mickey groused as he gingerly cleaned the blood from the woman's cheeks.

"What's the purpose in that?" he probed. "Her hair and clothing will remain caked until she awakens."

Mick's hand stopped its ministrations for a moment before resuming with calculated tenderness. "It's not a compulsion. I don't need to clean her off. I just...I don't want her to see her face like this."

"Nichol's scent covers her."

Mickey smirked humorlessly. "Yeah, well, usually it's Rhys's. She wears his clothes a lot during the day."

"She reeks of Boy's blood," he put forth, testing his second-youngest.

"And of you," Mick grimaced. "Audra carries more scents on her than any Tender we ever employed."

Satisfied with the cleanliness of her face, Mickey tossed the soiled towel into the hall and reclined on the sofa, one arm propping his head. The males sat in silence for over an hour, dawn coming and going with little more than a tremor through Mick's long limbs as Kai stood stoically, his mind occupied by the possibilities of Jagg's unknown whereabouts.

"Kaius?" Mick interrupted the quietude. "Was Nichol...I could feel how much he wanted...what were his intentions?"

"As he stated," he replied calmly. "His physical reaction to the touch of an attractive woman was no different than you or I would have. I regret that my interference caused more damage to the woman than Nichol would have caused had he been left to his own devices. Had I stood aside, he would likely have released his fangs on his own, yelled a lot, and left. He acted out of annoyance."

"Yeah, sure," Mickey scoffed. "It's annoying as all hell when a hot woman grabs your junk."

He chuckled. "Nichol has very strict internal guidelines. He'd only recently resigned himself to placing the woman into a slot outside the Tender box. For him, her wanton behavior tonight unbalanced his mental standards."

"She wasn't wanton," Mick frowned. "Audra was negotiating."

He cocked a brow. "Negotiating."

Mickey ran a hand through his hair, his tell that he was grappling with the situation at hand. "She offered her body and blood in exchange for not being sold."

"So a Tender."

"No," Mick mulled. "More like an arranged marriage of convenience. Audra offered exclusivity bound in writing."

He reflected on the information. "For what purpose? My understanding is she has a role within the haunt. One that ensures her security."

"Guess she doesn't know that."

****

Audra's eyes flickered open, her mind hesitantly examining her surroundings before recollection set in and her hands flew to her neck.

Soft.

Undamaged.

She ran her fingers down her body, feeling the stiffened fabric of the otherwise worn black singlet.

"If you could refrain from groping yourself right now, I'd appreciate it."

Rhys.

She guardedly swung her legs over the edge of the bed, recoiling upon seeing her bare thighs exposed. The track pants she had inadvertently inherited from Rhys landed in her lap.

"Thanks," she mumbled, pulling the sweats on

while trying to maintain a modicum of dignity. "What are you doing in here?"

Rhys stretched his tattooed arms across the back of the sofa and arched his brows. "You tell me. Look around."

She scanned the destroyed room, her memories of the previous night alternating between a fog and crystal clarity.

Nichol.

Mickey.

Her offer.

Their refusal.

Fangs.

Kaius.

"Oh my god," she gasped as images of the evening bombarded her head. "What have I done?"

"Meh," Rhys shrugged. "Had a few drinks, had a few laughs, tried to sell yourself to the highest bidder, manhandled the wrong vampire. You know, typical Tuesday things."

She dropped her head into her forearms.

"I assure you," Rhys said quietly, "the fault in last night rests entirely on my shoulders."

With the silencing of her hand, she bolted into the bathroom and away from Rhys's piercing stare.

She had screwed up epically.

With the exception of an obligatory glass of wine with clients, Audra and alcohol had not collided since her earliest years of college. The combination of dulled awareness and heightened libido had lost its appeal quickly, her disciplined mind recognizing the dangers such unrestraint could pose in her chosen profession.

Testing the shower water, she turned up the heat

and stepped under the burning stream. Pink rivers poured down her body, the crunch of bloodied hair softening and loosening under the punishing water. Wash, rinse, wash, rinse. She repeated the motions over and over until the steam of the shower overtook her vision completely.

She wrapped her black and turquoise hair with a towel, reaching blindly for the second one she kept for her body.

Gone.

Pulling the damp towel from her head, she began rubbing the water droplets from her skin. As her hand brushed against her stomach, her mind flashed to stone muscle under cool skin. Shaking the offending hand, she grew rougher with her drying ritual.

"You pain receptors may be altered from the excessive heat," Rhys called out unhelpfully. "I can hear your skin being damaged as I speak."

She exited the bathroom and glared at Rhys. "A moment of privacy, please."

He turned his back and averted his eyes. "Your door will be replaced later this evening. As will the dresser. We cleaned up what we could without disturbing you, but I'm afraid the area requires a good vacuuming."

Collecting her fresh clothing, she returned to the bathroom to dress. With her uniform in place, she got to work setting her hair into a sleek ponytail and applying her makeup. Her armor. With a quick nod of approval for herself, she exited the bathroom, the feeling of control solidifying as she walked toward the hallway and directly into Rhys's bare chest.

"Where do you think you're going?"

"I have amends to make," she retorted coolly.

"You may amend all you like. After we talk."

While most conversations she had with Rhys encouraged argument, his current tone held a contrition that brokered a temporary peace deal. The clicking of her heels soothed her as she sat primly on the sofa. Rhys joined her, his long legs spreading casually across the cushions while she cocked a brow expectantly.

"Ah. There you are," Rhys murmured before strengthening his voice. "I knew two months into your initial work with Molly that your skills would be beneficial to the haunt on a more permanent basis."

Oh.

"However, in my effort to avoid dealing with your shit on a constant basis, I may have failed to communicate that to you."

She felt her eyes narrow. "A failure to communicate."

"I really, truly despise you," Rhys responded cheerfully. "But you're good at what you do, and your abilities are of use now and in the future." He paused, as if collecting his thoughts. "I apologize if my inaction caused you to feel your position here was in jeopardy and you would end up back where I found you."

With a deep, stabilizing breath, she snapped at the contrite male. "You apologize? Rhys, I manhandled Nichol's…I manhandled him. And Mickey. I rubbed myself on him like a cat in heat, and you apologize?"

"So whiskey doesn't agree with you. It doesn't agree with a lot of humans."

She pinched the bridge of her nose. "Rhys. I made a demeaning offer to two males I respect based on a drunken, apparently unfounded, fear of death or sale. I treated them like bargaining chips."

"Technically you treated your body and blood as bargaining chips. You treated them like junkies."

She sank back into the couch, defeated. "So I still have my place, but I'm back to square one. Lower than square one. Lovely."

Rhys placed his hands behind his head, his repentance long forgotten. "Nichol will be harder to break. You did make a play for his dick, and all." She groaned in shame. "But he did almost kill you, so you can work that angle."

She shot him a glare and crossed her arms.

"Mickey will be easier. Just stay the fuck away from him and let him come to you. Don't be all..." He gestured at her. "Don't be all Audra on him. Keep your psychoanalysis bullshit to yourself. He has his issues, and everyone else's issues, to contend with all night, every night. He doesn't need your guilt infusion as well."

She nodded her understanding. "I should go check Molly and Dom," she muttered. "The loss of Amy as a roommate may affect her negatively."

Rhys stood and extended his hand. She eyed it for a moment before gripping it tightly and rising, her knees firmly together under her slim skirt. "You're a bitch," Rhys smiled fangily, "but I'm glad you survived the night."

She rolled her eyes and set off down the hall.

****

Glancing at the clock, Audra stifled a chuckle. Molly and Dominic rarely made it through a full session anymore before she became less of a psychologist and more of a voyeur. The couple canoodled on the sofa in the common room, their nonsensical conversation consisting primarily of movie quotes and song lyrics before hands began to wander.

She stood, excusing herself to deaf ears, and strode briskly toward the communication room. The halls were strangely lifeless, empty of the echo of baritone voices or heavy footfalls. Approaching the com room, she braced herself to face Nichol.

"Fuck off."

Well then.

"I'm coming in, Nichol. Like it or not," she called out, her strong voice belying the nervousness of her stomach.

Nichol stood tall across the room, his arms reaching upwards as he untangled a series of cables. With determination, she planted her spiked heels before him.

"Fuck. Off."

"I apologize."

"Fuck. Off."

She drew a deep breath. "I take full responsibility for my actions last night. You didn't deserve the assault and reacted accordingly. Please accept my apology and recognize that it will never occur again."

Nichol stepped back, moving further from her encroaching proximity. "It will never happen again, because alcohol has been removed from the approved purchase list."

She brushed her fingers over her mouth to contain a grin. "That's one way to make me more of a pariah," she stated.

Hazel eyes finally dropped to meet hers as Nichol ground his teeth quietly. "Your blood is not unappealing."

"Lovely. Help yourself," she said, lifting her wrist.

Nichol flashed his fangs menacingly. "I'm full."

She shook her head and walked from the room. "I'll be placing an order for approval later. No whiskey, of course."

Grunting in response, Nichol's voice carried down the hall. "I had no intention of killing you. Don't make me regret my restraint."

With a tentative peace reached with the most obstinate of the males, she made her way toward the bloodslave quarters in search of the guy who had saved her life. Boy, her captor for two years, walked swiftly through the cramped interior. His ash-blond hair hung long in his empty eyes as he moved his large body lithely throughout the space. While Boy's presence had always instilled a healthy fear in her, his actions didn't. He was methodical, precise in his intentions. He touched the humans under his watch only as much as required to withdraw their blood and he restrained even the most aggressive bloodslaves with an eerie serenity.

Boy was fascinating.

She stood halfway down the stairs and waited for Boy to acknowledge her with his eyes before she spoke.

"Thank you."

He stalked into her personal space, his long arms reaching toward her face. She held her ground, encouraging his assessment of her well-being as he lightly tapped her neck and scented the air. Apparently satisfied with his findings, he turned and disappeared further down the bloodslave quarters without a sound.

She slowly descended the final steps into the compound, the clean click of her heels at odds with the muffled whimpers and heavy clanking of the cell bars. Boy's blond head was visible at the back of the massive maze of large steel cages housing the humans, along the wall that held the blood-letting chairs.

Moving down the closest aisle, her aisle, she kept her eyes forward and followed Boy. Curiosity overcame many of the captive humans, and they eased closer to the cell doors to get a better glimpse of the woman walking freely through the quarters. She spared a glance at her old cell, noting there were four extra bodies in the tiny holding area and she instinctively assessed the size and muscle mass of the newcomers, mentally ranking their threat levels.

Had she not been pulled out by Rhys, those four extra humans would be her competition for food and water.

Boy was well aware of her presence as she approached the row of metal chairs. Three humans were strapped in, their arms connected to syringes and long tubes as their blood was carefully siphoned and bagged. She ran her manicured fingers along the straps of an empty seat, her inner arms itching as they remembered the pinching sensation that preceded every pint that was taken. Two of the humans in the seats kept their attention on the cement floor, their acknowledgement of her little more than a quick flicker of their gazes.

The third, however, met her eyes, staring at her with a lethal combination of hatred and defiance.

"Traitor," the man whispered as Boy carefully eased the syringe from his arm. The male was young, likely in his early twenties. His body had the gauntness of a bloodslave survivor, but his eyes held the fire of an alpha.

She took a step back.

The man smirked. "Sold yourself for a shower and a meal," he hissed before he spat at her feet. "Traitor."

Boy's long arm shot up from his kneeling position on the floor. The man's head was slammed against the back of the chair and Boy's blue eyes locked onto her in warning.

She wasn't one of them anymore.

****

At the exit to the bloodslave quarters, Audra took a moment to compose herself. Her nerves were shot, memories of her time in the compound flashing through her thoughts too rapidly to process. With a few centering breaths, she pushed the images back into the recesses of her mind and straightened her shoulders.

Survival was tantamount.

She resumed her trek through the haunt, walking quickly through the vampire wing when she was accosted by an extremely agitated Rhys.

"Follow me," he commanded, his boots thumping purposely toward the communication room.

The staccato of her heels kept pace with the decisive rhythm Rhys had established. The pair entered the communication room, greeted by a sea of tension.

"How accurate is the intel?" Rhys demanded.

"Impeccable," Kaius replied tersely. "DeChamplain's eldest witnessed the marking."

She maneuvered herself into the corner where Boy stood motionless. How he'd arrived before her was a mystery.

Damn vampires and their unnatural speed.

The male assessed her slowly and returned his attention to Kaius.

"That's fucking bullshit," Mick snarled. "How did he end up getting caught?"

Nichol joined the table. "The west coast has been amping their militia at a significant rate, given the ports of entry and high number of recognized haunts within the area. Small town, unknown face in the darkness, increased anti-vamp weaponry…"

"He's a fucking ghost when he moves," Rhys spat.

"Unless he is distracted or unfed," Kai qualified quickly. "Regardless of the why, we know where Jagger's being held. A rescue mission will be established tonight."

"What needs establishing?" Rhys snarled. "We go in, we drain the fuckers, we leave."

"In a pre-vamp world, sure," Audra interjected, stepping away from the wall. "But now? You go in fangs a-blazing, the media and congress will obliterate every one of you. You want Deepfryers in every county? Because that's how you get Deepfryers in every county. Picture it, Rhys. Those slick glass UV light enclosures on the steps of each courthouse in the US. Public executions. Vampires being burned alive for entertainment." Visuals she'd seen online years ago when she was free flashed through her mind, videos of vampires overseas alit in the shower-like death traps used as final punishments for the vampire sin of existing. "Dominic. Text Molly and have her and the Tenders meet us in here."

Dom pulled his phone out, quick to follow her suggestion.

"Put that away," Nichol barked. "We aren't taking orders from her."

She walked around the table, squaring off with

Nichol. "You need fresh ideas. You need people who have lived among the human population within the past decade. You need to hear reactions to the prejudices that have consumed pop culture. And if you're planning a cross-country trip, you need people who can run errands and, I don't know, walk into the sunlight in an emergency. Dominic. Call the others in."

She waited, staring down the misogynistic male and keenly aware of Kaius's presence as his unblinking blues measured her methodically.

She took a breath. "Rhys?"

"I'll brief them in the hall," he muttered.

Chapter Twelve

Waking in prison was frustrating enough without the permeating stench of excessive cheap cologne assaulting Jagg's enhanced faculties. The synthetic odor clung to his clothing and hair and coated his tongue. With his senses of smell and taste compromised, he was left to rely on touch and his flawless sight to navigate his limited surroundings. His ice eyes opened, alerting the guards to his awoken state.

Guards.

Boys playing dress up.

He kept his head low, allowing the cheap light bulbs to cast the shadow of his hood over his eyes so he could read the lips of his captors.

"Dracula's risen," the shorter one called out, snickering at his own joke.

The boys positioned themselves on either side of the cell and turned their faces from his sightline.

It would be so easy, reaching out. Tearing their heads from their bodies. Maybe removing a limb or two for effect.

So easy.

He closed his eyes again, effectively shutting off all contact with his environment save his sense of touch. The cot's linens were coarse and sturdy, stiff from lack of use yet already pilling across the midline. The dense foam mattress was uneven and unforgiving, mechanically shaped to lie square within the cot's frame without attention to even the smallest modicum of comfort.

The pillow was no better.

Though he could take his rest in any place from a cement floor to a shallow dirt hole, Nichol had outfitted the haunt bunks with bedding of the highest quality, and he had easily acclimated to the small luxury upon his return to his brethren decades earlier.

His current bed lacked contour and a warm body.

The vibrations of his cell bars alerted him to his inquisitors' arrival. The young guards fumbled for their keys as the pair of investigators assumed a position against the far wall. He sat up and pierced the detectives with his glare.

"He talk yet?" the pale man inquired of the guards.

"No, sir."

He flashed fang quickly in acknowledgement. In his four nights of captivity, he had yet to utter a word, and his lack of verbal response had led to a hastened judicial order authorizing his branding in a misguided attempt to ensure cooperation.

A manila envelope waved through the cell bars, its official seal breached. He eyed the paper, making no move to accept it.

"You're going in for marking tonight, vamp," the pale detective stated. "Unless I lose a copy of the order." A pencil was slid into the cell, rolling haphazardly across the uneven floor. "All I want is an address. You write it, I make this order disappear. Agreed?"

He stared down the man, pleased with the increased heart rate his unblinking eyes caused. The officer shifted his weight subtly, the stale odor of foot sweat penetrating the air with each movement.

"Address," the investigator barked, his patience for the humming male growing short.

Pulling his hood back up over his ears, he stretched back onto the cot and awaited the tattooing.

"It really stands out," the taller officer marveled, his thin lips gaping open slightly.

He resisted the urge to touch the identical brands. The mercury was slowly burning through every cell it touched, infiltrating each nucleus with its venom. How Rhys willingly submitted himself to the torment of tattooing was beyond his comprehension.

Hurt like a bitch, Rhys had once said when asked about his intricate designs.

Rhys had a flair for the understatement.

"All right, vamp," the pale man began. "Hood down." He complied without hesitation. As intimidating as he looked donning his customary hood, he knew the crystal of his eyes was unnerving for his more vocal captor. "We're going to play a little game."

The detectives' games had been rather boring. Every night, the pair would arrive with a new method to pull information from their prisoner. Last night had been the write-and-release game. The previous night was the good-cop-bad-cop game. The first meeting had involved a game of truth or lie.

He was beginning to question if the good detectives understood the word 'game'.

"I want your group's location, you want out of here. I can't release you until I check your house out. I get an address, you get your freedom. Yes?"

Sometimes, when speaking with humans he

enjoyed, he would blink periodically to soften his gaze and relax his company.

He didn't like his current companionship.

"So I got to thinking," the investigator continued, "that maybe you're under some strange compulsion. Maybe you can't actually give me the address. Your voice obviously works. So we're going to play a little game of hot and cold. Thumbs up, thumbs down if you prefer."

The lankier man unrolled a map of West Virginia, glancing at the cement walls before resigning himself to holding the large paper.

"See here? This is where you were picked up." The detective pointed at Vansburg. "This," he said, his finger tracing its way to Charleston, "is where you were spotted last week. I reckon you hail from somewhere in this area. Thumbs up?"

He remained stoically attentive to the bars of his cell, watching the detective's lips in his peripheral.

The interrogator frowned a moment.

"Maybe he has amnesia," one of the young guards suggested.

"Maybe," the detective mulled, "he hasn't got the right incentive to talk."

****

The amalgamated factions of the haunt had reached an impasse. Mickey watched as Dahlia and Justine sat silently in their chairs, backs straight and knees crossed as they feigned a polite interest in the arguments tossing across the table. Simone sat in Rhys's lap, her smooth thighs providing a warm resting place for the frustrated male's wandering hands.

"You cannot keep referring to the police as

criminals. It's establishing a negative mentality regarding their life value," Audra countered at Nichol's repeated insistence they drain Jagger's detainers.

"They're upholding laws created to destroy us. They. Are. Criminals."

"And you are the criminals from their point of view. Do you guys ever look outside your own perceptions?" Audra sighed in exasperation.

"Our goal," Kaius interjected in a vain attempt to direct the discussion, "is to get Jagger out."

"With as little bloodshed as possible," Audra interrupted.

"With," Kai side-eyed her, "as little violence as possible. Our goal is our endgame. No other agendas apply. Vengeance is not on the table tonight."

Molly's head rose from Dominic's shoulder. "Could we apply another agenda?" she asked. "Like, they already marked him. Why are they keeping him?"

"Until he gives up our haunt, he won't be released. Jagger won't turn on us, so we can assume he won't be released," Nichol stated with certainty.

Molly pursed her lips. "So, if he tells them where to find a haunt, he'll be sent home."

Mickey's eyes narrowed. "A haunt. Any one would work."

"We are not starting a civil war among ourselves by targeting our own," Kai warned.

"Where is Dovidas?" Molly said, her voice graveling.

"Chen haunt in northern Beijing," Louis replied. "It's not a bad idea."

Nichol's hazel eyes lowered in contemplation. "It would be intricate. I would need to tap into the FBI servers and gain access to their ground visuals. Reroute their servers to pass through ours. But it has the potential to gain intel on Dovidas and his cohorts indirectly."

Kaius nodded slowly. "Use one enemy to spy on another enemy for our benefit. The agenda has become significantly more complicated."

"And interesting," Mickey mused. "How would we communicate this to Jagg?"

Molly, obviously pleased with the acceptance of her idea, perked up. "We could send him messages through songs. Like Dommie did for me!"

Dommie. He would have to remember that for future harassment sessions.

Nichol stared blankly at Molly. "Songs."

"Yes!"

"Jagger is fucking deaf."

Chapter Thirteen

"I can't believe you still own that thing," Louis muttered, his nose wrinkling in distaste at the beige compact beater parked in the corner of the garage. "It wasn't cool then, it sure as shit ain't cool now."

Mickey grinned at his friend. "Whatever. You wouldn't know cool if it reared up and fucked you in the ass." Tossing a set of keys over, he patted his car lovingly. "Don't listen to the grumpy fuckwit. Daddy will take you for a good spin when he gets back."

Louis started Dominic's sports car, smiling at the healthy purr of the engine. "Dahlia on her way up?" he called, adjusting the seat.

He tossed his bag onto the pile of arsenal and blood stashed in the back. "I can hear her now."

The bubbly brunette skipped into view, her dark brown bob bouncing. "I'm here! Sorry, sorry, sorry! Mickey, where should I put my bags?"

Bags? Multiple?

He opened the rear passenger door. "I'll toss them in here," he offered, trying to maintain an impassive expression as he took in the large suitcase with two matching shoulder bags.

What the hell did this woman think she'd need?

As if reading his mind, Dahlia handed him the luggage before climbing into the back seat herself. "This is my first rescue," she squealed, "so I wasn't sure what I should bring. But I know I'll need a few pairs of shoes. In case one hurt my feet or gets damaged doing rescue stuff. And jeans, of course. Sweaters in case it's cold. Boots, too. My makeup and lotions, of course…"

Sparing a glance toward Audra and her single leather backpack, he nodded in feigned understanding toward Dahlia and left Louis to listen to the rest of her list while he joined Nichol and Boy at Kaius's SUV.

"We all set?" he asked, avoiding the woman who had joined the group.

"Should be," Nichol grumbled in distraction. "Kai is monitoring the com room with Dominic. Both have been briefed on their responsibilities and solutions to any problems that may occur. Audra has been outfitted with a tethered phone to allow her to speak only to us. Rhys has taken over for Boy in the bloodslave quarters…"

"And he's still understandably upset," Audra said pointedly, as it had been Mickey who suggested Boy would be beneficial to the operation. Rhys's close relationship to Jagger could be an impediment if tough decisions needed to be made, and without Kaius as a buffer, Mickey didn't have it in him to keep up with Rhys's heavy torrent of emotions, should things take a turn for the worse. "I have his number in this burner phone, so I'll update him frequently on our progress. Agreeable?"

Audra would do it whether the males protested or not, so they remained silent and tucked her small bag on top of Nichol's meticulously stacked equipment. As Nic climbed into the driver's seat, Audra and Boy had a quick stare-down before Boy folded his long limbs into the back seat and Audra took her place in the front.

He loped over to Dominic's car, content to sit back while Louis drove. The garage door lifted, and the first inter-species mission in Kaius haunt history officially began.

It was, to be frank, awkward.

Had it been just him and Louis, the stereo would have been competing for attention over the males' voices as they rehashed old conquests and laughed over past antics. They would have discussed current actresses and singers, explicitly detailing what they'd do to them given the chance.

Hell, the duo would have compared notes on the Tender currently fidgeting with the zipper on what smelled like her makeup arsenal.

The first hour of the drive passed slowly in the darkness. He adjusted to the muted din of emotions from his brethren, their peaks a dull hum while their valleys barely registered in the recesses of his mind. Louis was an apathetic bubble of relief. Despite the increasing distance between them, Rhys's worry-tinged anger remained steady and unabated. Dominic was bored and barely pulsing in his head. Nichol thrummed with annoyance, confusion, and apprehension.

Kai was silent.

He took the opportunity to reach toward Jagger.

Nothing yet.

He wasn't surprised that his brother remained outside his range. Jagg was a master at containing his strongest impulses and emotions, locking them in a box where Mick couldn't gain access. Ordinarily, Jagger's skill was a relief to him as he was little more than a buzzing in the background of his thoughts. In their current predicament, however, the inability to assess his brother left the hauntmates in the dark about Jagg's condition. He could be injured. Weakened. Starving.

****

Bored.

Jagger stared at the bag of blood sitting directly in his line of sight outside his cell, noting the liquid was thickening quickly and would soon be inedible. The detectives had been by earlier, tossing the bag down just out of his reach before silently exiting the room.

Apparently the new game was withholding unappetizing, spoiled meals.

Reclining back on his cot, he appraised his situation and the probable reaction of his hauntmates. By now, Nichol would have alerted the others to his disappearance. Information with the DeChamplain haunt would have been exchanged. He had recognized one of the haunt's younger vampires in the room when the marking occurred, the male's ovaled irises concealed with contact lenses and his fangs clipped neatly.

He wore a bright red Purifier Posse hat.

It was a nice touch.

So he waited for instructions, watching carefully for anything that stood out in his limited space. The room was relatively new, and he suspected he was the first vampire to grace the titanium alloy bars. His young guards were losing their giddiness, his lack of reaction to his situation proving less exciting than the recruitment videos likely promised. The detectives were unsure, often consulting a photocopied handbook entitled Navigating Vampire Detainment.

It didn't provide good advice.

The east coast had been an interesting mix of species hatred and living rights. While the police and military appeared to be enacting the recent laws with vigor, he had noted a high number of vampires walking freely among the human population. He had indulged in the freedom himself on a few occasions, surprised at how ignored he was by the general public in light of the growing anti-speciesism plaguing the news cycle and dominating politics as the Species Purifier groups grew louder. Sure, the odd person crossed the street when he passed, but overall it had been an enlightening experience as long as he avoided law enforcement.

Of course, he had been in the bigger centers at the time and disappearing into the crowds had been easy.

His captivity in Vansburg had been little more than being at the wrong place at the wrong time. Across the country, investigations into missing women had taken a sudden and disturbing turn. No longer were likely suspects being questioned or scrutinized. Fingers and accusations pointed to vampires, regardless of proof or logic. Those few haunts that had registered with the federal government found themselves raided with alarming frequency.

The resting places of vampires were being publicly exposed, the members marked in the name of safety. In Vansburg, the body of a local mother had turned up behind the high school days before his arrival in the town, and a fanged scapegoat was needed.

He was, therefore, the most likely suspect as he moved quietly down the streets at first dark, his intentions not much more than finding a quick meal before setting off toward Connecticut.

The mercury bullet passed through his ribcage with

little resistance, cauterizing the wound open as it moved through his body. Jagger spun, his irises narrowing into black slits when he saw the cop who'd shot him.

"I said, hands up, vampire!" a burly officer barked, his partner's weapon trained on his skull.

Out the corner of his eye, he could see eleven human observers cowering from the sound of the gunshot. Two officers he could take down easily without a trace. Eleven extra humans would be too messy and bring too much heat in an already volatile social climate.

He lifted his hands slowly, observing the cop's lips.

****

Mickey tried unsuccessfully to catch Louis's eye. The bastard knew he was aiming for subtlety, and he was flat out refusing to make it easy.

"So, Dahlia," Louis drawled, adjusting the rear-view mirror with a smirk, "tell me more about these reality television programs you're so interested in."

In that one sentence, he knew his friendship with Louis had finally run its course.

Not really. But very fucking close.

Five hours into the drive, and Dahlia had been talking for almost four of them. Louis, the traitorous jackass, encouraged her inane conversation with open-ended questions requiring essays for answers. Did she always talk this much? Had he just never noticed? Or maybe he never had to notice, what with his limited interactions with Dahlia confined to a bed or a sofa. Or a wall.

Staring forlornly at the SUV in front of them, Mick wondered how Nichol and Boy were doing. With Boy being mute and Nichol preferring silence to useless chatter, he bet it was a nice, quiet drive. Probably smelled better, too. Dahlia's stockpile of makeup had created a strange chemical scent combined with a faint moldy odor. Under the guise of interest, he had rifled aimlessly through the bag earlier, hunting for the offensive smell.

It was everything.

How had he never noticed how much this woman required to make herself look the way she did? What did she look like without all this crap? There were lipstick tubes, white powders, beige sticks, black sticks, pink sticks, an assortment of sparkly powders, and a ton of brushes of all sizes with residue on them. It was nauseating.

Once they returned to the haunt, Dahlia would definitely be off his meal list.

He pulled out his phone and fired off a quick text to Dominic, reminding him to feed within the next day or two. He then sent off a hopeful text to Nichol.

How far until we bunk

Nichol's response was as concise as he bet the conversations were in that vehicle.

two

He resumed his blank stare ahead, grunting politely in response to Dahlia, despite being unaware of what she said. Louis was grinning at his discomfort. That or he actually enjoyed Dahlia's blathering. Turncoat.

The night couldn't end quick enough.

Chapter Fourteen

"But if he was expecting us, would he not stash a key somewhere? This seems highly illegal," Audra stated, her arms crossed and foot tapping as she eyed the Missouri bolt hole.

Nichol's deft fingers popped the lock on the heavy steel door with ease and Mick smirked as the ancient male's shoulder heaved slightly in exasperation.

He held back as Boy led the group down the stairs. The descent far less painful than it had been during their last entrance into the hideout when they'd made a mad daylight dash down the stairwell, the seconds of sun exposure they endured leaving them blind, burned, and injured.

Checking the vehicles one last time before following the others, he pulled the newly replaced door tight behind him. As the crew moved toward the secure room at the end of the hall, the faint scent of bleach wafted over them.

Right. They had left a small mess of blood and bodies last time.

Boy's head remained down, his blank eyes obscured by his long hair as he propped the bolt room door open with one arm and waited patiently as the rest moved into the cement room.

"Here?" Dahlia questioned, her painted brows raised in surprise.

Audra was silent, her cat eyes assessing the emptiness of their accommodations. Mickey stood at her side, watching in fascination as her normally confident stance altered, her shoulders hunching slightly and knees bending as though preparing for a fight.

The rest of the males were quick to relieve their backs of the bags they had brought in from the vehicles. Nichol set to work establishing a temporary communication center while Louis pulled out an assortment of human food and blood bags from a cooler. Dahlia perched on the floor, sandwich in hand, and wrinkled her nose in distaste as she glanced around.

Audra quietly dragged a cord into the hallway in search of electricity for Nichol.

He and Louis emptied their duffle bags slowly in a pathetic attempt to make two beds for the women.

"We should probably pick up air mattresses or something for next time," he muttered to himself.

Louis examined the pitiful excuses for beds. "We suck at this."

Audra reappeared and wandered over, taking control of the mess and adding the contents of her own bag. "Done. There's a secondary hallway that was too dark for me to check. Why don't you two go make sure it's safe."

He frowned, rising to his feet. "That's one bed. One small bed."

Audra waved the males off, effectively ending the discussion and dismissing them.

The dark corridor led to another bolted steel door, a possible secondary escape route. Louis took his time wandering up the stairwell. "Nothing but an exterior door," he called as his footsteps descended. "I was almost hoping for something more interesting."

"More interesting than network television discussions?" he teased.

Louis grinned and led the way back to the basement room. "It's called foreplay. She talks, I pretend to know what the hell she's talking about, and I'll be spending the day with a warm vein."

Bastard.

Dawn approached quickly, its arrival echoing through the limbs of the vampires as they fired off a few messages to their hauntmates. Dahlia periodically rifled through the cooler for snacks as she debated loudly between removing her makeup or sleeping in it for the day.

He hoped she'd sleep in it. The remover smelled horrific, and there were no windows to vent the stench.

As Dahlia settled into the makeshift bed with Louis lounging beside her, Mickey noted Audra had made no move to eat or prepare for rest. "Maybe you should tell her to hunker down while we watch in shifts," he whispered to Nichol, too soft for human ears to hear.

Nichol glanced over at the woman who was leaning against the back wall, her eyes lost in space. "Audra. Eat. Now."

Mickey shook his head and grunted. "Helpful."

Boy observed the group, his blue eyes flicking between Audra and the cooler. He moved from his position at the door and pulled a sandwich out, walking it over to Audra. Her brown eyes held a hint of mistrust before she accepted with a quick bow of her head.

What. The fuck.

Once nothing remained but the plastic wrapping,

Boy took it from her hands and motioned toward the corner opposite Dahlia. Without a word, Audra moved swiftly to the spot. She sat against the wall, pulling her knees to her chest and closing her eyes. As her breathing slowed and regulated, he cocked a brow. "How the hell is she sleeping like that?"

Boy looked at him pointedly before turning his back and resuming his post.

Nichol stretched out on his back and flung an arm over his eyes. "Two years in the quarters, Mick. Who do you think controlled her eating and sleeping patterns?"

Hunching over his knees and staring at the sleeping woman, he felt an uneasiness overcome him.

The bloodslave quarters had supplemented the haunt vampires for decades. Imported from other haunts with questionable practices, the Kaius haunt took in bloodslaves who knew too much, humans who couldn't be released without placing the whole of the vampire species in further danger.

Bloodslaves had been instrumental in funding their existence and had saved the lives of hundreds of injured vampires over the years. The hauntmates themselves had turned to the bloodslave bags during missions such as the one they were currently embarking on.

The bloodslaves were necessary, especially with the current political and social climate. Rampant public feeding was becoming increasingly dangerous, and shipments of blood had removed many vampires from the streets, thereby reducing their chances of arrest or death.

They were necessary.

Hell, without the bloodslave bags, Dahlia and

Audra would be lunch for four males.

Logic wasn't helping him resolve the disquiet in his head.

Audra shifted her arms, wrapping them tighter around her legs without opening her eyes. He narrowed his gaze at her, as if attempting to gain a better view of her mind. Take charge, this and that isn't ethical, social construction Audra had become meek and obedient in the barren cement room.

No. Not meek. Not obedient.

She had gone into survival mode.

He closed his eyes and focused on Audra's expression as Boy approached her with the sandwich. She had assessed him, his motives. She had hesitated before accepting the food, as though she expected a sign of payment for nourishment.

A flicker of gratefulness when Boy offered her a corner.

With her spine to the wall, Audra was in a prime position to fight, her vision unimpeded and no chance of lurkers at her back. He opened his eyes and gauged her readiness, even while in sleep. Her breathing was steady, but shallow. Her weight remained balanced on her feet. Hunched forward with her head buried in her locked arms, Audra's face and torso were protected. Ebony and turquoise hair was pulled tight into a braided ponytail.

Two years was nothing more than a blip in the lifespan of a vampire, but for a human woman in her early thirties, it was a lifetime. "Nichol?"

Nic grunted.

"How long do most humans last down there? What's the turnover rate?"

Nichol lifted his head. "Six months. A year, if we're lucky given the state most of them come to us. Boy burns the dead once a week, so I'm guessing here. Rhys would know better."

He nodded and resumed his evaluation of the cool, collected psychologist.

Her sense of self-preservation was intense, calculating. She interacted with each male differently, tailored to each personality, yet she didn't put the same effort in for the Tenders.

They had no power over her wellbeing.

He reflected on his limited experience with the haunt bloodslaves. Their cells were cramped and stale, with the toughest vying for control over food and water. A bastardized experiment in Darwinism. The stronger humans shared a look, a gleam of war in their eyes. They were intelligent, manipulative, and observant.

They learned the schedule, the pecking order, and established dominance as new bloodslaves were brought in. They conserved their energy and spent their many hours of down time lying in wait, anticipating a time they might escape. However, even the most hardened of bloodslaves eventually succumbed to the same insanity he had witnessed among the general bloodslave population.

And none escaped.

At least none escaped unless they caught Rhys's discerning eye.

It was better for the rare bloodslave who was selected by the Tender trainer. Those chosen received opportunities for education, talent development, and lived their remaining years in luxury provided by wealthy vampires.

It had to be the better alternative.

"Nichol?"

Another grunt.

"How'd she end up in the bloodslave quarters?"

Nichol sat up, rubbing his neck. "She arrived with a small contingent from Vermont, pulled off an island by a young haunt during a ship docking. Newspapers determined her cause of death to be drowning from a fall overboard. My guess is the vamps who grabbed her pulled her boarding papers. But who knows. Human law enforcement rarely looks deeper than the easiest route."

"How do you know that? She tell you?"

"Internet, Mick. Try it for something other than downloading music."

****

A vibration rumbled through the metal frame of the cot and into Jagger's head. His eyes opened and he glanced at the guards.

"I said, get up, bloodsucker," the younger guard snarled, his bravado minimized by his refusal to get within an arm's reach of the cell bars.

He cocked a brow, turned his head away from the boy, and returned to his position of rest.

The tremor reached him again, indicating the kid was still attempting to gain his attention. Reluctantly, he sat up and swung his legs over the edge of the mattress, affixing his stare on the guard, who stammered momentarily.

"We…uh…you've been deemed a…uh…a hostile prisoner. Non-cooperation. So until you talk we…well…we have ways of, you know, making you."

He smiled pleasantly at the nervous boy, making

sure his fangs were on display.

The kid's partner appeared with a long black hood and a portable stereo.

"You need to stand up and turn around. No funny business. Hands behind your back. So I can get these cuffs on. Got it?"

He complied, interested in what new game the detectives had authorized for this evening and secure in the knowledge he could break through the handcuffs when he was done playing. As the cuffs clicked on his wrists, he stepped away and faced his guards, his eyes on their lips.

"If you could just...bend down...little closer...just gonna put this on your head..."

As the hood draped over his eyes, he recognized the game.

Backing up confidently, he resumed his place on his cot, hood in place. The vibrations of the stereo started immediately.

Had he been a young vampire, the sound overload would have made for an effective torture method. The vibrations were consistent and strong, indicating the volume of the noise was quite high. It held no discernible rhythm. Combined with the removal of sight, a young vampire would have had a difficult time assessing his surroundings and would be more likely to lash out.

He, however, was no newly-turned. And apparently his captors had yet to realize he was deaf.

The vibrations continued through the night and into dawn. They provided a slight discomfort in his gums, but severely lacked the impact the good detectives had surely anticipated. The elimination of the scent of pharmacy cologne spray filtering through the cotton hood led him to deduce that his guards had fled hours ago, their ears and minds unable to withstand the constant assault. He had managed to rest, recognizing the investigators had moved from passive to aggressive techniques and he may need to conserve his energy, remain at the top of his game.

He was curious how far they would go, given the precarious protection vampires carried among lawmakers. Loopholes, traditionally a vampire's greatest bargaining chip, were likely being applied and he was almost eager to find out exactly what those loopholes were.

Katja Desjarlais

Chapter Fifteen

Audra lifted her head from her arms, her neck stiff from holding its position throughout the day. Her eyes were quick to take in her surroundings, searching for threats to her safety and rank.

None.

Unless Nichol's mood counted.

She remained motionless, holding her position as she scanned the room and flexed each of her muscles in a slow, steady sequence. Nichol was wrapping cords into meticulous loops, his attention wholly focused on the task. Louis was cross-legged beside Dahlia, his eyes glazed over while Dahlia nattered away about why she preferred strawberry jam to raspberry.

Looking toward the door, she met Mickey's gaze. His arms were crossed as he leaned against the door frame and stared back at her, his expression unreadable.

Boy's slow approach at her right drew her attention from Mick. Boy crouched down in front of her and offered a hand. She instinctively recoiled, her arms wrapping tighter around her legs, her fingers gripping her inner arms to cover her veins.

Boy waited her out, not a single muscle twitching as she stifled the urge to fight against the vampire reaching into her space. When logic finally won out, she accepted the proffered hand and Boy assisted her to her feet.

114

She kept her back to the wall and massaged the tension from her shoulders, musing how nice a shower would be before rolling her eyes. How quickly she had grown accustomed to living a semblance of a normal life of showers and meals and bedding. With a quick shake of her head, she wandered over to Dahlia's nest and collected her backpack. A few makeup touchups and a spritz of vanilla later, and she was ready to face the long drive ahead.

"I'll take Dahlia topside and find a bathroom," she informed the males as they disassembled and packed Nichol's technology center back into the hard cases.

Nichol grunted in acknowledgement and the women strode into the hallway, Audra with her backpack and Dahlia with her multitude of luggage. Over the sound of Dahlia's pants, she could hear heavy boots trailing them in the dim corridor.

Boy.

She gave the mute vampire a quick smile as he fell into step behind the women. Something about cement walls and poor lighting had made Boy's presence reassuring, almost comforting.

The devil she knew.

As they breached the exterior door and stepped out under the lamplight, she turned and reached up to Boy. "May I?"

The male stilled and she used her fingers to comb his long bangs into his oval irises. "There. Don't look up and you'll blend right in."

The women took turns in the dirty gas station bathroom, Audra speeding through her routine and Dahlia taking significantly longer. Boy waited patiently outside, his head down while he catalogued every sound. She observed the slight twitch of his head as he pinpointed approaching vehicles and pedestrians, his nostrils flaring as scents she couldn't detect provided a wealth of information to the male.

He was fascinating to watch, having spent months exposed to the other haunt members. Boy was more attune to his surroundings, more feral in his movements. He had no noticeable human traits, no tells. Not a single eyelash moved unnecessarily.

Like Kaius, he was the perfect predator.

By the time Dahlia deemed herself ready, the vehicles were loaded and running, their drivers anxious to get the second leg of the excursion done.

"We should switch!" Dahlia exclaimed. "I'll ride with Nichol, you can ride wi…"

"Fuck. No."

Nichol's word was law, and soon Audra was sitting in the SUV, staring out the window at the blackened sky and wondering how long it had been since she had truly seen the light of day.

****

Rhys glared at his phone screen, simultaneously willing it to ping with information while resenting the woman who would be communicating the intel.

For such a wordy female, Audra sure was tightlipped when she texted.

Nimble fingers trailed up his calf, circled his knee, and proceeded to head north. He ran his hands through Simone's curls, gently straightening them before watching them bounce back to their unruly place.

"The colors look good, angel," he mumbled absentmindedly, admiring the tendrils of rainbow hues interspersed among the golden-brown locks. "Justine's work?"

Simone looked up at him from her position on the floor. "Of course, Master. She's amazing."

Humming in agreement, he flicked open his Solitaire app and began flicking through the virtual cards.

Leaving Kansas City

Mentally calculating the route, he growled in frustration. They wouldn't get within Jagger's reach until close to dawn tomorrow night. Too late to make contact.

Keep me posted on your whereabouts and if any changes are made to the plan

Minutes ticked by. Bright pink nails scratched gently along the inside of his thighs.

k

K. Fuck your k, he thought, unconcerned that it was one of his own common responses. He didn't know what reply he wanted, but k was not it.

"Master?"

"Hmm?"

"Should we continue my elocution lessons?"

Looking at his silent phone, he leaned back on the sofa and shook his head as he spread his legs a little wider.

****

"We'll make Louisville if we push it after this fill up," Nichol called over to Mickey as the males placed the fuel nozzles into their respective vehicles. "As long as the women don't waste too much fucking time."

He gestured in frustration at Dahlia and Louis.

Mick grinned. "At least you aren't driving with them," he groused. "I swear to god I'm losing years off my life thanks to them."

Nichol nodded slowly in understanding. "Boy. You and Mick switch."

Boy silently unfolded his long limbs and exited the SUV.

So did Audra.

"Well, that was rude," she chastised, her cat eyes narrowed and more feline than usual. Boy silently twisted himself into the back of Dominic's car as Audra's hands flew to her hips. "Boy," she called without turning toward him, "you don't have to move if you don't want, sweetie."

Sweetie?

He knew his mouth was gaping open but lacked the control to close it.

Nichol's fuel pump disengaged, and he replaced it before getting back in the car. "Get in."

Audra's lips pursed, but she obeyed. Mickey finished gassing up and gave a quick wave to Louis and Dahlia before he took Boy's place in the back of the SUV.

Audra held her tongue just long enough for Nichol to reach the highest speed he dared on a highway crawling with state troopers.

"You should be ashamed at how cliquish you guys are."

Nichol kept his eyes forward. Mick stared into the darkness.

"You'd think that after centuries of existing solely within your own kind, you'd be more accepting of each other. The way you boss him around and ignore him...it's no wonder he's so sullen. Why would you treat your brother so heartlessly?" Audra lectured, arching her neck to make eye contact with Mick.

Nichol scoffed. "He's not our blood," he stated.

"Neither is Louis, and you all treat him just fine."

He ducked his head low, allowing his hair to shroud his eyes as Nichol gripped the wheel tighter. "Boy is…" he began, unsure of how to respond. "He's just Boy. He's always been around, he's never spoken, and he's just, I don't know, just here."

"Well," huffed Audra, "I don't know why he stays around. Poor guy is so ostracized. Perhaps you two should think about that once we return home."

Home. He wondered if she noticed she used that word.

Nichol rolled his eyes and turned the music on, setting the volume on max.

The drive continued to the beat of Swedish death metal. As the faint lights of Louisville broke on the horizon, Audra lowered the volume.

"We should pull over at a gas station so Dahlia and I can use the restroom before we head to whatever cement tomb we're spending the night in."

"No need," Nichol replied tersely. "We will be in a motel for the day."

Confusion, a rare expression for Audra, crossed her face. "You're dropping us off?"

"Kentucky citizens are surprisingly tolerant toward us despite the movement in their government. We're staying at a motel that has a wing dedicated to vampires. It's come highly recommended by haunt leaders in the area who own a stake in the property."

As the convoy pulled into the sparsely populated parking lot, Nichol pulled a credit card from his pocket and handed it to Audra. "You'll check us in while Mick and I assess the area. Text me when you know our room numbers. We'll meet you there."

Audra's eyes flicked to the name on the card in amusement. "Yessir, Mr. Cam Pewter."

As she disappeared through the large doors of the motel office, he and Nichol walked the perimeter, noting exits and scenting the air. Boy escaped Dominic's cramped sports car and took position behind the wheel of Kaius' SUV, the absent haunt leader's vehicle noticeably more functional for road trips than the youngest member's road rocket.

A text came through from Audra, and Nichol motioned toward the arm of the motel that had steel doors and no windows. Mick held back while Nichol strode toward the rooms, his ears tuned in to the quick footsteps behind him.

They lacked the familiar click clacking.

Audra caught up to him easily, her breath coming out in short puffs. "There's a private security team that monitors the premises during the day, vetted by a haunt around here," she panted. "And a second door to each room that can only be locked and unlocked from the inside. I...oh, wow am I out of shape...I was impressed with the cleanliness of the front desk. It bodes well."

He ground his teeth, dulling any reaction he felt rising at Audra's heavy breathing and proximity as she passed the keys to Nichol and assisted Dahlia with her plethora of luggage.

"Mick, you and Louis will bunk together," Nichol instructed as he tossed a few cases onto his back. "The women will be in the middle room. Boy and I will take the exterior one. We'll coordinate daytime monitoring of phones and online intel through text."

He nodded and changed course toward Louis.

"Would you like me or Dahlia to take first shift?" Audra asked as she opened the second secured door to her room.

Nichol frowned. "Neither. We leave at nightfall tomorrow."

A manicured brow lifted. "We," she replied, gesturing to herself and Dahlia, "can leave the room in an emergency, whether that means sun-proofing the cars for an afternoon escape or picking up a gallon of milk. You," Audra drawled, flicking her wrist around, "are useless in approximately twenty minutes. Who. First."

Nichol growled, his back to the women. "Fine. We'll all coordinate daytime communication through text."

Mickey watched as Audra, apparently satisfied with Nic's adjustment, pushed the pin coded door closed.

Each male's phone buzzed moments later.

****

Establishing Nichol's rotation in the day watch was of utmost importance. Once his was solidified, he could continue to maneuver the chemical-laced Dahlia out of his sphere of contact. Content with the numeric code he had programmed into the security door, he pulled out his phone while mumbling to Boy.

"If we have one from each room on alert, it'll greatly reduce any threat that arises over the next fourteen hours and allow us to be updated if anything new comes in about Jagg," he muttered, typing quickly. "You'll be on first rotation, along with Dahlia and Mickey. I'll take the second and use the time to tear down the com equipment in preparation for departure."

Boy remained silent, reclined on one of the motel beds.

After receiving confirmations from Mickey and Louis, he glared at his phone as Audra's response came in.

Change of plans. Louis bunking with Dahlia.

His mind rearranged the schedule instantaneously before realizing the hitch.

Where are you staying

With Boy

He turned to the mute male behind him. "Audra is bunking with you today?"

Silence.

A knock.

He keyed in his code and opened the door to a less than amused Audra.

"Mick has agreed to move in here with you," she grumbled. "Boy, you and I are heading to the other room."

"That's not the plan," he stated.

"Yeah, well, I'm not sleeping next to a horn dog and her boy toy," Audra responded, her jaw set in frustration and face showing her weariness.

His eyes flashed in annoyance at the change in his schedule. "Fucking Tenders," he snarled. "Fine. Boy, you go to Mick. Audra, you stay here." He reached for her bag and tossed it on the bed furthest from the door. "Mickey can't read Boy since he's not of our bloodline," he said by way of explanation as Boy left the room. "And right now I'm too fucking annoyed to be that close to Mick without adversely affecting him."

As Audra moved toward the bed, he fired off a new

rotation.

First up Audra, Louis, Mick. Boy, Dahlia, me second

He pinched the bridge of his nose. Fucking Tenders. Both shifts were no longer optimized.

And he liked things optimized.

Audra glanced at her phone. "I'll hop in the shower to get myself energized, if that's okay. Once I'm out, you're free to rest."

He grunted his reluctant agreement.

Rest.

He didn't rest when humans were present. Especially female humans. His rest would consist of faking it and running fight sequences in his head until it was his turn to stand guard.

Steam from the shower poured from under the bathroom door, filling the small motel room with the scent of Vanilla.

It wasn't offensive. Strong, but not overpowering.

He completed his computer set up, testing the scramblers and establishing a secure connection to the haunt and Kaius. He activated the history application at last minute, in case Audra decided to do a little web surfing during her watch.

She emerged from the bathroom, her black and turquoise hair dripping onto the carpet. "We have a lack of towels in here," she griped, her tone testy. "I assume it's too close to sunrise to call room service?"

He nodded. "I'll make do." He vacated his seat at the computer, gesturing toward the chair. "Check in with Louis and Mick every thirty minutes. Your phone volume should be at max in case you drift off. If Kaius rings on the laptop, wake me immediately. If you need anything, wake me. If you suspect anything, wake me. And if you feel you can no longer stay up, wake me."

Audra hummed in acknowledgement, pulling a brush through her hair as she sat. "How do I wake you? Are you guys disoriented and in attack mode when you get up? Are you dead to the world and need a bucket of water thrown on you?"

"Unless it is an emergency, wake me…gently," he said, unsure of what to suggest as he hadn't been woken by a human in centuries. Not that he anticipated resting, but Audra had no need for that information. He could fake it. "State your name while doing it. I'll be less likely to take you down. If you scream or dump water on me, I will drain you and leave your body in a ditch."

With her thumb already flying across her phone screen, she laughed quietly. "Deal. No waterworks or hysterics. See you in a few hours."

He disappeared into the shower, his discomfort over sharing a room with her evident in his twitching muscles and tightened jaw. Standing under the hot stream, he catalogued every item in the motel room that could be used as a weapon. The furniture was crafted from a weak metal. The walls were bare of art in wooden frames. Only he knew the numeric code to open the security door.

He had already half-heartedly rifled through her bag when she'd been in the bathroom.

Satisfied with his safety, he contemplated telling her the code to exit the room, but quickly dismissed it. If she was in enough danger to require opening it, he better be fucking awake.

She may need food.

"Audra," he called out over the rush of water, "will

you require a meal soon?"

"Boy tucked a few granola bars in the front pocket of my bag yesterday."

Boy. He and Audra had a strange rapport. The silent, sullen male appeared to anticipate her physical requirements, and she accepted his help with gratitude. She didn't fight him or argue, as she did with Nichol and the others.

It was odd.

Once the water turned off, he was faced with an empty towel rack. He was standing naked, glaring at the barren metal rack, when the door flung open and she stood before him, mouth agape and a damp towel in her outreached hand.

It had been a long time since he had to lock his bathroom door.

Snatching the towel from her hands, he slammed the door closed. The steam heat was escaping fast and he was in no mood to be more chilled than he would be drying himself with the damp towel.

As he pulled his cargos on, he could hear Audra finally moving away from the door. He stormed barefoot from the bathroom and straight to his bed, avoiding looking at the female who was audibly stifling a laugh. Flinging his arm over his eyes, he ignored his roommate as long as he could, knowing damn well he wasn't going to rest.

"It's difficult to reconcile the bitter computer geek with the Adonis I just saw," Audra mused aloud.

He continued to ignore her.

"I wonder if that's solely a human trait," she continued, "the categorizing of individuals into preconceived physical groups based on their intellectual and emotional groups. Do animals see the physically strongest and assume he or she lacks intelligence? Or vice versa?"

He never should have agreed to change bunkmates.

"It's truly ridiculous, how our brains create the unknown details based on nothing more than stereotypes."

He moved his arm a fraction, peeking at the woman whose back remained to him.

"Of course, clothing conceals the finer details. Even some of the larger ones, depending on the cut."

He gained no amusement from her meanderings.

"So I'm at a loss now as to how accurate my mental vision is of the others, since I've obviously created a greatly flawed image in my mind of..."

"There is no circumstance now or in the future that would require you to devise an unclothed image of me," he snarled, eyes closed, and teeth bared.

The smile was evident in her voice. "Oh, Nichol. I no longer need to devise anything. Small or large."

She was fucking teasing him. Baiting him. He deliberated opening both doors and risking sun exposure to get the woman out of his room.

But the scent of burning flesh was more of a bitch to ignore than the current bitch sitting at his laptop.

Chapter Sixteen

Mick snapped his wrist, untangling his phone's charger cord. He and Louis had been practicing Louis's hypnosis skills through the motel room wall. Louis's casual comment that he was feeling strong and focused told him Dahlia had not gone straight to bed upon settling into their room.

Better Louis than him.

A slight buzzing sensation in his mind had been the most impact Louis had managed to make, but given their distance and physical wall, it was better than previous efforts. It gave both males hope that perhaps Louis's talent could become more finely-tuned than initially anticipated.

Distance vampire hypnosis would be very cool.

The training had kept his conscious mind occupied, his attention on his friend instead of on his own imaginings of what exactly Nichol's rolling moods meant.

They meant the bastard was still awake, he thought in annoyance.

So was Audra, judging by her precise texts every thirty minutes.

Annoyance.

Unexpected calm.

Frustration.

Pride.

Anger.

Resignation.

What the hell were they discussing?

Or doing.

As Louis's tingling sensation waned, he spared a glance at the motionless Boy before diving further into Nichol's river. A pang of guilt hit him as he waded through his brother's private emotions, but he pressed on, disregarding his own pulsing hostility. Avoiding Nichol's traditional waves of frustration, anger, and annoyance, he probed into the less common waves. Echoes of the calm Nichol had felt early in the evening remained, a steady undercurrent Mickey had come to associate with a physical reaction to a soothing external stimulus.

What the fuck external stimulus was Audra providing?

The thought flashed across his mind before he shook it off and continued his examination.

Pride.

That stream was common among his other brothers, but Nichol had rarely radiated pride without vexation. Mentally tracing the path pride took, he noticed it ran alongside the river of calm, swelling and abating along its banks, intermingling with annoyance but not being swallowed by it. Searching deeper, he attached himself to the pool of resignation.

The shores were lapping rhythmically, as though Nichol had accepted something throughout the morning that had integrated into his core with ease. Wading in, he dipped himself into the deep center before shooting back and pulling himself out of Nichol's thread with a jolt.

Adoration.

Admiration.

Amusement.

He ran his fingers through his hair in shame, checking to ensure his reaction had gone unnoticed by Boy as he fired off a quick text to his fellow guards and turned the shower on full blast.

His ability to trace deeply through his brother's emotions was one he had kept hidden from them. It was the ultimate invasion of privacy, an assault he had sworn off consciously committing against the males he fought alongside.

The water pushed his long hair into his eyes as he hung his head.

He was fucking jealous.

Jealous of his brother, who was currently shacked up with Audra in a room down the way.

Jealous of Rhys and his heated interactions with her.

Jealous of Dominic and his solidified connection to Molly.

Jealous of Boy and of Audra's unspoken trust in his ability to attend to her needs.

He rinsed the soap from his hair and squared his broad shoulders as he exited the shower. Envy was no excuse for the violation he had committed against Nichol. Especially when that envy was unfounded.

Nichol adored Audra.

Adored her as one did their best friend, not as a potential bedmate.

Given the pull of the undercurrents, he wasn't sure Nichol even knew it yet. But Mickey did, and his methods for extracting the information required an apology once Jagger was released and Nichol was free to exact judgement.

It would probably be very painful. Painful and memorable.

Laying back on his bed, he picked up his phone and chimed into the conversation, letting Audra and Louis know he was done his shower.

All scrubbed

Louis was quick to reply.

Signing out for a few to do the same ttyl

You guys have enough towels?

Confused, he reread Audra's message and stuck his head into the bathroom to check.

Yeah why

We had to share one

Eyes narrowing, he re-read those five words over and over before recalling his discovery of Nichol's feelings toward her.

Devil's in the details...

****

Audra grinned at her phone, well aware Nichol was still alert and observing her. She had maintained a quiet, steady, one-sided conversation for the past hour, realizing he would not be truly resting as long as she was in the room. In the motel mirror, she had noted slight shifts in his arms, flexes in his abs, and tightening along his jaw as he fought reactions to her musings.

She had pondered aloud about extending their roommate status once they arrived back at the haunt, getting "BFF" bracelets for the two of them, and a variety of other topics she knew would annoy, but not anger, Nichol. The longer she went without garnering a negative response, the more solidified her belief that

Nichol actually enjoyed her company.

Even if he refused to talk to her.

Truth be told, she had initially been mortified when she had flung the door open to give Nichol the sole motel towel. She hadn't been listening closely and had assumed he would be hidden behind the shower curtain, not standing there angry and naked.

Not that he should have been hiding.

Damn.

Strangely enough, she hadn't felt a single stirring when her gaze had taken in her roommate in all his natural glory. The guy was muscled, defined, and well-equipped.

It was also Nichol.

When he had exited the bathroom in silence and stormed across the room, she took a chance and made light of the situation.

Nichol didn't drain her.

Or threaten her.

She wasn't certain, but she thought he may have rolled his eyes under the strong arm draped over his face.

"Mickey wants details on our shared towel experience," she said, a glint in her eye. "But I feel that was too special to share."

Her ears perked up as Nichol emitted a quiet huff of air and sat up. "That's enough," he grumbled. "You. Sleep. I'll take over."

She grinned at him and crawled into her bed. The whir of the computer being brought to life lulled her as Kaius appeared on the screen and he and Nichol began softly discussing the mission.

****

The throbbing of his fangs centered Jagg, providing him with something to focus on as the detectives continued their newest game.

"Give up the location."

Two minutes of silence.

Thirty second flash of UV light.

The pattern had continued for hours, the foul stench of burning flesh permeating the room. He kept his eyes trained on the investigators, showing no sign of weakness. It hadn't taken the humans long to garner that his clothing offered little protection from the light, and they had stopped focusing their efforts on his exposed hands in favor of aiming the narrow beam at various other parts of his body. He could feel his skin healing slowly, only to have the wounds reopened as the light danced across his form.

Deprived of rest, he knew he would only be able to block his pain from Mickey for another hour or so before he would have to channel that energy into maintaining his stoic facade. Without fresh blood to energize his body, his healing was slowed significantly, leaving more and more raw holes in his body with every blast of light.

His retinas were slowly clouding.

It wouldn't be long before he lost his most powerful functioning sense.

With the bag removed from his face, he had subtly scoured the room for indications his hauntmates had arrived and attempted communication.

Nothing out of order, nothing different.

He scanned the room again, before the UV light destroyed what was left of his sight.

Nothing.

Different scenarios plowed sluggishly through his mind. The guard with the UV flashlight was extending his arm further into his sphere, emboldened by the physical damage he was witnessing. In his weakened condition, he calculated his chances of capturing the man's wrist, draining him dry, snatching the cell keys, unlocking the bars, and escaping before he was hampered by bullets and trapped above ground, blind and injured, during what was likely daylight hours.

It was unlikely he would survive.

The most logical solution would be to give up another haunt, a group of vampires who wouldn't be missed should the government go in guns a-blazing. He scoured his mind, steadying himself as another blast of light tore at his leg. Every haunt he had visited so far had been highly connected despite their solitude. And pissing off a haunt with ties to ancient vampires was never a wise move.

Two beams of light hit him simultaneously and he entered survival mode, all cognitive musings tossed to the side.

Chapter Seventeen

Nichol's eyes flicked to his buzzing phone, his hands busying themselves with wrapping speaker cords.

Back to back texts. Fuck.

Kai: Check Mick. Jagger injured

Boy: Mick convulsing. Advise

He pinched the bridge of his nose and growled low in his throat. They were a six-hour drive away from Vansburg, and four hours away from sunset. For Mick to feel blowback from Jagger's pain, it meant the torture was intense and potentially fatal.

Fucking fuck.

With every powerful contact the hauntmates had being confined to darkness, he was left with limited options. He glanced at the security door, calculating how long it would take to move through the sun's rays to Mickey's room.

He would face substantial damage. Healing time would be too great.

Fucking fuck.

"Audra," he barked, his voice harsher than he intended.

She stirred for a moment before sitting up, her eyes wide and arms moving frantically to disentangle herself from the sheets.

"I need you in Mick's room. Now."

Audra stood unsteadily, trying to get her bearings.

"Yes. Yeah, of course. What do I do?"

He fired off a text to Boy. "He needs fresh blood. Jagger is injured and Mickey is experiencing negative effects from it. If you aren't willing, I'll order Dahlia over."

Audra was already pulling her runners onto her feet. "Hand me my phone."

He passed her the phone and keyed in the code. "Go on three. Once you reach Mick's room, knock and give Boy time to shelter before entering," he ordered as he disappeared into the bathroom.

Then he waited.

Eighteen minutes passed before his phone rang and Audra's voice whispered through the device. "I think he's stable. At least, Boy seems to think so. What do we do now?"

He'd been racking his brain for eighteen minutes, trying to formulate a plan with his limited resources. "I'll listen to suggestions," he mumbled in defeat.

Audra took a sharp breath in the silence. "Three way us with Kaius. He'll need to approve my idea."

As he brought Kai into the fold, Audra began explaining her thoughts in a hush.

It was risky, with many variables that the hauntmates couldn't fully explore in their short timeline.

But it was better than nothing.

****

Audra sat on the floor of the bathroom, her free hand stroking the long, matted hair of the blond vampire on her lap. The sight of him contorting in pain on the floor echoed in the forefront of her mind. If Mickey was affected this strongly at such a distance, what was Jagger experiencing?

Her plan was flawed, a game she had played in the past when little more than reputations and careers were on the line. It was a game of chicken, usually played out in the media, not in the cells of jails.

She motioned for a pillow, slipping it under Mick's head as Boy assisted her to her feet. Boy had carefully monitored Mickey's feeding since the vampire was too far gone to know what was happening to him and around him.

So much strength lying immobile on the tile.

"I'll be back within the hour," she whispered to Boy, shoving her phone into her back pocket along with Cam Pewter's unreturned credit card and the SUV keys Boy had pushed her way.

Boy typed in the code and vanished as she stepped into the sunlight for the second time in years. Her eyes blinked in protest against the blinding rays and she lost her balance for a moment. Using her hand to shield her eyes, she moved quickly to the vehicle and started the hearty engine.

She was free.

Sunlight and freedom, an intoxicating and overwhelming combination.

She gripped the steering wheel, her eyes adjusting to the brightness as she moved onto the street. She could keep driving, passing the mall on her left and continuing straight to a police station. She could reverse her death certificate, appear at her estranged mother's house and beg to be welcomed back. She could return to her profession, her world of manipulation and manicures where the game stakes were reputations and revenue, not torture and death.

The engine cut with a rumble in front of a pharmacy and she tucked the keys into her back pocket. She moved quickly through the aisles, filling her basket with an assortment of beauty products and treats she had long forgotten she enjoyed. The cashier didn't even glance up as he took Cam Pewter's card from her hands, barely acknowledging the signature as Audra collected the receipt and pushed her wrist through the bag's handles. Tossing the purchases into the back of the car, she continued her mission.

Her mission.

Shoving the thought into the back of her mind for later, she veered into a higher-class clothing store, flipping through the racks quickly and waving off any assistance offered by the clerks as she loaded her arms with her selections. Skimming the shoe display, she added several complementary heels to her pile before tossing Cam's credit card on the counter. The salesclerk eyed the card suspiciously for a moment before running the purchases through.

No wonder credit card theft was such an issue, when sales obviously trumped security, she mused.

As she doubled back down the road, she caught sight of a secondhand military gear store, its faded sign barely visible from the street. Pulling into the empty parking lot, she contemplated requesting Nichol to outfit her properly when they got home.

Home.

Shaking off the stray thought, she marched into the dilapidated storefront, exiting ten minutes later with a bag of clothes and combat boots on her feet.

****

Nichol listened as the SUV's engine cut out. The

light padding of Audra's sneakers had been replaced by a louder, thumping rhythm. Her footfalls bypassed his door, moving swiftly to Mickey's room. Less than a minute ticked by before his phone rang.

"I'm back. I'll need an hour to look the part. Did you set everything up on your end?"

He grunted in agreement. "You returned."

A soft chuckle preceded the deadening of the connection and he finished packing and wiping the room down, eliminating any proof he or Audra had been present.

****

"I'll never get used to the whole not-breathing thing," Audra muttered as she passed by a motionless Mick to access the bathroom. He was now lying on one of the motel beds, his long legs dangling off the edge. She popped a piece of chocolate into her mouth as she carefully outlined her eyes, dusting shadow across her lids. Within the hour, Audra Verdi would be reinvented as Meredith Abernathy, Attorney-At-Law.

Her former life and likeness would be swept from the internet and replaced by an alternate history, one that would hold up to even the most scrupulous investigator. With her hair in a reserved chignon to hide her telltale turquoise strands, she applied the new makeup color palette carefully, downplaying her distinct eyes with muted shadows before donning a pair of weak reader glasses.

It wasn't much, but Nichol figured that in the unlikely scenario anyone from her past ever began sniffing around, Jagger would be free, and she would be a phantom once again.

At least, that was the plan. The only plan they had.

Meredith's wardrobe was significantly brighter than Audra's, her cream-colored suits and pastel blouses looking surprisingly cheerful laid out neatly on the bed.

She glanced down to check on Mick, who lay immobile on the bed. "I'm going to duck into the bathroom to change. Come get me if he stirs."

She stripped quickly, folding her jeans and plain shirt neatly before pulling on one of Meredith's lilac blouses and shimmying into the fitted cream pants. Slipping her feet into the four-inch matching pumps, she slid her arms into the suit jacket and walked out, handing Boy her phone. "Text a picture to Nichol. Tell him I'll be there in two. Be ready to roll at sunset."

****

Rhys sat hunched in his chair, his tattooed arms draped over his knees. He had joined Kai and Dom in the communication room on Kaius's command during the early afternoon and had held position as the boots on the ground came up with the plan that now had his eyes scanning the internet for Meredith Abernathy.

Simone had swung by the room with Justine and Molly a few hours earlier, anxious for any information they could get and quick to offer their wrists to the tense males.

"Nichol's a genius," Dominic breathed as he watched over Rhys's shoulder. "Articles, photos, social media tags? How did he do all this?"

He flipped between the open tabs on the laptop. "Some kind of photoshopping program, I'm guessing. The glasses were a perfect addition. Hides the most identifiable part of her."

Kai leaned over to get a better view. "Does she

139

look darker to you in these old photos?"

Pulling up an enlarged photo, he examined Audra's skin in a photo obviously taken many years ago but doctored to add in the spectacles. "That's a tan. Shit, Kai. You really need to get out more."

Kaius merely returned to his position and continued to hunt for aerial photos of the Vansburg police station.

The anticipation of sundown and preparation for Audra's mission had been significantly tampered by Dominic's soothing pheromone, for which Rhys was begrudgingly grateful. His focus on his task had improved significantly, as had his mood, after Dom had offered to assist. Without Mickey close by to pull the hauntmates down, he was recognizing how much he and the others had become dependent on Mick to boost their control.

"Any update on Mick?" he asked as Simone laid her head on his thigh.

Kaius nodded. "Boy has maintained contact. Mikhail is resting and quiet. Jagger has become more muted once again. I can only assume he is also resting."

Dominic resumed his seat beside Molly and grasped her hand. "What do you think they're doing to him?"

"Jagger has a high tolerance to pain," Kaius said quietly. "Considering our distance, I believe whoever has him has access to Deepfryer technology. Or a tanning bed. Though I suppose that would present some security issues..." He trailed off momentarily. "His pain was intermingled with hunger. He was disoriented."

Rhys lifted his hand from Simone's hair to avoid

accidentally injuring her in his frustration. "So he's likely starving, injured, and regressing. Does Nichol know this? Is Mick seriously going to be traveling the rest of the way? The closer he gets, the worse it'll be. Why don't they leave him behind with Dahlia and Louis. Or Boy."

He stood and began pacing the room. "Why the fuck didn't you send me? They need age and strength, not goddamn women. Now Mick is essentially injured and useless as long as Jagg is, and I'm here staring at a motherfucking computer screen."

His chair shattered against the wall, leaving crumbling drywall in its wake.

Kaius's hardened gaze fell onto him as a surge of calm filled the small space. "This," he said gruffly, gesturing toward the demolition work, "is why you're here, and not on the mission. One of those goddamn women holds the greatest chance of rescuing Jagger without resorting to an all-out species war. You've been here for hours. You've sat through the discussions. You're well aware of our choices and our reasonings. Now either you get yourself under control, or I'll put you in the dungeon for the duration of this affair."

****

Jagger sat motionless in the far corner of his cell, his back tight to the walls and blinded eyes staring straight ahead into blackness. His fingers ghosted the cold floor, feeling for vibrations in the cement. The stench of burnt flesh filled the room, overpowering every other scent in the small space and coating his tongue with its residue.

Minutes passed. Hours. Time was irrelevant as his body warred with itself over which injury to heal first.

When the detectives had vacated the room, he'd retreated to the back of his cell like a beaten dog, a wounded beast among predators.

It would be humbling when his mind pulled itself full from his core, the predator becoming the prey.

Heavy vibrations against his fingertips alerted his consciousness to an approaching foe. He kept his unseeing eyes forward, no longer able to hide his infirmity from his jailers. His core pulsed and slithered, attaching its all-consuming tendrils to every splinter of his intermittent cohesive thoughts.

One muscled arm swung out, cutting a swath before him as it reached toward an unseen threat. In the far reaches of his cognizance he felt himself becoming feral, a snarling mutant in a cage flailing against ghosts.

The burning began again, welding the wall to his sentient mind shut.

Chapter Eighteen

"Don't you dare hang up on me, Nichol!" Audra's voice hissed through the speaker as the phone disconnected.

Nichol gripped the steering wheel tighter, his teeth grating in irritation. "Again," he barked to Dahlia, prompting her to reach her wrist toward Mickey's exposed fangs.

"I think he's taking too much," the chemical-scented Tender whispered after a few moments. Reluctantly acknowledging her weakening heart rate, he reached his arm into the back seat and located Mickey's jaw. Using his fingers to unhook Mick's fangs, he rammed his own forearm into the snapping mouth, grimacing as his brother bit down hard and released with a howl.

The fuel stop at Huntington couldn't appear on the horizon fast enough.

The convoy had been driving toward Vansburg for less than twenty minutes when Mickey's stagnant body suddenly arched in the back seat, a roar of agony sending Dahlia shrieking against her door.

"What the hell is going on up there?" Audra demanded, her brusque voice replacing Louis's mellow drawl on the speaker.

"Mickey is having another episode," he growled, his eyes darting between Mick and the road. "And this

Tender needs to calm the fuck down before I toss her on top of the rabid vamp in the back seat."

"Pull over. I'm trading with Dahlia."

"No, you aren't," he snarled, his hazel eyes glaring down the Tender beside him.

"Nichol," Audra commanded, "pull your damn car over. I can calm him."

"You, we need," he stated, his foot getting heavy on the gas pedal. "The Tender is expendable on this mission." With a firm grasp, he angled the woman's arm into the back seat and toward Mick's elongated fangs. The Tender flinched as her skin was pierced but brokered no argument.

"Slow your ass down!"

Audra's voice held a slightly frantic pitch, one he didn't relish. He lifted his foot slightly, allowing the car to resume its lower speed. "We'll fuel up in Huntington. Louis, stay behind me and at the ready should I need to stop beforehand. Boy, ensure Audra rests. She has much to do when we reach Vansburg."

He had hung up, his attention required within his own vehicle.

Audra had called back eleven times since.

Mickey's rhythmic panting in the back seat was reassuring for him. His brother was fighting to retain some control over his mind and body, refusing to fall completely into the depth Jagger had breached.

With one eye on Dahlia, he spoke quietly to Mickey.

"Soon, Mikhail," he muttered softly. "We're less than three hours from Jagger. Every piece you pull from him now will keep him fighting that much longer. Keep him sane that much longer." He paused. Jagger was almost twice Mickey's age. Perhaps it wasn't Jagger's sanity that was at risk.

"I once recommended to Kaius that he put you down. You were in your fifth decade. I had just returned from acquiring information from Johann Ritter and was trying to replicate his experiments without frying myself in the process." He smirked, thinking back to his crude laboratories from centuries ago. "Granted, I shouldn't have been working during the daylight. So perhaps it was partially my fault. I had been standing on a chair, tapping a thin rod into the roof so I would have a sliver of sunlight to work with. You were supposed to be resting and I was less alert than I should have been. To this day, I don't know what possessed you," he mused.

"Where in your head did it make sense to knock my chair legs out with a pumpkin? I heard the damn thing come across the floor, but I was so close to getting that pinhole. I can still hear you cackling as I lay on the floor in defeat, my rod snapped, chair legless, hammer wedged into the piece of roofing that had ripped down and exposed my carefully-crafted experiments to much more than a pinhole of UV light. Light that was quickly igniting my legs and burning my favorite pants."

He chuckled softly. "I experienced defeat that day. That pumpkin mocked me, not a dent in the goddamn thing. And it was carved to look like me, down to the freckles. You really were a pain in the ass."

He continued to murmur to his younger brother until the lights of Huntington breached the horizon.

****

Audra gingerly escorted Dahlia to the back seat of

Dominic's car, helping the depleted woman take her place beside Boy, who was quick to adjust his position to provide her with more room. She briefly met the unaffected gray eyes of Louis as he filled the gas tank.

Nothing but a flash of mild concern. No guilt. No questions.

With Cam Pewter's card still tucked in her hand, she grabbed her bag and headed back into the convenience store, ignoring Nichol's gaze the entire time. The questionable cleanliness of the restroom had her changing her clothing slowly, ensuring not a single thread grazed the sticky tile floor. After she laced her combat boots, she returned to the fuel pumps where Nichol and Louis were finishing up.

"Why have you changed?" Nichol inquired, frowning. "We'll be in Vansburg in just over two hours."

She lifted the hatch of the SUV and carefully laid her work attire on top of the electronics cases. "I don't want to get blood on them."

"You will not—"

"I will," she interrupted while she ducked down to move the front seat as far forward as it would go before placing her bag on the seat. "It's not up for discussion."

Nichol growled low in his chest as he watched her proceed to climb into the back with Mick, using the hump in the middle of the floor as a perch. He replaced the gas cap and checked that Louis was ready to leave. "If you insist, you will ride up here where his access to you is limited."

She ignored him, her hand brushing Mickey's hair from his face as his muscles twitched and jerked. She reached into her bag and pulled out a bag of blood.

"That won't be effective," Nichol warned. "Jagger's injuries have surpassed the usefulness of bagged blood. I believe that's what's driving Mikhail right now."

She tore a small hole in the plastic before pinching a small amount onto her fingers. "Why is that? Why is fresh better than bagged?"

"Oxygenation," Nichol replied tersely. "Fresh blood carries oxygen more efficiently, making it the better option. Bagged eventually improves, but it's slow to achieve the level required for healing."

She placed a bloodied finger in Mick's mouth, allowing him to taste the offering on his tongue. When he stilled, she repeated the action. "I never considered that. The blood carries the oxygen you need. Not your lungs. That's actually very cool."

Nichol grunted as he increased his speed on the highway. "That won't satisfy him for long."

"Better than draining Dahlia," she retorted, her fingers staining.

"Dahlia is expendable. You aren't."

She clenched her teeth. "How can you guys be so callous about the women you sleep with? Basic decency aside, there must be some part of those ice hearts that feels something for the Tenders after a while."

With a glance in the rearview mirror, Nichol's hazel eyes met hers. "I don't sleep with the women in our employ."

She used her bloodless pinky finger to move a stray blond lock from Mick's forehead before she resumed feeding him. "But you never leave the…are you celibate?" she asked incredulously. The idea that such a highly sexualized species would elect to avoid sex was intriguing. More so given how well-equipped she knew the angry vampire was.

Nichol remained silent, his eyes trained on the road ahead.

Shaking the conversation from her head, she returned to her initial complaint. "Regardless, you do feed from them. I would think you'd have some level of tie to them, some tiny grain of compassion."

"As you feel for chickens?"

She laughed quietly, ever aware of the panting vampire under her hand. "Humans aren't chickens. We have emotions. And cognitive thoughts. And language."

"So because you can communicate to me that your feelings are hurt, your value in the food chain is superior. Yes?"

She frowned. "Well, yes. It's like cannibalism. You used to be human once, too."

"But I am no longer. My molecular structure is as different from yours as a cow's would be. Therefore, it's not cannibalism and you are like a cow on my plate."

Taking a deep, centering breath, she refocused her efforts on Mickey. "I think I know why you're celibate."

Time crawled as Mickey twisted and turned in the cramped space. His movements were slow enough for her to anticipate, her fingers having only been grazed once along his fangs.

Despite the twinge of guilty voyeurism she felt, she used the opportunity to examine him. His blue eyes had flickered open intermittently but showed little more than a swirling torment. There was no sweat on his forehead when she ran her pinky over his brows. Over and over, she alternated between placing blood on Mick's tongue and trailing her clean fingers over his features in an attempt to soothe him. A particularly intense convulsion brought Mick's fangs close to her eyes, and she marveled at the length of them before curiosity overcame her and she reverently ran a bloodied finger over one.

Mick stilled, the tension in his muscles reducing a fraction. She continued to stroke the fang, watching the blood from her hand as it covered the faint silver glimmer. She changed her angle, fluttering across the sides to better examine the slight curve of the canine. It was reminiscent of a viper, serving a dual purpose of puncture and hooking. Becoming more daring, she ghosted her fingertip across the tip, flinching away as the razor sharpness sliced cleanly across her skin.

"That's a dangerous game," Nichol said quietly. "Your blood is palatable. Much more so than the swill you're feeding him."

She moved to wipe her bleeding finger on her cargo pants and hesitated, reaching her arm into the front of the vehicle. "You want?"

In the mirror, she could see Nichol's hazel eyes darken slightly as they zeroed in on the crimson droplets. She waved her hand a little, knowing the scent of her blood would further entice the reticent male. When his mouth opened slightly, she grinned and cocked her finger toward his tongue as he closed his lips around the wound.

"Isn't this nice," she conversed cheekily. "You, eating. Me, not dying. No screaming, no death. Just sharing a meal like best buddies do."

Nichol rolled his eyes but didn't release her finger.

"We could make it a weekly thing. I'll snack on popcorn, you can snack on my finger. We could watch a cheesy rom-com. I'll tell you about some loser I'm dating, you can bitch about work. Besties."

Nichol opened his mouth, freeing her hand and freshly-sealed wound. "Fine. But we're watching zombie movies."

****

Rhys drank deeply, reveling in the warmth of Simone's body. Her arm muscles had given out ages ago, leaving it up to him to hold her flush to his chest as he rocked inside of her. Her cries for harder and faster had dissipated an hour earlier as Simone's voice became hoarse, her Boston accent making a resurgence as she lost herself to centuries of skills.

He threw his head back, gripped her hips, and pounded into the woman, hunting for one more release before he skulked back to the communication room. The sheen of sweat on Simone's lithe body made her skin glisten in the lamplight, the scent of her body cocooning him against reality.

As her body clenched around him again, his thrusts increased in intensity and speed until he felt Simone's walls fluttering around him, pulling his own orgasm from him with a curse.

He pulled out of the warm body and patted the smooth skin of Simone's ass before he strode naked toward her shower. The hot stream beat on his tight shoulders, doing little to relax the knot that had formed over the past week. His self-imposed banishment from the com room early yesterday evening had done nothing to soften the edges of his temper. Dominic had stopped by shortly after sunset to inform him the boots on the ground were mobile.

And that Kai was struggling to hide his outward reactions to Jagger's assault.

He wrapped a towel around his hips and left Simone's room, the woman giving him a faint smile when he passed her. Her price would be high, he mused as he entered his own bunk in the Tender quarters. Higher if they could nip the accent, but there were a few potential buyers who would find it a charming quirk. Once Jagger was returned to the haunt, he would be placing Simone among the haunt Tenders to make room for a new trainee.

Or two.

With Simone out of the training room and Molly living almost exclusively in Dominic's bunk, he would have the space to house two potential Tenders. It had been a long time since he had taken on two women at once, but it had been an effective method in the past. Word on the grapevine was that there was a pair of Tenders being considered for surrender up north.

And the Tender pool in the haunt was depleting at a rapid rate.

His feet bare, he padded through the dim hallway toward the communication room. Molly met him outside the door.

"I did a run to the mailbox today," she said by way of hello. "A few boxes didn't fit into the minivan, though, so I'll head back tomorrow."

He cocked a brow. "Who are the boxes for?"

"Jagg, mostly," she replied, her feet moving quickly toward the garage. "Little help? Dom and Kai are busy on their computers."

He hooked his thumbs in his cargos and strode

after Molly, catching up quickly. "I wonder if that's the Deepfryer he was anxious to purchase," he mumbled quietly. "He's waited months for it to arrive."

The hatch to the Tender minivan was open. And packed.

"You got all this in yourself?" he asked in amusement at the precarious balance of the boxes.

With a grin, Molly pulled a few long packages out and passed them to him, swatting his hands away from assisting. "I know how I put them in. You'll screw up the system if you touch it."

Molly's system was as scattered as her mind, the pile in his arms growing taller and less stable with every addition. "I'll put these in his office and come back for the rest."

The air mail stamp was a clear indication Jagger's Deepfryer had finally arrived. Judging from the multitude of boxes, it had been completely disassembled for undercover transport. He took his time arranging the packages in Jagger's work room, a small enclave off the sparring room.

In it were subtle reminders of the inhabitant.

Hooded sweatshirts hanging on the chairs.

Dozens of blades scattered on the work bench.

Sloppy diagrams pinned haphazardly to the walls.

The place was an organized disaster.

When he returned to the garage, Molly began loading his arms again. "I hope Audra gets back soon," Molly chattered. "It's so quiet around here, what with Amy gone, then Dahlia and Audra. Simone's cool, but we don't have much in common. She's pretty you-focused. And I don't like you much."

He chuckled as Molly smiled cheekily at him.

"She'll snap out of that soon enough. It's a normal facet of the training. Not that you'd know." He bared his fangs at his worst trainee, who proceeded to pile another box to his already unsteady load. "What about Justine?"

Molly frowned. "I get how this Tender thing works. I do. But…"

Peering over the packages, he urged her on with a look.

"She's all over Kaius. I'm not saying it's bad, it's just weird because she and Jagger seemed kind of like a thing. Like Mick and Amy. Though I guess that's not a great example. Anyways, she hasn't really been interested in hearing any updates on anything. It's like Jagger's not here so he's out of sight, out of mind."

He adjusted his grip and walked out of the garage. "Give me a minute and I'll be back."

He moved swiftly through the corridor. He had also noticed Justine's lack of interest in Jagger's well-being, her involvement in any discussion beginning and ending with an offered wrist to Kai. He had ignored it initially, pleased his Tender wasn't avoiding his antisocial, ancient creator.

However, with Molly recognizing the same indifference, Justine's behavior was odd given Molly, Audra, and Dahlia's enthusiastic participation. He deposited the packages with less care and made his way to the Tender quarters.

"Justine?" he called outside her bedroom door as he rapped his knuckles on the wood.

The door opened quickly, her blond hair messed from sleep. She scanned the hall briefly, thrown off by Rhys's unexpected visit.

Walking past her, Rhys took a seat on her sofa, his eyes never leaving her face. "Audra will be moving forward during daylight today," he began. "With luck, Jagger will be back here within the week."

Justine nodded. "Good to hear."

"He'll need a pretty constant blood source if his physical damage is as bad as anticipated."

"Of course. Dahlia and I can see to him. Simone as well, if you're willing."

He leaned back. "He may need someone to stay with him consistently for the first few weeks."

"I'm sure we can work out a rotating schedule that meets his needs."

Frowning, he tilted his head. "You wouldn't want that responsibility?"

"If you feel I should."

A tattooed arm stretched across the back of the sofa. "You have no affinity for him at all, do you?"

Justine looked taken aback. "Of course I do. Just as I do for you. And Mick and Louis. And Kai. Nichol and Dom, too."

"But nothing extra for Jagg," he stated.

Justine's eyes narrowed in confusion. "It's not my job to develop preferences. I'm here to respond to need. And right now, Jagger doesn't need me as he once did. But Kaius requires sustenance."

He stood, his comprehension of the situation complete. "You're right. Keep Kaius sated. It's much appreciated. I realize he can be somewhat intimidating."

The perky blonde gave him a bright smile as he left.

Justine. Amy. Even Gabby. Perfect Tenders

molded to be ideal companions and blood sources among the hauntmates. It had been an immaculate system, one that kept the members of the Kaius haunt content.

But when placed side-by-side with the volatile Molly, the headstrong Dahlia, and the authoritative Audra, the perfect Tenders were coming up short in places he had never considered.

Placid obedience was fucking boring.

After they left his training bed, his role with each Tender morphed. As he incrementally relinquished control of the females, he was no longer the women's sole provider.

They became functional members of the haunt, with Rhys being relegated to a supporting role in their lives as he moved on to a new challenge, blessing his brothers the exquisitely crafted women until a sales agreement was reached. And Justine had fashioned her personality into precisely what Jagger needed, a quiet companion to stave off boredom and curb the loneliness he had carried since his return to the haunt.

He crept up the garage steps, moving stealthily so he could observe Molly without detection. Her long black hair fell in tangled waves down her back as she crawled gracelessly into the back of the minivan. Her smoky voice grumbled creative curses while she maneuvered a heavy box out of its awkward spot. With the box finally shoved to the hatch's opening, Molly sat beside it, her legs spread slightly as she inelegantly contorted to scratch her back.

He moved himself into her view and she greeted him with the flip of her finger. "Nice timing, asshole," she snorted. "I think I pulled my ass muscles getting this thing out."

No, Molly and perfection were not a cohesive match.

"You were gone forever. Did you talk to Justine?" she asked, moving over to make room for him to sit.

"I did," he responded. "She's doing her job. Precisely, to be honest."

Molly hummed, but he couldn't tell if it was in agreement or disagreement.

"When you finish the mail run tomorrow, come get me and I'll unload it for you. Sound good, cupcake?" he asked as he hoisted the last box up.

"Cupcake?" Molly snickered. "Take that one off your rotation. It's terrible."

Chapter Nineteen

"That wasn't the plan," Nichol snarled at Audra as she sat half-naked beside him. Her legs were navigating their way back into the cream suit Meredith Abernathy needed, the faded cargo pants tossed carelessly onto the gear shift.

"Plans change. She's far too weak to be in there. She would be more of a liability than a backup," she countered as she held out her hand for her blouse.

He thrust the garment at her angrily.

The argument had been steadily heating up since they had arrived in Vansburg. "Then we put it off until nightfall. You're not going in there alone. We won't know if anything goes wrong for hours, and by then it could be too late. You will wait."

With a laugh, she shook her head. "You will wait. Okay there, dad. You know damn well I need to get in there as soon as possible. I promise to keep my phone on me at all times, and I'll have the wire on me. It. Will. Be. Fine. Now help Louis get Mickey into the SUV and get your asses to the DeChamplain haunt before the sun comes up and you all fry." Glancing at the car's clock, she frowned. "You have thirty-seven minutes to get inside."

He passed over her shoes, taking the combat boots and setting them below Mick in the back seat. "You're tired. You haven't rested enough to have a clear head.

Your reflexes and observations will be affected. I'm not happy with this."

Flinging her door open, she walked over to Louis to request his assistance. A low rumble of annoyance reverberated through Nichol's chest while he stormed out of the vehicle and opened the door where Mickey lay cramped in the back, his eyes shut tight as he panted heavily.

Pushing her way in front of Nichol, she ran a hand along Mick's brow. "Poor guy can't take much more of this," she murmured as she attempted to soothe Mickey. "Be gentle getting him out."

Nichol hefted Mick out by the arms as Louis swooped in and grabbed his legs, carefully folding Mick in the back of the sports car and wedging him upright between Boy and Louis.

Nichol got into the driver's seat and called to her quietly. "Getting Jagg out is secondary to keeping him and yourself safe right now, got it?"

With a final salute, she drove off.

****

"I'm here," Audra said softly, knowing Nichol would pick up her whisper. The lack of verbal confirmation from his end was unnerving, but they had decided an earpiece would be far too noticeable and could impede the mission. It also left her on her own to read the situation as it evolved and react as she saw fit.

It was, in a word, stressful.

The stone building was smaller than she had envisioned and finding a parking spot had been far less of a hassle than she had anticipated. With her falsified documents and identification in hand, she marched into the station. A balding man in his mid-fifties glanced up from his desk, unimpressed with the early morning interruption.

She pulled out her ID, sliding it across the counter. "Good morning. I'm here on behalf of a vampire prisoner being held here."

The man's brows raised in surprise before he schooled his expression. "We don't have any vamps here," he lied, his eyes flicking to a door at the end of the short hall.

She steeled her expression. "My name is Meredith Abernathy, and I'm a lawyer representing a Mr. Luciano Othario. Witnesses have placed his last known location in the custody of your law enforcement." She placed a folder on the counter, opening it to reveal a perfectly forged photo identification for Jagger, aka Luciano Othario.

The officer picked up the paper, squinting as though trying to place the face. "Lemme check in the back and I'll be right back. Take a seat over there."

She collected her papers and nodded, refusing to sit on the dingy sofa as she looked around casually, noting the single exterior exit and three solid doors leading out of the reception area. The balding man returned quickly, a pale man in an ill-fitting suit following hot on his heels.

He sized her up with his dark eyes. "Detective Whitman. You are?"

With a firm shake of his hand, she stared the man down. "Meredith Abernathy, attorney. I'm here representing Luciano Othario."

"No one here by that name," the detective stated, his hands shoving into his pockets.

Pulling the identification photo from her file, she

pushed it into the man's line of sight. "If not that name, how about that face?"

The detective swung his head back slightly. "He's in custody."

"What are the charges?"

Walking behind the desk and pulling a folder out from a cabinet, Whitman sneered. "Refusal to register. Refusal to disclose. Non-cooperation. Assaulting an officer."

She narrowed her eyes. "Why was he apprehended in the first place?"

With a smile, the detective closed the file and returned it to its place. "Suspected murder. I'm sure you understand. Strange vampire, dead woman. Dots connect."

"When can I see my client?"

He flinched slightly, his hesitance swift but notable. "He's resting now, but if you want to make an appointment to see him tonight, I'm sure it can be arranged."

She chuckled low. "No. I'll be seeing him immediately. You see, Detective Whitman, I have it on good authority that your men have been pushing the laws of interrogation past the legal line. Into the Geneva Convention zone, as a matter of fact. Escort me to my client now, or I bring the media into it. And I assure you, sir, it will not end well for you."

The detective's lips pursed as he contemplated how serious she was. She could see the man's mind working, attempting to calculate the damage his career and reputation would receive if the media threat came to fruition. "Follow me, Ms. Abernathy."

Her heels clicked against the cement steps as they

descended into the basement. An overpowering stench of decay and death permeated her senses, watering her eyes. She grit her teeth. "You're the lead detective, I assume?" she inquired, the hostility in her voice palpable.

"I oversee, but my men are independent in their investigations."

Rat bastard, she seethed. Already laying the groundwork to shift blame for Jagger's treatment on to his subordinates.

A security door opened to reveal two young guards warily eying a barred enclosure. She glared at the detective before advancing on the cell.

"You'll want to stay back, Ma'am," one of the guards warned. "He's a violent one."

Peering into the corner of the darkened chamber, she could see the remains of what looked like a mattress strewn across the floor, a malformed metal frame blocking her view from a shadow hunched in the corner.

"When did he last eat?" she demanded, her voice strong despite the tears threatening her composure.

Detective Whitman stared hard at the young guards. "Last night. Gentlemen, this is Ms. Abernathy. Our resident vampire is Luciano Othario. Ms. Abernathy is his lawyer."

The guards shared a quick look of concern. "We tried getting the broken bed out of there, ma'am, but it's just not safe. You should stand back. He's unpredictable."

She straightened her back. "Open the cell."

Detective Whitman moved to her side, shaking his head at the guards. "I can't allow that. Your client is exhibiting violent behaviors. I can't guarantee your safety if you go in there."

"I can smell the burnt skin from here," she hissed. "Bring me some bagged blood and unlock the cell."

A guard cleared his throat. "We don't got any blood here, ma'am."

Her eyes fixated on Jagger, she snarled. "Then get some. Because I know starving a prisoner is definitely not on the approved list of interrogation techniques, am I right, Detective Whitman?"

The detective murmured to the guards briefly before both young men raced up the stairs. He brought the key to the cell over and unlocked it, rattling the lock more than necessary. "I assume you understand the risks of cavorting with clients such as yours," he sneered. "Blood has been ordered. Might be a bit, though. Priority is human usage, of course."

She carefully nudged at the cell, steeling herself to face Jagger. As the gate swung open, Jagg's arms swung out, knocking the warped metal frame away from him. Her eyes were adjusting to the low light, Jagg's form slowly becoming more detailed.

The clang of the cell door closing and locking barely registered.

She crouched down and removed her heels, shuffling forward with deliberate motions to avoid sudden movements. The extent of Jagger's physical damage was unknown, so she approached him as one might a wounded lion, extending her hand and wiggling her finger slightly in the hopes her scent would cut through the foul stench in the cell.

Nothing.

She turned slowly, her control nearing the breaking

point. "My client has been, for lack of a better word, tortured under your watch."

"Funny loophole," the pale man mused as he sauntered toward the security door. "Vamps are their own species. Not human. You may have a case of animal abuse on your hands, but even that would be a stretch, Ms. Abernathy. I'll give you and your client some privacy. Good luck."

Animal abuse.

Audra squeezed her eyes shut, shaking the thought from her head.

Nichol had heard that.

Louis.

Kaius and Rhys.

Strong, proud males labeled as animals in the eyes of the law.

Below animals.

The hooded sweatshirt Jagg wore was shredded, holes and singed edges revealing open wounds in flashes when he pulled his large frame further into the corner. His cargo pants were in slightly better shape, the sturdy fabric charred but holding together. Her heart clenched as she realized the cell was absolutely silent, save her ragged breath.

The absence of Jagg's trademark humming tore at her.

She skimmed further into his space, her wrist an offering of blood and help. Jagg remained motionless, his eyes obscured by the hood of his shirt. She reached her other hand into her jacket pocket, pulling a small vial out before discarding the jacket behind her. With her eyes on him, she popped the cap off and dipped her finger into it before extending her arm closer.

Seconds passed as the two remained inanimate. Then, with a labored jerk, Jagg's head lifted, his fangs fully extended. His nose twitched slightly, scenting the rancid air. She held her position, her anxiety reducing with every passing moment Jagger didn't attack. His arm lifted, heavy with effort, and reached in her direction. She fought the urge to further close the gap between them and allowed the injured vampire to search the empty air until his hand brushed hers. His long fingers toyed with her own, inadvertently transferring the blood from her finger to his own. His hand retracted toward his face, drawing her eyes to Jagg's.

Opals.

The cloudy whites of his eyes blended seamlessly into the damaged white haze of his irises, creating a haunting, soul-tearing stare. He wasn't unfocused, because nothing recognizable remained to be unfocused. Silent tears rolled down her cheeks as she fully accepted the brutality Jagger had faced in the human jail. She watched him gingerly bring his bloodied finger to his nose before running his tongue down the length of it.

She ventured forth, her movements smoother as all care for the cleanliness of her clothing disappeared. Jagger tensed, sensing her approaching form. She dipped her finger into the vial again, a peace offering. Jagg caught the scent quickly, his aim more true as he sought out her hand and brought it to his mouth. Her finger cleaned of blood, he slowly turned her hand, bringing his other arm up toward her face. She closed her eyes as Jagg ghosted his fingertips over her features, examining her chin and cheekbones, her brows and nose. He ran one hand carefully across her hair and the other down her neck.

"Aud…"

Taking his fingers quickly to her lips, she mouthed into his fingers, willing them to read her warning. "Shhhhhhhhhhh."

The movement was subtle, barely visible to the eye, but Jagg nodded. Sealing the vial, she pressed it against his palm, locking her gaze on his pained motions. The imperceptible speed of his blade work seemed like a memory from a thousand years ago as he struggled to coordinate the opening of the vial before putting it to his lips.

Nichol had prepared her for the worst, providing a tube of his blood in case Jagger was unable to recognize her scent. Nic rationalized that at his significant age, which he stubbornly refused to disclose, his blood would amp whatever stagnant meals Jagger received, and would double as a message of safety for her to pass along to Jagg. The male retreated back slightly, turning his head away from her view.

"What the fuck," she whispered, leaning forward to peer at Jagger's profile. She stretched toward his blinded eyes, entranced by the markings now adorning his once pristine skin.

Tattoos.

Her fingers skimmed the slate-colored design briefly, pulling back as Jagger lowered his head further from her reach. Taking his hand in both of hers, she helped him lead her wrist to his fangs, silently encouraging him to feed. He balked at the offer, angling his head away and she repeated the action, pressing her skin against the razor tips.

"Come on, Jagger," she whispered to deaf ears as she scored her skin on his canines, forcing the issue.

The pain was intense, causing her stomach muscles to tense and contract. Her balance wavered momentarily until his long arm steadied her against his side, his strength propping her until the hurt turned into a pulsing ache. He adjusted his bite, his fangs no longer buried to the hilt in her veins. As the minutes crawled by, she whispered into her mic.

"He's been badly burnt. All over. His eyes are completely white. He can't hear or see, so I can't communicate. Nichol, if you're listening, the blood was a spectacular idea. Jagg's eating right now. And it fucking hurts. Remind me to thank Mick for having smaller teeth. Because damn. I'm waiting for the guards to return with blood, but he needs so much. And Mick took so…I don't think the good Detective is eager to let him go anytime soon."

With a deliberate movement, Jagger released her wrist, his hand wrapping around the puncture wounds as he lay his head on his knee. The pair sat motionless in the dim light, Audra fighting the exhaustion of blood loss as Jagger's opal eyes stared into the abyss.

Chapter Twenty

The coarse cement scratched across Audra's back as she was unceremoniously shoved behind Jagger. The male was on his feet, crouched and snarling toward the cell bars.

"Glad to see you still among the living, Ms. Abernathy," Detective Whitman called out, his voice oozing with contempt. "Your client doesn't appear any more cooperative with you than he was with us."

She stood, fruitlessly brushing the dirt from her pants. "He's been remarkably cooperative," she snarked. "Perhaps he doesn't care for your communication methods, Detective."

The pale man moved closer to the bars, peering around Jagger. "Visiting hours are over."

Placing a staying hand on Jagg's shoulder, she moved past him to collect her suit jacket. Jagg's growl grew louder, but he remained stationary. She took her time, picking up her folder of papers, adjusting the sleeves of her shirt, slipping her heels on. "That blood on its way, Detective?"

"Like I said, it takes time. Priorities and all."

She faced Jagger, placing both hands on his shoulders to center his attention. His opal eyes dropped to her level and he cocked his head. "I'll petition the courts for your release," she said loudly for Detective Whitman's benefit. "And will return tonight." As she spoke, she brought her fingers down and traced a message on his chest. "I. Will. Return."

The cell lock clicked, indicating the good Detective was becoming impatient. Seething, she allowed him to lead her up the stairs into the waiting room before she launched into him.

"What do those markings mean?" she demanded. "You tagged him like a goddamn farm animal."

The detective smirked, his hands shoved deep in his pockets. "The law states all vamps must be registered, physically marked with the government-designated symbol, and must provide their address to law enforcement for verification. Your client was unregistered and has refused to cooperate. He gives up his location, we check it out, and he goes with you on his merry little way. But until I have a verified address, he's mine."

"You're willing to make a deal," she stated. "A bigger target, perhaps? A little bump for your career? Small town cop takes down a big-time vamp ring?"

The detective's eyes remained impassive. "Return tonight with some useful info, and maybe I'll find some flexibility."

She turned on her heel and out the door. Her mind knew she needed to get to the DeChamplain haunt, to meet up with the others and establish a plan. But the guilt of leaving Jagger behind tore at her composure. Once she was on the highway, she pulled out the burner phone Nichol had handed her mere hours ago.

"I'm here," she said, her voice wavering as she assessed the area for other vehicles. "Where to?"

Committing Nichol's directions to memory, she listened in silence.

"Audra?" Nichol's voice called through the speaker. "Confirm."

She took a deep, focusing breath. "Got it. I'm hanging up and taking off the wire."

"The wire stays," Nichol growled. "Until you arrive."

"Nichol. Kaius. Whoever else is listening. I am going to have a good, long cry. Then I'm going to drive to you, eat, give my report, and go to bed. In that order. A few minutes of privacy right now would be much appreciated."

****

"She's injured and not telling us," Nichol hissed furiously. "Boy. You will fix her when she arrives."

"Perhaps one of the DeChamplain Tenders could go pick her up," Kaius suggested over the speaker. "Blood loss compounded by an injury may affect her ability to drive."

"I'll send one of them," he replied, bringing the phone with him as he moved quickly toward the staircase leading to the main haunt in search of a Tender. "I suspect her body may be going into shock. Human systems are significantly more fragile."

Rhys's voice, distorted over the phone connection, chimed in. "She's fine."

"She is not fine," he barked, motioning to a short brunette. "This has been going on for well over fifteen minutes."

The petite woman was quick to Nichol's side. DeChamplain had been extremely accommodating to the Kaius hauntmates, offering shelter, food, and the use of his Tenders for any unexpected errands during daylight hours.

"She's crying it out," Rhys stated. "It's a common thing for women. Instead of killing something or beating on someone, they release frustration through crying."

He frowned. "Audra isn't a Tender."

"She is a woman, though," Rhys chuckled. "And frankly, I'm way more in tune with how women work than either of you."

Shaking his head at the brunette, he returned to the office where he and Boy had taken up position. "You assure me there is no injury. She's unable to answer her phone." He had dialed Audra's burner phone repeatedly over the past ten minutes. The mic she wore transmitted every ring in stereo, barely audible over the sobbing that had overtaken the small room.

"She's able," Rhys retorted. "But she doesn't want to. And she is going to be all sorts of pissed-off when she finds out you didn't respect her request and turn off sound to the microphone."

Though faint, he was certain he heard Dom snort. "There's no need for her to know," he said gruffly, settling back in his chair. Boy remained at his back, a statue in the corner. "How long will this continue?"

"Could be five more minutes, could be an hour. I've sat through a few that lasted longer, but those women weren't part cyborg like Audra," Rhys offered.

He ran a hand through his hair and grit his teeth.

Seventeen minutes.

He motioned for Boy to continue monitoring the situation and went to the adjoining room to check on Mick. Louis was propped against the sofa Mickey inhabited, both males resting. Dahlia had disappeared shortly after their arrival, the DeChamplain Tenders bringing her into their fold and assuring them she would be cared for.

Mickey had stabilized as Audra united with Jagger, serving as a secondary confirmation the first part of their plan had been successful.

Nichol's blood had been a last-minute addition, a safeguard for Audra should Jagger be too far gone to recognize her scent. The small vial would provide little healing assistance but would serve to boost whatever bagged blood reached Jagger prior to his release.

Feeding Jagg hadn't been a part of Audra's assignment.

They had discussed it.

He had commanded her to secure blood bags, as she had given Mickey more than she could spare without detriment.

He growled in frustration.

He suggested. She balked. He commanded, she conceded until she was out of his domain and he was powerless to argue.

And now they were entering their twenty-first minute of crying.

Deferring to Rhys's expertise on women was his only beacon against the overwhelming feeling of helpless frustration that had lapped at his psyche since the sobbing began. It was a discomforting state for him, hearing the distress of what he was quickly categorizing as his female counterpart. Only the most critical of injuries elicited any outward reaction from him, and he had just assumed Audra's poise would be affected likewise.

Minute twenty-four brought with it silence. He glanced at Boy but was met with the same empty expression the vampire had worn for centuries.

The sound of an engine starting.

"I should be there in ten," Audra said, her voice strong but wavering. "I know your controlling ass wouldn't let you turn off the mic, Nic, so hello, I'm good now, and do not mention this. Ever."

****

Rhys, Kai, and Dominic re-examined the satellite photos, scrutinizing their every angle and comparing the information against the ground maps that various GPS companies had compiled over the years. Kaius had relaxed infinitesimally once Audra's breakdown was over, his gaze no longer distracted by the offending speakers of the com room. Dominic had remained unaffected, almost amused by Nichol's reaction. Of course, he was bunking with Molly and had had a crash course in dealing with human female emotions.

"Once we make this information available, it will be a declaration of war," Kaius mused. "Are you prepared to face the fallout?"

Nichol's voice broke through. "If Chen and Dovidas are working together against our kind, war is our only option."

"We have allies," Rhys put forth. "And in the unlikely chance Chen is unaware of Dovidas's intentions, he may end Kaspars long before we bring it to his doorstep."

"Bringing human law enforcement into our battle will expose the discord within our species," Kaius warned. "It may be used against you."

"Worse than being legislated below animals?" Rhys scoffed. "If I'm going to go extinct, I'm going down fighting. I'd rather be taken out by Chen than by humans any day. And what's with all this 'you' talk?"

Kaius stilled.

"You're fucking kidding," Nichol snarled over the connection. "We have humans, Dovidas, and possibly Chen on our asses with this move, and you're leaving?"

Rhys stared at his creator, his jaw set. Kai's stoic silence confirmed Nichol's accusations. "We'll make better use of Boy from here on out," he stated, averting his eyes from Kaius. "With Jagger home, Mick will recover quickly, and our numbers will be back on par. I'm disconnecting now but call back once Audra is ready for debriefing."

With the flick of a few buttons, Dominic, Rhys, and Kaius were separated from Nichol's mission.

"Why didn't you warn us before Audra walked in there?" Rhys demanded.

"I received word this morning," Kai replied. "After she had entered Jagger's cell. I'll be leaving at dusk."

Kaius's comings and goings had been a bone of contention among the hauntmates over the centuries, never knowing where, when, how long. Nichol was affected most acutely, his age putting the burden of the haunt's safety squarely on his pissed-off shoulders. Rhys was next in line. Between their combined personalities, they had managed to hold the group together during the long absences, taking over the training of new brothers as they arrived and integrating them seamlessly into the fold.

At almost twice his age, Nichol had initially been reticent in embracing him as both a brother and a comrade. On his own for large chunks of his first six centuries, Nichol had developed an isolationist mentality he was unable to fully escape despite the addition of four younger brethren.

"Will you be reachable?" Dominic inquired.

"Periodically."

The hauntmates had speculated over the years that it was Kaius's own creator who called him away, but none of them had ever happened upon the elusive Khthonios in their travels. None of the males were even certain of the sire's continued existence. Kaius himself was ancient, a rarity among vampires. Few survived their first century, with fewer surviving their first millennium. At well over two thousand, Kaius was a legend, and his children reaped the benefits of his power through allies and name.

He leaned back in his chair, crossed his arms, and glared at the table until the laptop screen sprang to life, and Audra's cat eyes filled the screen.

****

A dainty brunette answered Audra's knock, her smile welcoming her into the DeChamplain haunt. The woman was quick with pleasantries, a soft British lilt to her speech. The offer of food and a shower trumped her desire to discuss the day's events with the males, knowing she would feel more prepared to relive the experience once she was fed and clean. Staying in the upper floors of the house, she regrouped and rejuvenated before descending to the lower levels.

She had to shake the confining cell from her mind. Had to push back the memories the thick metal bars had conjured. Had to wash the foul stenches from her skin before she could take on Nichol's ire.

Squaring her shoulders, she pushed the basement door open and came face-to-face with Nichol. He scented the air, his hazel eyes assessing her face and body for damage.

"You are well."

And with that, the duo made their way into the makeshift communication room.

"Mick's good?" she inquired as the computer fan spun to life.

"He's better. Resting next door with Louis."

"And Dahlia?"

"Resting upstairs."

She tightened the string of her sweatpants and faced the camera. As Kaius, Dominic, and Rhys appeared on the computer screen, she launched into a detailed retelling of what occurred in the Vansburg jail. The males were mostly silent, their agile minds likely creating databases for the information she provided. They probed periodically for further details, their voices flat and unaffected as she described Jagger's physical state. When she described his feeding, Nichol interrupted.

"You were instructed not to feed him."

She rolled her eyes and attempted to continue.

"I explicitly forbade it."

Rhys's brows rose, amusement dancing across his dark features and radiating through the computer screen.

She turned from the camera and looked long and hard at Nichol. "And we both see how effective that was. Continuing on."

The hauntmates began discussing the blatant communication issue she had with Jagger. "He's played his hand well," Audra explained. "I don't believe Detective Whitman has any idea Jagger is deaf. However, with his vision also gone it may become noticeable quickly. I had to resort to drawing on his chest to tell him I would return. How does he not know sign language?"

The males were silent until Kaius took the reins. "Much like humans, vampires watch for anything they can use to their advantage when facing an adversary. For some, their youth is a detriment. For others, it's a lag in strength or speed. Survival is dependent on being able to overcome our personal challenges, to mask them from others who may use them to their advantage, learn to adapt them into our arsenals.

"Jagger is a talented lip reader, and that skill has become quite a weapon for our haunt over the past few decades. His quiet disposition provides a strong cover for his lack of response when he is out of range."

"Perhaps a secondary form of communication would be beneficial for Jagger, and for all of you, to learn once we return," she stated harshly, Jagg's current condition still fresh in her mind. "What do I do tonight when I return? I assume braille is also out of the question."

Kaius stared unblinking. "We have a secondary form of communication, one Jagger is extremely familiar with. Morse Code."

With a huff, she leaned back. "Some of us weren't alive in the 1800s. I don't know Morse Code."

Nichol's fingers tapped rapidly across his phone. A small printer fired up. "Cheat sheet."

She lifted a manicured brow. "Nice. Now on to getting him strengthened. I'm not sure I can feed him again—"

Ignoring him, she continued. "If one of the DeChamplain Tenders can act as my assistant, we can get her to serve as a fresh meal."

"Not going to happen," Louis interjected as he crossed the room to the camera. "DeChamplain's Tenders are active in the town. Too easily recognized. It'll have to be Dahlia."

"She's too weak," Audra argued. "Rhys. Say something."

Rhys averted his attention from the screen.

"Rhys."

His navy eyes looked up, then over to Louis. "Dahlia goes. Sorry, Audra, but we have two guys down right now. The town's too small for Louis to do his mojo on a local woman, and we can't afford to step on DeChamplain's toes. If Nichol is willing to donate a bag of his own blood, Dahlia won't have to give up much. Are we in agreement?"

Quiet murmurs of approval rumbled across the speakers and through the small office as she sighed and nodded her acquiescence to the plan. The males took over the conversation and she slouched down in her chair.

Chapter Twenty-One

Each paper lay precisely atop the next, their corners matching perfectly to create a visually appealing stack. Nichol tucked the meticulously ordered sheets into Audra's file and set them by her shoes. Boy moved silently behind him, adding his own potent blood to the collection before ghosting out of the room.

"Stealthy bastard," Louis muttered from the sofa. "Gives me the creeps every time he's around."

He grunted in agreement. "I want eyes on her location tonight," he ordered. "Mick is stabilized. You'll drive the women there and watch from a distance."

"Sure thing," Louis said as he stood. "I'll go get Dahl ready. You going to wake the bear?"

His eyes flicked to Audra. "I would prefer not to."

He had known the moment Audra had fallen asleep, her breathing low and steady to match her heart rate. The males had discussed strategy after strategy, following each path until they could see the end result.

Every road led to casualties. With human and vampire politics at play, there was no move the Kaius haunt could make that would escape ramifications from either end. A takedown of the jail would be bad publicity at a time when vampires were demonized in the media, and the likelihood of Jagger's face making front page news as a fugitive could cause a witch hunt. Or bring bounty hunters.

Neither choice was palatable.

Bringing human law enforcement down on the Chen haunt would be viewed as an act of war among vampires but could serve as a rallying point against Dovidas and his accomplices.

"If Dovidas is overseas, do we continue to view him as a threat to North American haunts?" Rhys put forth. "If we yank Jagger out, we do little more than up the pressure from humans. A fight on our own soil, against one enemy. If we engage Chen, we bring another front into the fray. And Chen is fuckloads more dangerous than humans."

He mulled the thought over. "If Dovidas is adding Deviants to his retinue, every month we hold off only adds to his strength. Rumors of Chen purposely creating Deviants have been rampant in that area for centuries. If we force them out, force them to relocate, we may buy some time. I believe the Deepfryers are a means to an end for Dovidas. What's his end game?"

Dominic sat back, his eyes dark. "Amass an army, take over the world? You say Chen is over four thousand? Powerful, but probably really out of the modern age. Dovidas is obviously embracing human technology and understands the political climate. Could be a scary combination."

Kaius rose to his feet, his blue eyes scanning the room before landing on the screen. "Nichol, final decisions will defer to you. However, I believe your hauntmates have very valid, very plausible assessments. I will contact you shortly."

He clenched his teeth and ran a hand through his

short hair. Audra hadn't moved in hours, her awkward position holding steady despite raised voices, low growls, and barked orders. He approached her as one might a rabid wolf, prepared for whatever illogical reaction she had to him stirring her. He used one booted foot to nudge the chair. Again. He lifted his toe to the arm rest and jiggled the seat gently. When she remained motionless, he kicked the legs with more force than intended.

Her body tensed, limbs shooting out to steady herself.

"The hell!" she yelled, her eyes scanning the room before falling onto him. "A simple tap on the shoulder would have sufficed, Nichol."

"You need to be ready in ten minutes."

Glaring at him through smudged eye makeup, she stormed from the office to prepare for her evening.

****

Audra listened to Nichol's logic as she rolled her stockings over her knees. Her mind calculated the timeline, cringing when she reached a final number.

"You seriously believe Jagger will be fine with that?" she demanded through the door. "This was supposed to be quick. Another week or two gives that smarmy detective more time to figure out I'm not a lawyer. How long do you think it will be before he puts two and two together and realizes I'm working for vampires? One screw up and we expose the DeChamplain haunt."

"Jagger is useless until he heals, and as long as you can access him, we can feed him. They won't release him until the Chen haunt is positively identified."

"And if they back out of the deal?" she probed.

"We make an example of Vansburg."

She breathed out as she pulled a coral skirt over her hips. "The government will bring in Deepfryers with or without Dovidas," she said quietly.

"It's not the Deepfryers we're stopping," Nichol said, his voice muffled through the door. "It's whatever Dovidas is using them to achieve. We were too slow to the game and have no organized assistance. Allies, yes, but a coherent plan of defense, no. We strike now, we may buy a few months to join forces with others. Dovidas is ambitious. A war profiteer. And he's now hooked up with one of the oldest haunts in the world."

She opened the door. "If he plays his cards right, the humans will do his dirty work for him? Is that your thought, to beat him at his own game?"

Nichol nodded and walked alongside her as they exited the house, passing her a small cloth bag that held two bags of blood. Louis and Dahlia sat in the car, watching her expectantly. Accepting the pile of folders and blood from Nichol, she arranged herself in the back seat. Dahlia looked pale, her trademark perkiness lacking the vibrancy her presence usually brought.

"Let me do all the talking," she said to Dahlia. "I'm tossing as much jargon in as I can right now, but Whitman seems suspicious."

Louis met her eyes in the rear-view mirror. "I could help with that."

"Nichol and I considered that," she stated, "but we worry about the paper trail that exists already. And then there's the guards. The officer at the desk. I'm not sure how many people work in the building, or how much communication has been made with the FBI vamp division. An unsanctioned release would be questioned and could bring a lot more heat to haunts in the area."

The vehicle slowed to a stop around the corner from the police station and she assisted Dahlia out of the car. Louis motioned toward a secluded alley a few hundred feet away and waved the women off.

She and Dahlia were greeted by an older woman at the desk. Her graying hair was held back with distractingly juvenile monkey barrettes.

"How can I help y'all?" she asked in a sweet lilting accent.

She rested her elbows on the counter. "I'm the lawyer representing the vampire you have in custody. Detective Whitman is expecting me this evening."

The woman smiled, her straight teeth bright against her pink lipstick. "Ah yes! Leonard mentioned you would be arriving. I'll go let him know you're here."

Dahlia sat quietly on a faded chair, her hands folded neatly in her lap. The cheery woman reappeared with a wave. "Leo will be out shortly. He can take you down to the holding cell."

She nodded and moved to a corner of the small reception area, her eyes scanning the room for recording devices. Minutes passed. The woman at the desk clicked away on her computer, pausing to smile at her intermittently. As the twenty-minute mark approached, the receptionist finally broke the silence.

"I was thirty-six when the exposure occurred," she opened, glancing toward Whitman's closed office door. "My children were all school age by then. I remember thinking what a magical world they would be inhabiting, one where these mythical creatures would live alongside us ordinary people." She paused, her eyes softening.

"It was an exciting time, wasn't it? You would be too young to remember when they were nothing more than fairy tale monsters, I suppose. But me? I grew up watching movies and reading books about vampires. I never dreamed they would be real."

Audra adjusted her stance. The woman was correct. She had just turned twelve when the first reports broke across the newswire. The fascination and fear was palpable across the globe, but in the eyes of a young girl, vampire existence was still in the realm of possibilities. It had only been two years prior that she had learned the truth of Santa Claus.

She had still been on the fence about the Easter Bunny.

"I've never met a vampire," the woman mused aloud. "I've seen them on television. Perhaps passed them on the streets while visiting the bigger centers. But living up here, we don't see much outside traffic."

She smiled at the woman. "Until Luciano Othario, of course."

When the woman's head shook in denial, her barrettes clanged quietly. "Leonard and James were quick to confine him downstairs. I've seen him, but that's very different from meeting him, isn't it?"

"Perhaps Detective Whitman will allow me to introduce you," she said, her mind cataloguing the openness of the elderly lady.

"I would love to," the woman breathed. "I realize I should be petrified of Mr. Othario. But he was quite the handsome beast when he was brought in." She blushed, causing Audra to chuckle as she caught Whitman's door opening.

"He's definitely a hottie," she whispered with a

wink.

The woman beamed, her cheeks pink with excitement. "Well, honey, my name is Clarice. And I would be honored to meet your client."

"Meredith," she said, walking over to shake the woman's hand.

Detective Whitman emerged from his office, his pale face sporting a sour glare. He strode over to her as his eyes moving suspiciously between her and Dahlia. "No visitors."

"She's my assistant."

"No. Visitors."

Her eyes narrowed at the miserable man. "Fine. Take me to him. Dahlia, you wait here and hold my phone."

She followed the detective down the back steps, tapping her foot impatiently as he disarmed the security door. She pushed past him, ignoring the young guards as her eyes adjusted to the dim lighting.

Jagger had resumed his crouched position in the far corner of the cell, his face shrouded by his hood. "Has he fed?" she demanded as she set the blood bags down, removed her suit jacket, and hooked her unusable glasses into the breast pocket.

The guards shared a glance. "No, ma'am. The medical clinic in town said blood is fo—"

"Humans, yes," she barked. "Withholding nutrition is against the law, Whitman."

The detective gave her a tightlipped smile. "Against the law to starve a human or animal, Ms. Abernathy. And we established yesterday that your client falls into that little gray area."

She looked pointedly at the lock.

"First, we deal," the detective said, dismissing the guards with the wave of his hands. "Then you can go in."

"Present your terms," she posed, crossing her arms.

"Hand me a bigger target," he stated. "Something for me to pass on to the big guys. Once they confirm it, your client is free."

She rifled through her folder, passing the detective an agreement Nichol had drawn up in anticipation. "Sign this, and I hand over information on one of the oldest groups of vampires in the world. Once I fax a copy to my office, you can phone in your intel."

Detective Whitman's eyes lit up briefly as he scanned the papers. Nichol had made an impressive copy of an official document, his attention to detail immaculate. Whitman moved toward the security door. With a quick glance at Jagger's immobile form, she followed.

****

Nichol stared intently at his young brother. He and Boy had relocated Mick to the floor of the office so he could maintain a continual monitoring of his phones, fax, computer, and younger brother. Mickey had become restless, shifting aimlessly on the floor since shortly after Louis had texted his scouting location. One of the DeChamplain Tenders had come by after Audra left, offering her wrist for the injured male. Although a few drops from her scored skin had made it down his throat, Mick had turned his head away, refusing more from the unknown woman.

The fax machine whirred to life, spitting out page after page onto the floor. He collected the papers, scanning them for a signature.

Detective Whitman was an ambitious man.

Audra's precise handwriting graced the papers, each change to the original document sloppily initialed by the detective.

Nightly visits from Luciano Othario's lawyer until his release.

Unobstructed nightly feedings under Meredith Abernathy's supervision.

All communication with Luciano Othario to be carried out through Meredith Abernathy.

Discontinued use of enhanced sound interrogation on Luciano Othario.

Discontinued use of sensory elimination techniques on Luciano Othario.

Discontinued use of UV light on Luciano Othario.

He snarled.

Audra had done a spectacular job of identifying the outside forces that could impede Jagger's recovery. He flipped through the pages, his eyes hunting for the detective's signature alongside the most important part of the document, the promised release of Jagger within 24 hours of a confirmed haunt location, with a maximum retention time of one week from the date of signing.

He smirked as he saw Audra's precise addendum alongside the release clause. Jagger was to be released between the hours of 10pm and 4am, a guarantee he would not be sent into the sunlight in retaliation. Firing off a quick message to Rhys, he settled in his chair and began working on hacking into the FBI vamp division communication lines.

****

Detective Whitman worked quickly to release the

lock on Jagger's cell, the documents he needed to locate the Chen haunt held tight in his fist. With a bag of blood in each hand, Audra inched past the foul man and listened for the clicking of the lock and his retreating footfalls. Jagg's fingers twitched along the cement floor as she stepped closer to him, pausing to remove her shoes and watching while his head slowly turned in her direction.

The milkiness of his damaged eyes had turned mercurial, the hue replicating the color of the tattoos now adorning his face. Jagger rose to his feet, his body primed for attack. She punctured one of the blood bags, held it out, and shook the liquid slightly to encourage the scent to reach the tense male. Dark brows furrowed in confusion for a moment before a hand reached out. She placed the bag in his hand, careful to run his fingers along the lacerated opening, then watched as Jagg brought the bag to his lips and haltingly emptied its contents into his mouth.

"Boy," he muttered, his voice rough.

Assured of his cognizance, she brought Jagger's hand to her face and waited until he had identified her before lowering herself to the floor at his feet. Jagg followed, his sterling eyes staring blankly ahead. They sat together for over an hour, still and silent, before Jagger adjusted his position. His hands roved up her body, settling on either side of her head.

"Are we alone?" he whispered.

She nodded, covering his hands with her own.

"May I speak freely?"

****

Jagger could feel the graveled vibration of his voice as he spoke. His fingers wrapped into the hair of the woman before him, reveling in the warmth her hands provided over his. The scent of Boy's blood had thrown him temporarily, leaving him unsure as to the identity of his visitor until she had forced his hands to her features. The intake of Audra's blood earlier had jump started his healing, with the worst of his surface burns transitioning from debilitating pain to a persistent thrum. Small flashes of light had pierced his mind as evening approached, signaling an improvement in his destroyed eyes as well.

Audra answered question after question about the mission, with him fighting off the frustration of being limited to yes and no inquiries. Her initial attempt at Morse Code was valiant, but pathetic. It took her forever to tap out the most basic responses, leaving him to revert to feeling the nods or shakes of her head after each question. When her head remained still, he would rethink, rephrase, and search for greater details on his rescue.

Specifics of the mission were difficult to ascertain, but he was relieved to discover that his hauntmates were trading information on another haunt's location in exchange for his freedom, as negotiated by Audra. Every so often, she would provide a slow, labored answer to a question, her fingers tapping his palm gently. Within the week, he would be out of the cell and away from the pale detective's interrogation techniques.

"You'll bring blood every night?" he inquired, his desire to heal amplified by his impending release.

A nod.

Audra's hands left his, her head turning slightly away from him before the telltale feel of plastic brushed his fingertips. He scented the air, his fangs running long as he recognized his eldest brother's blood. He gulped the bag down greedily.

Nichol and Boy's offerings intermingled in his body, surging forth to repair his charred flesh and seared retinas. He sat back against the wall, his balance compromised as the aged blood of his hauntmates flowed freely through him.

Audra's arms reached around him, attempting to steady his position.

"I'm fine," he muttered quietly, basking in the elevated mood washing over him. "You would identify this as being drunk."

In his hazed mind, he could sense Audra pulling back. His arms searched the air for her, bringing her tight to his side as he began humming. The shaking of her shoulders and raising of her cheeks against his ribs told him she found his condition amusing.

He was okay with that.

****

Nichol glared across the room, his teeth bared.

"Put him in the shower," he snarled at Boy. "A cold shower."

Mick grinned as Boy hoisted him up off the floor. "You joining me?" he called out to Nichol as Boy dragged him away, Mickey's feet barely keeping up.

He rubbed the back of his neck. If vampires could feel muscle knots, that is precisely where it would be. Audra's wire sat on the desk, mocking him for his lack of attention to detail.

A half hour had passed since Mickey woke, his eyes focusing for the first time since the hotel room in Louisville. Boy had been quick to bring a few bags of blood from the cooler while Nichol assessed his brother and brought Rhys up on the laptop.

Moments later, Mick had delved into complete lunacy.

"What the fuck is he doing?" Rhys demanded, his eyes trained behind Nichol. He glanced over to see Mick sitting with his back against the wall, knees bent, rolling his head back and forth against the plaster.

"Hey Rhys!" Mick called out, his fangs laying long on his lip. "Where's Dom? Dommie. Dominator. Dominatrix…" He trailed off, chuckling to himself.

He eyed Mick warily as Rhys began muttering under his breath. "Nichol. Fucker's blood-drunk."

"Impossible," he retorted, hazel eyes narrowing as Mickey began mumbling about Audra.

Dominic appeared on the screen. "Molly gets like that after too much wine," he offered. "I had no idea we could get wasted." He looked over at Rhys accusingly.

"This is bullshit," Nichol barked. "Mick. Get up."

Mickey grinned, his blond hair flopping into his eyes as he fought himself to his feet and thumped backwards against the wall for support.

"Nichol," Rhys began slowly. "Is this him, or Jagger?"

He stared at the empty doorway where Boy and Mick had exited. The combination of his blood with Boy's was a risk factor he should have anticipated. At Nichol's age, his blood was far more potent than that of a vampire centuries younger. Add that to the elusive Boy's blood and Jagger was probably experiencing a high unlike any he had ever had.

Mick was receiving the residual.

And Nichol knew better.

He knew better than most what ancient blood could

do.

He turned to his monitor, his jaw set. "Rhys. Can you think of anything that will lessen this? If Mikhail is this incapacitated, Audra may find Jagger to be far more than she can handle.

Is there a risk to her safety?"

Chapter Twenty-Two

Audra closed her eyes, sighing in annoyance as she relaxed against Jagger's chest. Without her phone, she was unsure how many hours she had been held hostage in the firm cage of the seemingly intoxicated vampire. Her only hope of escaping the nuzzling at her neck was dawn's impending arrival. Fleeting thoughts of calling for Detective Whitman to unlock the cell had danced across her mind, but in Jagger's inebriated state it was too great a safety risk.

So she stayed put, her arms and legs intertwined with Jagg's limbs.

Every so often, she would crane her head to look into his mercurial eyes, marveling as the pupils and irises began to emerge from the lightening gray. Jagger took every opportunity to graze his fangs against her elongated neck, the sharp points never breaching her skin. He tolerated her half-hearted swats at him with a smile ghosting his face before he'd pull back and reposition her at his side.

Heavy footsteps broke over Jagger's lilting hum.

"Time's up," Detective Whitman called as he passed through the security door. Jagg stiffened at her side, pulling her impossibly closer to him.

She brought his hands to her head as he leaned into her ear. "You have to leave."

She nodded.

"You'll return." A nearly imperceptible slurring of his words.

Another nod as she disentangled herself.

Detective Whitman sneered at her through the bars, the disgust at her position evident on his pale face. She ignored the miserable man, patting Jagger's shoulder quickly as she exited the cell. They stomped up the stairs, her heels clicking loudly in the enclosed space.

"I assume you've made contact with the FBI," she said as she strode into the reception area.

Detective Whitman grunted. "You can return tonight. No visitors."

Making her way to Louis, she was pleased to see Dahlia sleeping soundly in the back seat of the car and she dropped into the vehicle, exhausted.

"Everything okay?" Louis asked, his eyes searching her face.

"Why wouldn't it be?" she mumbled, rubbing her eyes.

"Nichol was concerned. How did communication go this time?"

"I suck at Morse Code."

They sped through the night, anxious to beat the rise of the sun. As they pulled into the DeChamplain haunt, she stormed inside, leaving Louis to rouse Dahlia. The petite brunette Tender from the previous day smiled at her and motioned toward the shower, handing her a pile of clothing. Making quick work of it, she was scrubbed, dressed, and tearing downstairs to confront Nichol before Louis had a chance to tuck Dahlia into bed.

"Tell me you didn't know what that blood would do to him," she snarled at Nichol as she stomped into the office.

"It was an oversight I take full responsibility for," Nichol replied, his hands fisted into his auburn hair. "I didn't realize the severity of the effect until Mickey woke and you were without a communication wire." His eyes held a strange look. "You are…well?"

She flopped into a rolling chair, her wet hair dripping across the fabric. "I'm fine," she grumbled. "Hungry and tired and sick of being touched, but fine."

A low rumble began in the corner of the room, amplifying as two more tones joined in. She opened her eyes and scanned the room. Boy was approaching her with an apple, his empty eyes providing no clues as to why a soft growl was emanating from him. She brought the apple to her teeth and zeroed in on Mickey slouched in the far corner of the room. His blue eyes were trained on hers, fangs on full display.

"Oh, for heaven's sake. Put those away," she snarked as she bit into the fruit. "You too, Nichol. And stop that noise."

Nichol's arms crossed his chest as the sound lessened. "Touched how."

She rolled her eyes at him. "Jagger likes to cuddle. Did you know that? I sure didn't. I've just spent five hours being sniffed and squished by a drunken, humming vampire. I'm tired. I'm hungry. Let's get this debriefing over with."

With a few taps of the keyboard, Rhys and Dominic appeared on the laptop screen. Nichol moved to crouch by her side, inching away when she stared him down.

"Audra," Rhys called out through the speakers. "You're good?"

"Jesus," she muttered before updating the hauntmates on Jagger's condition and the negotiations for his release.

"Those flashlights," Rhys interrupted as her report drew to a close. "Did they look specially made?"

She shook her head. "He had three in his office. One had a sales tag still on it. You guys debate that. I'm heading to bed." She looked pointedly at Mick, who had been staring at her cockeyed throughout the narrative. "And keep this guy away from me. I'm not snuggling any more of you bastards."

****

Holy fuck she's beautiful. Beautiful and smart and nice and beautiful, Mick ruminated as Audra's hazy form disappeared through the doorway. His pristine vision was blurred, but he could make out the swell of her hips in Rhys's sweatpants as she left.

"Don't you dare," Nichol growled at him. He glanced back, becoming vaguely aware of his movement toward the door. Halting his progress, he grinned at his older hauntmate and took up residence in the office chair.

In his current state, he was barely registering Nichol's irritation. Rhys and Dominic were little more than whispers in his head, distance and Jagger's influence trumping their impact. The muddying of his senses was an incredible reprieve from the agony he had awoken from. Snippets of the past few days bounced around in his head.

Consuming hunger.

Fear punctuated with helplessness.

Pain interspersed with confusion.

Soft skin against his cheek.

195

A faint scent of vanilla.

A gentle voice promising he wasn't alone.

He arched his neck and sniffed the fabric of the chair he was sitting in.

"That's just creepy." Dominic's voice broke through his fog. "At least when I was doing it, I was connected and had an excuse. Mick, man. You look like an idiot."

He flexed his arms behind his head, turning away from the screen with a lopsided grin as he decided to go off in search of Audra.

"Don't. You. Fucking. Dare."

Nichol's large form blocked the exit, arms crossed, and fangs bared.

"Mick," Rhys's voice called out over the speaker. "Maybe you should sit back and relax until the buzz wears off. By dusk, you should feel under control again. If you still want to go after Audra, then maybe we can okay that. But right now, Nichol and Boy are doing you a huge favor."

Rhys's advice resonated in the recesses of his mind. "Fine."

With his feet struggling to cooperate, he returned to the chair and slumped into it, half listening as Nichol and Rhys discussed the upcoming nights. His murky thoughts were jumbled and tangled, becoming little more than a wall of static as he stretched his senses out, searching for something tangible to grasp as Jagger's blood-high coursed through him.

A heartbeat.

He forced himself to listen to the steady beating rhythm, its strength breaching the host body and echoing in his ears. With each pump, he become more focused, more determined to cling to the solidarity it provided. Beat after beat, the haze faded away as the clarity of the sound intensified. He closed his eyes, picturing the owner of the beat. The long black and turquoise hair brushed sleekly down her back. The peculiar brown eyes that caught every nuance. The flex of her calves as she walked in those sky-high stilettos.

The curve of her breasts visible through the arm holes of Rhys's ill-fitting tanks.

"Damn," he muttered, his mind zooming in on the visual.

****

Audra stood in the doorway of the office, a brow cocked. Boy was standing upright against the wall beside her, his eyes open but unseeing. She had witnessed it from him in the bloodslave quarters periodically, an almost alert state of rest. It was as freaky now as it was then.

Nichol lay sprawled across the desk, one arm tossed over his eyes. The tension held in his body was gone, his lethal form bordering on vulnerable as he lay exposed. She squinted, noting the youthfulness of Nichol's features when his expressions weren't ravaged with hostility.

A frat boy, she thought with amusement.

She dropped her gaze to Mick, who looked ridiculously uncomfortable with his long limbs draped over the chair. His blond hair was spread across the back of the seat, stray strands clinging to his cheekbones. One arm hung limply toward the floor, the other resting comfortably on his manhood. With a roll of her eyes, she tiptoed toward the sleeping laptop, tapping it lightly to bring it to life and stifling a giggle as Rhys and Dominic appeared on the screen, both heads-down on the communication room table.

While the past week had been exhausting for her, she had been inattentive to the resting needs of the vampires. Reflecting back, she couldn't pinpoint a moment Nichol or Boy had slept. Mickey had been at the mercy of Jagger's emotions and assaults for days, his energy depleted. Every time a call had been made, Rhys and Dominic had responded instantaneously.

The poor guys were dead tired.

With dusk on the horizon, she squatted beside Mickey, anxious to read Jagger's condition through him. The intense stillness of vampires when they rested was disconcerting, their chests not rising and falling, their eyelids motionless, their muscles void of movement. It was like staring at wax statues. Beautifully crafted wax statues with toned arms and hardened abs.

Mickey's inactivity boded well for Jagger's current status, his mind no longer siphoning Jagg's lows or highs. She moved slightly closer, watching the darkened lashes for any sign of distress.

"Hey," Mick's voice whispered into the silence.

Blue eyes snapped open, destabilizing her gracelessly until a long arm gripped her waist. She blinked slowly, locking her gaze as she scrutinized Mick for any sign of agitation.

"That's pretty unnerving," he whispered.

"No more than you not blinking," she hushed back with a smile. "How are you feeling?"

Mickey stood, flexing his shoulders while running a hand through his mop of hair. He motioned toward the hall, smiling briefly when she led him out.

"I'm good," he said quietly, his eyes darting back toward the room where his hauntmates slept. "Jagger's resting. He's muted right now. Probably a good thing."

Her head tilted. "Are you or Jagger hung over? If there is such a thing?"

An amused chuckle rumbled from Mick. "No lasting negative side effects," he replied. "I've heard of blood-drunks, or blood-highs, before, but that was definitely intense." His eyes darkened, the blue irises obscured in the dim hall light. "How was it for you? Jagg wasn't himself."

Placing her hands on her hips, she looked up at the large male. "Tell me what you felt from him."

"Tell me what he did."

"He snuggled."

Mick stared down at her, his eyes searching for mistruths. "It was pretty muddled. A real mess. But if I had to name the streams, I'd say relief and contentment were the biggest waves. A little sadness. Light bursts of lust." He muttered the last word, breaking eye contact.

"You can feel all that? And you can follow it, even in that state?" she asked softly, her curiosity barely contained.

Mick backed up slightly, his shoulders hunching. "Yeah. I can get deeper if I want to. Or need to."

"Nichol mentioned you were funneling what Jagger was experiencing. Tell me?"

The split-second look of surprise at her query wasn't lost on her. Mick ran a hand through his hair, allowing more strands to fall forward. "I can drain it. Pull it off the guys and drain it out so they don't get overwhelmed. It sounds cooler than it is."

"Where do you drain it?"

Mick frowned. "Can we not talk about this?"

She raised her hands in surrender, a smile on her lips. Pushing Mickey to discuss his abilities was never her intent, but the opportunity had been too great to pass up. She reached up to push his hair from his eyes, an instinctual response to the flash of vulnerability that crossed his face as she pressed for information.

He tensed, his arctic eyes holding hers as his head turned slowly toward her hand, his lips brushing against her palm. She recoiled, intent on pulling her arm into her body before Mick grabbed it, returning her hand to its position against his skin.

Her teeth clenched as he leisurely trailed open mouth kisses across her wrist and down the inside of her forearm, never once breaking his gaze while he entwined his fingers with hers. Her eyes narrowed in suspicion as he repeated the actions with her other arm, the sensitive skin of her pale wrists sending tendrils of electricity through her core. As his lips travelled along the inside of her elbows, she inhaled sharply.

Blood-letting scars.

Her muscles twitched away impulsively, halted by the tightening of Mick's grip. He ran a finger across the tiny puncture scars that peppered her inner arms, his jaw flexing as he examined the evidence of her time in the quarters. His blond head shook quickly, and he continued his journey across her shoulders, his fangs grazing her collarbone as he captured both her wrists in one large hand.

"I've hated this shirt since day one," he whispered, almost inaudibly. "I love the view, but fuck. It reeks of Rhys, no matter how many times it goes through the wash." Mickey's free hand traced the neckline of the shirt, hesitating briefly before drifting down her cleavage and resting on her hip as he knelt down. One finger hooked into the precariously loose band of the sweatpants and followed its path across her stomach, the soft ghosting of his skin against hers causing her hips to sway toward the light touch.

He lifted his head from her sternum and rose to his full height, his eyes hidden behind locks of unruly hair. He released her without a word, sidestepping her in the hall without looking back as he walked into the small room adjoining the office.

She took a moment to collect herself, breathing deeply to counter the rising heat of her body. Her lips pursed and she turned on her heel.

"I don't reek," she hissed as she entered the room and saw Mick lounging on the sofa, his long arms spread across the back. She padded over to stand between his knees, her hands gripping her hips.

A smirk passed his lips. "You do. You always reek of my brothers," Mickey said as he blatantly appraised her figure.

"I just showered."

"Doesn't matter," he said, adjusting his speech as his fangs ran out further down his lower lip. "Jagger is all over you. Especially your hair. A little Louis tossed in there. Nichol is pretty strong. A lot of Boy in your bloodstream. And, of course, Rhys." His blue eyes left her legs and locked on hers. "You're a regular vampire cocktail."

"But not you?"

"Oh, I'm on you, too," Mick leered, flexing his arms behind his head. "Not nearly as much as I'd like, but I'm definitely on you."

She crossed her arms under her breasts, unsure if she was insulted by Mick's breakdown of her scent. His eyes dropped to the swell of her chest, his hips adjusting slightly on the sofa. The pair stayed their positions as Audra focused on controlling her breathing and keeping her gaze away from the growing evidence of Mick's arousal.

She searched his eyes for any indication he was being swayed by Jagg's intoxication the night before, uncertain how many of Mickey's actions were driven by his own emotions and how many were piloted by those of his brethren.

His arms dropped to his splayed knees, his head inches from her waist. When she didn't move, his hands hesitantly rose to her hips. He waited, as though expecting her to push him away. When she remained still, he began his exploration of her form, trailing his fingers down the outside of her thighs and running them up again, avoiding the heating juncture between her legs in favor of feeling the curve of her hip bones. She kept her arms firmly crossed, refusing to give in to the shudder of anticipation she felt in every nerve.

He resumed his expedition, reaching his long arms around her to apply a soft pressure to each vertebrae, winding through the lines of her ribs. His fangs were a breath away from her breasts, refusing to make contact as her inhalations grew shallower, stubbornly denying them both the sensation of his lips on her body.

In a blink, Mickey was back to his sprawling position on the sofa. Her eyes narrowed in confusion and annoyance.

"Audra? How long do you need to be ready?" Nichol's voice called from behind her a moment later.

She exhaled loudly, her arms dropping to her sides. "Twenty."

Chapter Twenty-Three

"Who's this Finetree jackass?" Rhys muttered over the speaker. "Where did Whitman disappear to?"

Mickey shrugged. "When Nichol gets out of the shower, he might fill us in."

Audra's voice cracked slightly through the wire as she exchanged scripted pleasantries with the man, the clicking of her heels faintly echoing in the background. The heaving of a door opening signaled her entrance into Jagger's holding cell.

"I dunno, ma'am," the man's voice mumbled. "Detective Whitman didn't say anything about leaving you alone down here."

The rustling of papers preceded Audra's voice taking on its characteristic authority. "Everything you need to know is detailed in this. Complete with Whitman's signature. You may return an hour before dawn."

Mick shifted in his seat at the command in Audra's voice. He glanced over his shoulder at Boy, hoping he hadn't noticed the effect the commandment had on him. Bringing his attention back to the small speaker dedicated to Audra's wire, he flexed his fingers, willing them to forget the firmness of her thighs and softness of her skin.

Thinking of forgetting them didn't help his situation.

"You picking up anything from Jagger?" Rhys asked, his thumb tapping across his phone.

"Aside from embarrassment?" he grinned. "I'm guessing he's taken notice of Audra by now and is actively ignoring her in an attempt to save face after last night's snuggle session."

Dominic barked out a laugh alongside Rhys. "I don't know what's more terrifying, Jagger pissed or Jagger snuggling."

Now that he had full control over his mind, he had traveled from furious, to mildly annoyed, to accepting of Nichol's error in judgement the night before. His rest-deprived brother pulsed with anger and self-reproach as he took an extended shower, the forgotten wire and the combination of the blood of two extremely old vampires weighing heavy on the meticulous vampire's mind.

Had it been any of the other hauntmates in that cell, Audra may have returned to the DeChamplain haunt significantly worse for wear after spending the evening locked up with a drunk, injured vampire.

If she returned at all.

He monitored Jagg closely, delving deep through the interwoven emotions pulsing from the male as Audra's voice murmured in the background. Jagger was contrite, the embarrassment over using Audra as his personal stuffed bear apparent in his refusal to interact with her.

"Look at me," Audra demanded, the shifting fabric against the microphone indicating she was moving.

Rhys scoffed at her tone.

"Don't touch me," Jagger growled. Mickey zeroed in on Jagg's stream, ensuring there was no aggression hiding among the self-loathing and shame.

"You can see me now?" Audra barked. "Good. Then I won't feel bad telling you to stop acting like a little bitch and get off that floor."

A loud snarl sent feedback through the speaker and Nichol bellowed from the shower. "Turn it down, Mick!"

Adjusting the volume until the offensive sound dissipated, he continued to hold tight to Jagger, pulling as much frustration and humiliation off him as he could safely remove. Nichol appeared at his side, a large towel wrapped snug around his hips.

"What the fuck is she doing?" Nic demanded. "She wants to die. That is the only rational explanation of her actions. She is a suicidal thrill-seeker hiding in a composed package."

Rhys grinned, his fangs peeking out from behind his lips as Audra's hissed words crackled over the mic.

"Don't you dare turn your nose up," she ordered. "Either you drink it, or I will personally pour it down your throat."

"Back off, woman," Jagger growled, the low rumble still distorting the speaker sound. Nichol barked at Boy to bring him his pants, holding out his hand as he cocked his ear toward the sound system.

"It's Louis's," Audra stated. "Neither of us need a repeat of last night. Drink, then we talk."

"What are you reading from him?" Nichol demanded to Mick as he pulled his pants on and tossed the towel in Boy's direction.

"He was pretty embarrassed earlier, but now Jagg's got more of a hate-on for Audra," he said with a frown. "Is there any way to tell her to stand down?"

"Let her go," Rhys interjected. "Jagger needs a tongue lashing to get his ass in gear when he gets like this. Otherwise he'll sit in that cell and go completely static on us. He won't do a damn thing to her. He should, but he won't."

Mickey nodded slowly. "Fine. But I'll keep a bead on him. Drain as I think he needs. That good with everyone?"

The hours ticked by, Jagger remaining completely silent against the intermittent barrages from Audra.

Rhys had been right. The stubborn guy refused to feed, refused to speak, and refused to acknowledge Audra, judging from the tirades unleashed every thirty minutes. Her insults and goading were deliberate, phrased carefully to pull Jagger from his well of self-pity and push him into action. Mick maintained a tight rein, siphoning the bursts of humiliation and rage while allowing the focused anger to remain.

Any lust erupting from Jagger was purged quickly and effectively.

"He's been injured worse than this," Dominic said a few hours in. "What's his problem?"

Nichol huffed in frustration. "He's a stubborn jackass who cannot handle a woman helping him?"

Rhys, Dom, and Mick exchanged a look.

****

Lucidity returned in a haste, the mingling odors of his hauntmates infiltrating his senses and providing a much needed grounding. Jagger maintained his hold but loosened the grip he had on Audra's mouth and arms. The puncture wound in his thigh was healing, his body pushing the offending article out while Audra's lips moved against his hand. He pressed against her a little harder, ensuring he didn't block her airway.

The taunting had been easy to ignore, Audra's words filtering through his vision without hitting their mark. He recognized her game. It was the same one Rhys had played in the past, needling him to recover, to use the misery inflicted on him as a launching pad for revenge and escape. His pride was his Achille's heel, his greatest weakness when it was wounded.

Behaving like a feral animal at the hands of humans had been disgracing. Being at the mercy of lesser beings was humiliating. Knowing Mickey had felt it and Audra had witnessed it made things infinitely worse.

His inebriated mauling of Audra had been the final degradation.

The wooden pencil Audra had stabbed him with fell from his leg with a soft clamor.

The only physical reminder of his blindness was the slightly blurred haloing around the perimeter. The potent combination of Boy and Nichol's blood had worked to restore his vision, leaving little to repair the burns peppering his body. It was within the hazy outlier that Audra had moved, catching him off-guard.

"I'm well within my rights to draw equal blood," he hissed into her ear, his hands pressed tight to her lips. His eyes were drawn to the tiny microphone nestled in her cleavage and he tuned into the rapid emptying of rage and hostility from his mind.

He dropped his head, releasing Audra from his grasp with a mirthless chuckle at the obvious invasion into his emotions. "All right, Mickey. You can stop. Audra, say something to the guy."

Audra brushed her pants off deliberately, bending

to pick up a pair of glasses he didn't remember seeing back at the haunt. "Jagger is floundering for his balls," Audra enunciated toward her chest. "But since floundering is better than drowning, you can back off, Mick. Tell Louis I'll be street side shortly."

He straightened his spine and righted his hood. "You're leaving."

"I'll return tomorrow," she said, adjusting the spectacles on her face. "And when I do, this bag will be empty, and you will be ready to discuss a contingency plan. Get your shit together, Jagger. I have little patience for warriors posing as pussies."

With that, Audra kept her back to him until the detective arrived to remove her from the cell.

****

It was only the confines of the door frame that kept Mickey from standing to his full imposing height as the car came into view. With the night affording a few more hours of darkness, Louis's approach was cautious, his headlights catching Mick's stance in the darkened stoop. Audra's door opened before the vehicle came to a full stop, her long legs swinging out and propelling her forward. She avoided eye contact, staring past his shoulder as he blocked her entrance into the haunt.

"That was fucking stupid," he stated, his calm voice belying his anger.

She merely lifted a finger to him, silencing the berating he had planned. "I'm going to shower. I'm going to eat. Then, if I feel like it, I'll deal with you."

Deal with him.

He snarled, allowing her to push him aside and watching as she disappeared down the main hall.

Deal with him.

Louis approached warily. "Word of warning, my friend. She's in a bad, bad mood."

"That makes two of us," he spat, storming down the steps toward the guest rooms and pacing the tiny room he and Audra had inhabited only hours prior. The faint vanilla scent of her lotion clung to the room, further aggravating him.

Stupid, headstrong woman.

Despite the apparent effectiveness of her unexpected attack on Jagger, the outcome would have been fatal had Jagg's instinctual ferocity not been yanked from him. He walked the short length of the floor over and over, untangling Jagger's rage from his own before determining that yes, he was just as pissed as his brother was.

His ears pinpointed the padding of her bare feet down the hall before he heard her voice.

"Not now, Nichol!"

Determined to confront her, he stomped into the hall to intercept her path.

"Move, Mick."

When her hand pressed against his chest this time, he held his ground.

Audra sighed and rolled her eyes.

Rolled her fucking eyes.

"It was a risk, it worked," she huffed. "He's out of his Pitiful Pearl mood, primed to recuperate, and getting back his control. Now move."

"A risk," he said quietly. "What made you decide stabbing him would be a good fucking idea?" He stepped into her space, leaving less than an inch between them and forcing her to look up at him. "If I hadn't drained him, he would have torn your throat out."

"It was just a pencil," she argued back. "Maybe if you hadn't been funneling his anger for the first few hours, it wouldn't have come to that."

He could feel his vision sharpening on his prey. "You're laying your own poor judgement at my feet?" he hissed through his lengthening fangs.

Light brown cat eyes refused to break contact. "I'm merely pointing out that your brothers will never learn how to regulate their own emotions if you continue to do it for them."

"You would be dead thrice over if I didn't interfere," he snarled back.

"Oh, come on," Audra scoffed, her hands lifting to his chest once again to shove him off. "I can handle it."

He caught both of her hands in one of his, spinning her to the wall and holding her immobile with his body in an aggressive reproduction of their earlier tryst. He lowered his head to her jugular, reaching around to silence her lips.

"Is this how he restrained you?" he whispered in her ear, his irises darkening as she squirmed in his hold. "From behind? I didn't hear a sound out of you, Audra. Not. One. Smart ass. Word."

Audra's lips fought against his palm, her vocal cords taut and silent from the sharp curve of her neck. "Tell me," he hissed, "how did you handle it? Did you overpower him? Manipulate him? Reason with him?"

The fluttering of her heartbeat pounded in his head, her body's reactions betraying the calm she tried unsuccessfully to maintain. "Do it," he murmured. "Escape me like you did him. Prove me wrong."

Audra pushed against him, her muscles tensing and

flexing against his iron grip. Not a drip of fear coursed through her.

She was furious.

"You're going to have to do better than that," he taunted against her lobe, desperate for her to understand the potentially fatal position she had put herself in that night. Jagger's savagery had been swift once the weapon pierced his flesh. Audra's mic had picked up the sound of the bone strike, the telltale wet crunch of a puncture wound Mickey's only warning of the onslaught of rage Jagg unleashed in an instinctual reaction to an armed attack.

He froze.

A soft wetness brushed the palm that lay over her mouth as Audra's tongue lapped at him. His grip relaxed a fraction in surprise, enough for Audra to buck back against him, sending his extended fangs into his lower lip while simultaneously and painfully butting against his manhood. His hold tightened reflexively, adjusting to her new position facing him.

"That," he snarled, feeling the twin blood trails running down his chin, "is how you get yourself killed. If you cannot injure a vampire enough to incapacitate him, do not. Fucking. Bother."

"I'm in a better position now," Audra countered, her chest heaving with exertion against his.

He closed his eyes, willfully ignoring the droplets of his blood that had fallen along the neckline of her shirt. "I'm going to release you," he muttered as he realized exactly how dangerous a position he had put them in. The vision of his blood on her skin was trickling through his body. "I'm going to release you, and you're going to walk away, clean up, and head topside to rest."

"And if I don't?" she challenged.

He opened his eyes to give her the full view of his predatory side taking control, his emotions intertwined with the frustration and rage pulsing through his brothers.

She blinked slowly before bringing both hands to his jaw. He pulled his head back, cursing his body as it swayed a fraction toward her. Her hands returned to their position, undeterred as her fingers lightly caressed his jawline, her examination breaking only with each blink, the whirring of her mind evident in the clenching of her teeth.

"I knew you would do it," she suddenly whispered, her voice holding a touch of surprise. "In the back of my mind, I knew if I miscalculated his response, you would fix it." She stepped back and shook her head. "I used you. Just like the others do."

Chapter Twenty-Four

Audra awoke with a start, her arms flailing out to catch herself from an imagined fall. Blinking into focus, she was able to make out the slouched form of Boy standing against her door and she slumped back into the mattress.

Her temper had ruled her last night, altering her decisions and making her more impetuous than was prudent. She'd encountered many men like Jagger in her career, men who were unable to break past their shattered ego and rise past their temporary moment of weakness.

Some never recovered, becoming compliant shells and living out their corporate existences as second-rate yes-men. Others became bitter, negative cretins with a penchant for unnecessary cruelty, reliving their self-destruction in a continual loop and requiring all around them to suffer for it.

And some just needed a boot to the ass to reassert their power and position.

She had correctly placed Jagger into the latter category. When she had entered his cell to see the powerful vampire crouched in the corner, something inside her snapped. She had witnessed his eyes healing the night before, Nichol and Boy's blood repairing his mightiest sense as he drunkenly sniffed at her hair.

Jagger was no longer fighting blind.

214

He was also no longer fighting.

Coddling was ineffective in these cases. It only mutated the feelings of helplessness into resentful inadequacy. Jagger's aversion to looking at her when she entered the room proved that her presence during his weakest moments had made him hostile toward her.

So she took that hostility and ran with it.

She goaded him, spurred him to react with anything other than apathy and self-loathing. Small fires would light behind his eyes, only to be doused as his fuel was siphoned. When she saw a forgotten pencil lying in the corner of the cell, she went with her gut and forced a reaction from Jagger that Mickey would be unable to anticipate and absorb.

But he had.

And it was Mick's lightning response that kept her head on her shoulders.

The realization that she had subconsciously put her faith in Mickey to extricate her from danger sat heavy in her mind. Her independent nature was piqued by the blind trust she had witnessed from the Tenders when they spoke of Rhys.

Molly, a woman who suffered immensely at the hands of a vampire, turned to Dominic and Rhys for reassurance and assistance. Even the vivacious Dahlia relaxed trustingly as Louis belted her in to deliver her to the cell of a starving male.

Never, she had thought to herself. Never would she fall in alongside the haunt Tenders who blindly acquiesced to the hauntmates time and time again, refusing to question or examine.

She had questioned everything, complying only when she knew all the facts and creating contingencies in the inevitable case the males failed her.

Except Mickey, apparently.

The hypocrisy of her ideals against her actions was shameful.

She groaned into her pillow, forcing the blue-eyed demon from her head. She refused to think of the long fingers trailing across her spine. Refused to remember the ghosting lips on her collarbone. Absolutely refusing to acknowledge the lethal beauty of his fangs stained with his own blood.

His intent had been to warn her against impetuous actions, to prove how easily one miscalculation could end her.

And her traitorous body had led her brain astray, the coolness of his body doing little to tamper the heat of her skin as he restrained her against the wall.

She was a terrible pupil.

"I know you're watching me," she mumbled into her pillow. "Why are you even in here?"

She rolled over and looked pointedly at Boy. He turned briefly toward the door, then back to face her.

"Well, thank you," she said as she stood. "I'm up and ready to take on my next pissed-off vampire. You can go."

As Boy slipped through the door, she noticed the shadow of his feet under the door. Dressing in one of Meredith's pastel suits, she arranged her hair in a neat bun and hooked the glasses in her lapel, determined to behave like the rational, intelligent woman she was.

Boy followed in the shadows as she strolled through the basement halls, subtly checking each room for signs of Mick. Having no luck, she ventured upstairs, sneaking past Nichol in the office. An apology was in order, and she wouldn't feel right until she spoke with him.

Unlike the Kaius haunt, the DeChamplain Tenders resided above ground, the kitchen and living room windows open to the sunlight during the day. Nightfall had brought with it a poorly lit interior, the soft bulbs providing enough light for the resident vampires, but barely enough for the human occupants. She peered down the hallway where she'd seen the petite DeChamplain Tender disappear, her mood lifting momentarily as she watched Mick exit one of the rooms, his broad back to her.

"Will you return at dawn?"

The soft lilt of a female voice sent ice through her veins while Mickey grunted in affirmation before he pulled the door shut. He turned, halting in place briefly and averting his blue eyes from her, angling his torso away from her as he passed. She didn't need superhuman senses to identify the tangles in his long hair and the wrinkles in his trademark t-shirt.

With a deep, centering breath, she followed the vampire into the communication room and forced her brain to become engulfed with Nichol, Rhys, and the plans for the evening.

****

Mickey stood in the corner of the office, his arms crossed defensively as he silently observed the casual interactions between Audra and his brothers. Louis and Dahlia had joined the group shortly after Audra's arrival, eager to remain updated on the mission.

Nichol had managed to break into the FBI vamp division servers, pulling classified emails and orders onto his laptop screen with a tap of the keyboard. "I've bridged the security line to the Chinese outpost," Nichol announced with far less pride than Mickey believed he was due.

"Agents have been deployed to the area we identified. They're currently scouting the location, monitoring any movement in or out of the compound." He pulled up a grainy video. "There's our target. This drone took flight three hours ago. It's maintaining a consistent orbit around the area. When the feds breach the line, we will know."

Louis crouched beside Nichol, his head shaking in amazement with every tab Nichol pulled to the forefront. "You're an actual genius," he said in awe. Audra's laugh permeated the room.

It was fucking painful.

Audra plucked the tiny mic from Nichol's desk, her fingers dipping between her breasts to secure the line along her bra. In the corner of his eye, he memorized her movements as he continued to stare blankly at the laptop, feigning interest in the multiple emails flashing across the screen.

Louis stood, offering a hand to Audra as she pulled on another pair of stilettos. He definitely didn't time how long his friend's hand stayed in contact unnecessarily. As the pair exited the room, Nichol instructed Boy and Dahlia to fetch him a few bags of blood from the DeChamplain coolers.

"Go shower," Nichol instructed, hazel eyes narrowed in his direction.

He cocked a brow.

"You reek of cheap strawberry lip gloss and regret. It's distracting."

Growling in response, he stormed toward the door.

"Rhys told me to let you know you're fucking up epically, his words, and Dom has deemed you a lost cause. Again, not my phrasing," Nichol called after him.

He seethed as he stalked down the hall, ignoring the faint vanilla scent that wafted off the wall. The steam of the shower filled the tiny bathroom quickly, fogging the mirror and giving him a reprieve from the miserable bastard reflection.

His body remained wound, despite the hours he had spent sitting on the floor of the Rhys-trained Tender's room, grumbling about Audra and her absent survival skills.

Lathering himself up, he was bombarded with an image from mere hours ago, the dainty Tender with the large doe eyes who sat cross-legged on her bed and listened while he muttered on and on about another woman.

His pathetic attempt to push Audra from his thoughts had started and ended with a single kiss, the scent of the Tender's lip gloss sending him as far from her as he could get in the small room.

Every Tender Rhys trained was different from the scores before her. It was Rhys's ability to bring out and develop the women's talents in all areas that created a virtual army of perfection. The DeChamplain brunette had an amazing ability to listen with what was probably feigned interest, asking all the right questions and murmuring agreement in all the right places. Mick was four hours into his musings before he even realized how much he was unloading on the stranger.

Leaning on the shower wall, he shut his eyes tight and zeroed in on Audra's expression when she'd caught him slinking out of the Tender's bedroom, holding the image until the water ran ice cold.

****

Clarice's giddiness was contagious, her fingers toying with the giraffe clips in her graying hair as she followed Audra and Detective Finetree down the basement steps. Finetree, Audra discovered, was significantly less stringent than Detective Whitman. She had arrived shortly after the sun set, a large tote filled with cloths, towels, soap, and a fresh change of clothes.

"It's inhumane to allow him to fester in those burnt clothing," she argued when Detective Finetree hesitated at her request. "The odor down there is horrific. A few pails of warm water and a little privacy are all I'm requesting."

Shooting a dubious glance at Whitman's empty office, Finetree agreed with a stiff nod.

The young guards begrudgingly brought down a few buckets of slightly warmed water, making themselves scarce once Finetree unlocked Jagger's cell and watched warily while she dragged the washing supplies past the metal bars.

"We should be done here in thirty minutes," she called out, effectively dismissing the detective as she carefully unfolded the large towels from her bag. She kept track of the man's retreat through the security door before addressing the fixed glare from the corner.

"You reek and you look like a demonic vagabond," she stated, pushing a pail toward Jagg. "I want a nonviolent plan in place should Whitman back out of the deal. And to do that, you need to look as regal and charming as I know you are. This," she gestured across his form, "screams 'psychopathic serial killer'. It's not a good look."

Jagger reached out silently, accepting the bundle of clothes and towels.

"What's your plan, then?" he asked quietly. "Who am I going to impress?"

She grinned. "Clarice."

Jagger cocked a brow as he removed his torn sweatshirt. "Of course. Clarice."

Her hands busied themselves with the unwrapping a bar of soap and popping the lid off a bottle of shampoo. "She's the secretary upstairs," she explained, averting her eyes briefly as Jagger removed his bloodstained singlet. "Older woman with romanticized ideations of you brutish beasts."

A small smirk appeared on the handsome vampire's face. "You believe she'd open the door and let me waltz out of here."

"I believe she has an innate sense of justice and morality," she countered. "And I intend to use that if the opportunity arises. Now get on your knees and bend over."

Jagger stilled for a moment before realizing her intent. He assumed the position, flipping his black hair forward over the lukewarm water. Cupping her hands to wet his locks, she proceeded to scrub the blood and grime from his hair, washing and rinsing twice to ensure the scent of the shampoo would overwhelm the waning stench of decay. Covering his head with a towel, she gently prodded Jagg to stand, hiding her pleasure at the return of his mellow hum.

"Scrub up," she instructed, exchanging the soiled water bucket with two fresh ones. "I promised Nichol

I'd collect your nasty clothes for him to examine the oomph of the UV light they were using."

She strode around the cell, shoving the dirty towels and sweatshirt into her tote and collecting the tattered cargo pants as they were tossed aside. She joined in the unknown tune Jagger was humming while he sloughed the filth off his skin, her mood lifting.

"I should've brought some hair gel," she called over to Jagger before remembering to face him, freezing when she caught site of his very taut, very bare backside. She tilted her head, shamelessly scouring his frame for injuries as he continued to wash up. Her eyes were drawn to the slate-colored rings extending up from his ankle. Mickey had similar markings, though his didn't extend as high up as the muscular calf she was currently eying.

"You may want to stop staring at my ass," Jagg warned, his focus remaining on the task at hand. "I'm about to turn around and grab a fresh towel."

She dipped her head, providing him with the illusion of privacy as he turned toward her, dried off, and pulled on a fresh pair of black jeans. Satisfied that Jagg was appropriately covered, she lifted her head to give him a good view of her lips. "So are all vampires built like this?" she asked him, handing over the emerald button-down shirt DeChamplain had donated.

Jagger grinned, his nimble fingers closing the shirt quickly. "Of course not. Kaius picks good stock."

"Obviously," she mumbled, motioning Jagger to bend to her reach. Using her fingers to untangle the knots of his hair, she twisted and combed the short black mop into a passable style. "There. You smell good, you look good. If I can convince Finetree to allow Clarice down here, be charming."

"Got it."

A few imploring looks from the elderly clerk, and Finetree was leading the women down to Jagg's cell. The guards were significantly more relaxed without Detective Whitman's gruff presence, their spines curved to the wall as they chatted casually. When the small group passed through the security door, she smiled.

Jagger was leaning against the cement wall, bare feet crossed nonchalantly, and thumbs hooked in the belt loops of his jeans. His slight slouch dropped damp black strands across his forehead, framing his ice blue eyes and giving him a roguish, approachable appearance. He ignored her in favor of focusing his piercing gaze on Clarice, who tittered at her back.

"My, he is a looker," she whispered to Audra, blushing furiously when Jagger smirked at her compliment. He strode to the cell bars, stalking them like the predator he was and sending the woman's hands a-flutter. Finetree moved to Clarice's side in a gallant attempt to provide unneeded protection, earning a flippant wave of her ring-adorned hand.

Despite her reddened cheeks, Clarice refused to take her eyes off Jagger while he slowly draped his forearms through the bars and tilted his head slightly.

"Clarice, I presume," Jagg finally said, his voice husky and low. He adjust his stance slightly, drawing her attention to the strong straddle of his thighs.

Clarice's cheeks flushed more as she reached her hand toward his and shook it. "Yes, yes. And you must be Mr. Othario."

"Luciano," he purred, bringing the woman's hand

to his lips and ignoring Detective Finetree's sudden tap of his weapon. "Ms. Abernathy said you might have some questions for an old badger like myself."

Audra fought the roll of her eyes as he poured it on, standing aside while Clarice questioned Jagger on all sorts of things from his favorite music to his memories of early American settlement. Jagg answered each question thoroughly, interspersing his answers with subtle shifts in his position to draw the woman's attention to the lethal sensuality of fairytale vampires. He spoke respectfully, tossing in old idioms and terminology with ease and sending Clarice into flutters with the odd casual 'm'lady'.

He was damn good.

Detective Finetree stood guard throughout, his hand on his holster, until his patience grew thin. "All right, Clarice. We need to get you back upstairs."

Clarice reluctantly nodded, a final question on the tip of her tongue.

"You may touch, if you'd like," Jagger rumbled, correctly deducing the woman's hesitance. He parted his lips, drawing them back to give the woman access to his fangs. Finetree huffed a warning, which Clarice promptly ignored, her fingers brushing the silvery enamel quickly before she curtsied a farewell and followed the detective and guards upstairs to give Luciano and his lawyer some privacy. As the security door slammed shut, Audra approached the cell, applauding slowly.

Chapter Twenty-Five

"Can you isolate the images and enhance them? I'm seeing it, but not getting a bead on it," Rhys stated tightly, his profile visible on Nichol's laptop as Rhys and Dominic strained toward their own computer screen. "There are how many agents around and not a single reaction. Could he be one of theirs?"

Nichol's fingers flew across the keyboard, segregating the frames and adapting the sharpness. "No way Chen is unaware of the FBI. They're moving like elephants across the grounds. Whoever that is has to be connected to Chen or Dovidas. Those pictures helping at all?"

Dominic flung himself back in his chair and out of sight of the camera. "Tall guy in black. Might be a tall woman in dark blue. This is fucking pointless."

He had to concur. Their constant monitoring of the Chen haunt through the FBI's own drone had finally had some action when a figure cut clear across the no-man's zone and disappeared into the haunt entrance. The grainy footage provided no clues outside of the movement, leaving the Kaius hauntmates angered and frustrated.

With a come-hither crook of his finger, he acknowledged Audra's arrival in the increasingly cramped office space. Her damp hair and the odor of canned soup explained her absence since Louis had entered an hour earlier. He extended his arm toward her, accepting the tiny microphone and placing it atop his desk. "We have communication solidifying an ambush in seven hours," he grumbled as he continued to manipulate the blurry footage. "But we have a surprise visitor at Chen's, as well. Just trying to identify the bastard now."

He noted the intentional, awkward tilt of Audra's head as she leaned in and examined the pictures, using her hair as a shield from Mickey. After rewinding the video a few times, she righted herself. "Didn't you mention Jagg could do that? Move undetected by humans when he wanted?"

Rhys cupped one hand behind his head, the other resting on the curled hair of the new trainee. "Good call. So I think we can assume the new addition is a vamp. But if he can leave without being noticed, why enter a haunt under surveillance?"

"I don't like this," he mumbled, turning to Audra. "It went well. You read the woman correctly."

Audra laughed, graciously accepting the vacant seat as both she and Nichol ignored the surprised look from Rhys. "I would expect no less from an Elizabethan male," she said, her voice lighter than it had been in weeks. "Jagger almost had me swooning. I think he even managed to endear himself a little to Finetree."

"I'm amazed you managed to tear your eyes off his ass long enough to remember the plan," Mick snarked, his arms crossed over his chest as he slouched against the corner.

Audra's cat eyes blinked slowly. "Don't you have a Tender to fuck? Shoo. Let the big kids talk."

The world moved slowly for vampires. It took

practice to reduce their brain processes enough to eliminate the stop-motion appearance of their environment. Nichol had struggled with it in his youth, switching between observing the world at a human rate and that of a vampire rate. The ability to categorize the events and pull from his surroundings at both speeds had taken even longer to master.

He knew that the insult could not go unrecognized in the vampire world as the intent behind it was not one of playful jibing. He reluctantly allowed Mickey to take Audra down, her body brought to the floor with purpose and control, her head cradled in his large hand to prevent pain or damage. It was Boy's movements in defense of the woman that were his priority, since adding another male's scent and proximity to Mick would only escalate the matter.

He placed himself squarely between Boy's advance and Audra's prone form, his hands up in a sign of command briefly before he turned on a heel to observe. Rhys's whispered curses crackled through the speaker as Mickey's fangs came a within a fraction of Audra's lips.

"Say. It. Again."

The thrumming of Boy's strength at Nichol's back matched the tension in the room. Louis was crouched behind Mick, ready to intervene if he attempted to cause injury to the smart-mouthed woman.

Audra took a deep breath, an action he had often witnessed when she was processing the precarious situations she found herself in. "Shoo."

The formation of the single word brought her lips to Mick's fangs.

He was mildly impressed with the blatant challenge

the woman provided and he steeled himself to pull Mickey off of her.

Every male in the room, as well as those watching over the camera feed, stilled in anticipation as Mickey froze a moment before his head dropped toward Audra's neck, his lips brushing her earlobe.

"Do you feel this?" he whispered in her ear, perfect control pressing the points of his fangs against her throat without puncturing the fair skin. "This is Dominic's hunger. He hasn't fed off his connected in several days out of some twisted sense of protection and honor, and it surged to the forefront when he watched me take you down."

Nichol tensed.

"This," Mick continued, pressing Audra's wrists to the ground in a pulse that threatened to break the bones with each squeeze, "this is Nichol. His frustration waxes and wanes constantly while he works, amplified every time you disobey his orders and put yourself in danger."

Mickey's eyes flicked to the space he'd maintained between his chest and hers. "That would be Louis. The distance he appears to maintain so fucking easily but is actually propped up by an undercurrent of fear and hatred over what he is."

Louis growled low but was ignored by all as Mickey continued.

"Jagger is probably the one keeping you alive right now," Mick hissed, crossing his fangs under her chin. "He's drowning in self-loathing, but it's nothing he hasn't radiated for over a century straight. The disgust he holds over his own perceived failures keeps him, and by extension me, from gaining enough desire to finish the kill."

In his peripheral, Nichol noted Rhys on the monitor, removing his hand from the Tender trainee at his knees.

As Mick's hips ground sensually against Audra's, Nichol took a step forward.

"Rhys is trying," Mickey murmured, nuzzling Audra's cheek. "He's trying so fucking hard to rein in his incessant desire to connect with the women he screws. But it never. Fucking. Happens. Except once. Right, Rhys?"

Nichol's attention flicked to the computer screen as Rhys sat back in his chair and crossed his arms defiantly.

Mickey's body slithered across Audra. "What Rhys doesn't get right now, is that it isn't just his lust I'm being bombarded with. Is it, Nicky?"

He snarled, his fangs elongating in anger.

Audra's eyes fell on him briefly before Mickey gripped her face and redirected her attention. "He doesn't want you," Mick spat. "He wants everyone and no one, isn't that right, brother? You think I don't suffer for your self-imposed celibacy? How do you think you've maintained it all this time? Your impeccable control?" He dropped his head into the crook of Audra's neck as the room peaked with tension. "And none of this fucking shit is me," he whispered, almost inaudibly.

Mickey pushed himself off Audra and stormed from the room.

Louis was first to move, lunging forward to assist Audra from the floor and place her in a less vulnerable position. Boy watched Louis carefully, returning to his silent repose by the door until Louis led her out of the room, the mute servant trailing them. Dominic had disappeared from the screen, likely heading off to feed under Rhys's instruction and leaving Nichol and Rhys to decompress.

He focused on returning the room to rights, replacing every item to its exact position prior to the disruption. He minimized Rhys's window but kept one eye on the monitor, watching the grainy drone footage for signs of movement.

"Poor bastard." Rhys finally uttered. He brought the tab with his brother's face to the forefront of the screen. "Mick actually unleashes about all the shit we bury him under, and we respond by drowning him with guilt immediately afterwards."

With a grunt, he sat. "Perhaps I should have intervened right away. Mikhail will be greatly bothered by some of his actions tonight." His mind pulled up the image of Mickey grinding his body against the restrained woman. Mick's own guilt would likely be overpowering any his hauntmates unwittingly provided.

"Probably better you didn't," Rhys mused. "Audra's mouth will get her killed if she uses it on the wrong vamp at the wrong time. She knows too much to ever be released, which unfortunately aligns the rest of her existence with ours. Mickey may have taken it a little too far, but he did no permanent damage and I saw no fear in her after the initial takedown."

"That's because she has a death wish," he grumbled.

****

"I don't need a babysitter," Audra snarled, annoyed at the invasive proximity of Boy.

He'd escorted her inside her room, refusing to stand guard outside the door. Her body was still vibrating with the adrenaline rush she'd experienced at the very large, very lethal hands and fangs of Mick. The initial jolt of fear had dissipated quickly when she felt his cradling grip on the back of her skull. Had he truly wanted to end her, he would not have brought her to the floor in an instinctive protective position. He would have reveled in the hollow sound of bone smacking against carpeted concrete.

It was still a jerk move.

She knew the objective impartiality she'd clung to as she negotiated her new circumstances was evaporating. The clinical manner in which she assessed and analyzed the guys during her first months was no longer possible to uphold as she become more intertwined with their lives and their incomparable personalities. Even Boy, with his unheard voice and all-seeing eyes, was becoming less of a subject for study and more of a comforting presence.

Except when he refused to allow her the privacy she desperately craved.

Mickey had been primed to attack the moment she had stepped through the office door. Her flippant dismissal and insult was little more than the clichéd straw, one she'd felt instantly guilty over as the words left her lips. He'd been a hair's breadth away from imploding long before she had arrived back at the DeChamplain haunt that night.

Imploding.

That was precisely what she saw as she stared into those storming arctic blue eyes. She had latched on to them in fascination as he pulled the emotions of each hauntmate to the forefront. The color, shape, and depth of his irises changed as each impulse was exposed, reflecting for a moment the male they represented within the mind of the immersed vampire. She had wanted to freeze each change, align them with the eyes of the soul from which they originated. She wanted to eliminate the changes one by one until she was left with Mickey.

Just Mickey.

Dawn came and went. It wouldn't be long before the Chen haunt invasion went down, and she was determined to bear witness to the event for Molly's sake. The faint hope that Dovidas's cowardly body would burst from the haunt in flames played like a macabre fairytale in her mind as she settled into the bed for a nap.

****

They were at a standstill.

Perfectly matched determined eyes.

Evenly elongated fangs.

Toe to toe, head to head.

The revelation over their similarities would have had an impact on Mickey had it occurred during a less charged moment. But squaring off in the dim hallway of another vampire's haunt was definitely not the time for the long-haired males to pause and reflect.

His refusal to back down had as big an impact on Boy as Boy's refusal to relent had on him.

All because of the infuriating, hard-headed siren resting behind the wooden door.

The ancient vampire maintained a position of readiness, a position he didn't require due to his age and strength. Mick was smart enough to recognize it as a sign of respect as he stared down a vamp who could end him in a human blink, Boy's steadfast protection of his charge a noble endeavor from a mere slave within the Kaius haunt.

He stepped back, extending his wrist toward the vampire. "A guarantee," he said, his voice graveled with the solemnity of the offering. "I'll bring her no harm. I just need to…" Explain? Beg? Apologize? Fight?

He ran through the possibilities in his head. He had fucked up epically, as Rhys had warned, and both his mind and body were compelling him to do penance.

Boy's gaze slid to the blood offering, a deep understanding of the seriousness of the statement evident in his eyes. He stepped to the side with a nod, allowing Mickey to pass.

Reaching for the doorknob, he contemplated if it would be wiser and easier to provoke the ancient male to kill him before he prostrated himself at the feet of a wronged female. "Maybe you should have a quick sip," he muttered, not turning around. "Then you'll know if I'm in danger."

Boy didn't move. But he was almost certain he received a hint of a smile.

He entered slowly, closing the door behind him as he took in his surroundings. There were plenty of weapons at her disposal, he noticed. Nothing fatal, but dangerous enough to provide some serious injury.

Stilettos. Pens. Makeup brushes. A lamp.

As if sensing his presence, Audra stretched, emitting a long moan when she rolled onto her stomach. She lifted her head, opening one eye.

"How did you convince the Praetorian guard to

trade places?" she demanded.

"He was in the hall when I arrived."

Audra closed her eye and lowered her face into her pillow. "Waiting for you, no doubt. You're approaching the wrong bed. You want the hallway on the top floor."

He pushed his hands into his pockets, restraining them before they betrayed his controlled facade and allowing Audra's subtle jab to roll off him. "I'm sorry."

Sitting up on the bed, she regarded him curiously. "I accept."

He frowned. "You don't know what I'm sorry for."

"Yes, I do," Audra said, standing up. He trained his eyes on her face, ignoring the dangerously low pull of her neckline and the temptingly loose hang of the sweatpants. She stopped in front of him, hands on her hips. "I can see it in your eyes. You've chosen a time of day when you're tired, when you need rest. Yet you've come here, because this is when the assaults are at their quietest and you want someone, anyone, to acknowledge your actions as pure." One hand came to his jaw and he pulled away more violently than necessary.

"Leave your degree on the floor," he muttered, his hands close to puncturing through the seams of his pockets.

"Fine." Audra took a small step into his space. "You're sorry you attacked me. You're sorry you intended to frighten me. You're sorry you don't know how to respond to a woman who hasn't been tailored to be the perfect vampire companion. You're sorry you were too weak to block out Jagger. You're sorry I've seen you powerless and mindless. You're sorry you have a freaky, debilitating gift that you believe makes you a liability. You're sorry you can't identify who or what you are anymore. Have I missed anything?"

The urge to lash out in anger rose quickly, tempered by decades of controlling sudden onslaughts. His hands clenched at his sides, his shoulders rigid. "How about I'm sorry I came by? Can we add that to your notebook?"

When Audra's hand lifted to his face again, he held firm. She'd witnessed enough weakness from him. "I see you," she said softly, her light brown eyes squinting, searching. "Now that I have, I'll look for you. And make no mistake, I will know you." She grabbed his hand, cupping it in both of hers. "And I'm sorry, too. I'm sorry I used you when I was in that cell with Jagger."

"You didn't use me," he countered, easing out of her grip and backing toward the door. "You trusted me. Probably not the best decision, but there's a difference."

She watched him as he opened the door. "You're right. I trusted you. And I happen to believe it was a great decision, since I'm not dead yet." Waving him off, she sat and tossed her blanket over her legs. "Now off to bed, young grasshopper. The next few days will be long."

Chapter Twenty-Six

It was a mere two hours before Audra's prediction came to fruition. She awoke to Nichol's bellows in the hall for the others to join him. Scrambling into the small office on the heels of Louis, she came to a halt in the doorway.

The room sounded like a battleground, the staccato bursts of gunfire echoing in the enclosed space. Three cellphones were lying haphazardly on the floor, wiring connecting them to various speakers and recording devices. Nichol was laying awkwardly under the computer desk, his long legs shimmying him backwards into the nook to hastily fasten a few more connectors.

An extra monitor had joined the electronic chaos and was perched precariously on the crammed desk, rocking with every move Nichol made. Boy stood motionless, a smartphone aimed steady at the laptop screen, recording every blurry image.

"What the fuck?" Mick barked, attempting to turn the volume down on one set of speakers only to have another set amplify with frantic shouts. She scurried between Nichol's legs, accepting a cable from him and attempting to insert it in into the correct monitor.

"Phones out. Pick a conveyor to record," Nichol snarled, reaching into one of his black bags and tossing a handful of devices onto the floor. "Audra. Get this one fired up and bring Rhys on."

She moved quickly, tapping at the laptop skillfully and breathing a sigh of relief when Rhys's dark eyes appeared on the screen. Nichol stepped in front of her, taking over communications with Rhys and Dominic while growling orders over his shoulder.

Despite the lack of information, the Kaius hauntmates moved like a well-oiled machine, their single focus obeying the orders of their commander. She stood back, unsure of her role as she marveled at the speed with which the others adapted to the events unfolding on the screens and phones, relaying between each other succinctly and slipping into each other's places as new orders were given.

Flattening herself out of the way, she watched Mickey as he meticulously aligned recorders and phones together, providing buffers to reduce background noise. His eyes swirled between the varying shades of his brethren, his fingers gripping the electronics slightly tighter in bursts as Nichol began reviewing the events of the early evening.

"All our intel had the FBI boots going in at nine our time to make max usage of daylight weakness. Chen and his brood were to be taken alive and brought in at dusk." Nichol adjusted the clarity on his laptop. "The guys at the top want trophies. Judging from the weapons recommendation we looked over yesterday, they were more than equipped to go in."

"Then what the hell is all this?" Louis demanded, gesturing toward the mayhem on the screens. She moved closer, her presence acknowledged by Nichol as she peered at the monitor.

"That would be a Deviant army."

****

With the initial frenetic atmosphere dying down in the office, Mickey quickly funneled the rampant anxiety and confusion. His vision zeroed in on the blurry images. "Impossible."

The scenes flashing across the screens and echoing from the recordings rivaled the highest budget monster films in production.

He became acutely aware of Audra, her face paling. Cutting past Boy, he righted a forgotten chair and guided Audra into it, bracing his hands at her back as he took in Nichol's intel.

Nichol had a few hours to spare before the raid, so he had begun playing with his various toys, connecting and disconnecting wires to create a theatre-like feel to the invasion. He wanted to ensure they caught every detail, recorded each aspect for analysis, going so far as to establish a congruent streaming line for Dominic and Rhys, one that would transmit the same visual and audio cues while another ran live between the two groups.

Dawn hadn't yet broken in Beijing when the first blast went off. The Chen haunt had lit up like a funeral pyre, flames shooting hundreds of feet in the air as the earth shook with underground explosives. After securing the continued recording, Nichol had pulled up the thermal imaging footage of the initial blast. The ground had ignited, its reach surpassing the broad circle of the FBI agents and lighting several on fire, their green and blue forms suddenly alight with thermal yellows and reds.

Nichol replayed the heat imaging video alongside the grainy gray footage of a drone and sat back to allow the others to watch. The terrain appeared sturdy and untouched before a flash of white suddenly engulfed figures previously hidden among the brush.

Audra leaned forward, a shudder passing through her as she studied the images. He placed a reassuring hand on her shoulder, his own tension waning when she didn't flinch away.

"Here," Nichol said as he pointed to the dark movement streaming from the flames of the haunt. "They exited from several points, in or out of the ground I don't know. None are alit. You can see the speeds they reached as they descended on the agents. If you look here," his finger traced an imperceptible line along the boundaries of the haunt, "you can see the precise timing of the exit." Nichol rewound the footage, slowing it. "The first wave began within seconds of the initial detonation, looks like fifty of the freaks. With each explosion, another group emerges until the grand finale. Here," Nichol froze the image, "I would estimate the numbers at over two hundred, making a grand total of approximately four hundred Deviants."

Louis released a needless breath. "How does a vampire accumulate that many? It's physically taxing enough turning one. How many sires would be involved in this?"

Rhys's eyes blackened, the set of his jaw visible through the laptop. "Didn't our sources say Chen was a prolific creator? How many of his children have been actually seen? My bet is some of those Deviants have been alive for centuries."

The hauntmates hummed in agreement. The secrecy of the Chen haunt had been interrupted by small, inconsistent accounts of the ancient sire and his growing brood. Rumors were rampant, but reliable intel was negligible.

"Those mutants at Dovidas's house in Memphis, the night we pulled Molly out? I'd wager Kaspars learned a lesson or two from Chen on how to create an army," Mickey added, cognizant of Audra's erratic heartbeat.

Nichol forwarded the recording, closing in on the moment the hauntmates had joined him in the office. "Seventeen minutes after the first explosion, the sun rises. The final blast occurred four minutes prior. The last agent is killed two minutes after the sun breaches. These movements here," Nichol ran his finger around the scope of the screen, "are all Deviants. Their heat signatures are weak, so it's hard to get a bead on exactly how much sunlight each tolerated before igniting."

The recording was sped up to real time. "I haven't seen a single movement in the area in eleven minutes. I suspect reinforcements are arriving from the FBI shortly, but as of right now, I believe there are no humans or Deviants left alive in the area."

"What exactly are Deviants?" Audra inquired, her light brown eyes wide.

He squatted beside her. "In essence, turnings gone wrong. Not enough blood transferred, not enough taken, too close to death...there are a lot of ways things can go wrong. Most new sires screw up once, but something of this magnitude is pretty insane."

"What usually happens to Deviants? They obviously don't die on their own," Audra said, her eyes saying she knew the truth but needed to hear it.

"They're put down. Like the runt of the litter," Mick likened. "Deviants have no impulse control, erratic brain waves, and function solely within the id. The stress on the sire's mind is often too intense to allow Deviants to survive longer than a week. The odd creator tries to hold on longer, but in those cases both usually end up dead."

Her eyes narrowed. "How the hell has this been kept from humans?"

"It hasn't," Rhys commented. "Zombie stories have been circulating for eons. Lucky for us, the first documented sightings occurred in areas where religion dominated. Voodoo and blood magic was blamed, and we sure as hell aren't correcting the misinformation now."

"Zombies are real," Audra stated quietly. "Of course. Why not."

Nichol gave her a tight nod. "And they will remain untied to us. I interrupted the feed through the FBI main servers once the first wave came. Whatever documentation they have will be attributed to nothing more than a large vampire haunt."

The group sat in silence, digesting the events and monitoring the screens for signs of life. Or undeath. Mick stayed at Audra's side, too wound to fight the desire to remain close to her. He could feel her eyes assessing him, but refused to look her way, keeping his gaze straight and hoping his stoic face would give her no more insights into his mind.

Nichol was compulsively checking his phone. "Kaius is aware of the turn of events," Nichol muttered, one eye on his array of computers, another on his phone. "He recommends holding tight until we determine exactly what has gone down."

"What are your thoughts, Nichol?" Audra asked,

her voice stronger and face less ghostly.

Sitting back, Nichol tented his fingers on his abs. "Until I rerun the footage a few more times, I'm merely tossing out blind suggestions. But given the timing, this was a planned thwart of the FBI invasion to avoid capture. Our mystery guest is likely tied to it. The Deviants were sent off on a suicide mission. The haunt entrances were completely collapsed in the explosions, leaving them exposed to the sun shortly after their assault."

"Who the hell has four hundred disposable Deviants?" Louis mumbled, shaking his head. "Working under the assumption Dovidas is a Subduer, Chen would have to be as well, right? To avoid the Deviant insanity? The only way a sire could handle that many is if he could dampen the links to his own mind."

"And where is Chen?" Audra suddenly interrupted. "Buried under all that debris? Alive?"

The males stilled. "I'll keep one line on the site, but we need to start examining the video now. Rhys, you and Dom can do the thermal, we'll do the drone," Nichol ordered. "Audra, the sun has set. Wire up and head to Jagger. We need him informed. You'll be on your own. Yes?"

Audra nodded and stood.

"Not happening," Mick said, rising alongside her when he realized Nichol was serious. "I'll drive her in and scope the place. Just give me a few minutes to humanize myself."

****

Audra cocked a brow when Mick finally exited the DeChamplain haunt. "Creepy."

And it was. Mick's arctic eyes were covered with

brown contact lenses, rounding out the trademark vampire oval irises. His blond hair was fastened back through the opening of a ball cap, making him appear significantly younger than her. The cargo pants and black shirt uniform had been swapped out for faded jeans, a concert shirt that had seen better days, and a plaid button down.

He looked like he had stepped straight out of the 90's Seattle grunge scene.

"It's my hunting gear," he grinned, flashing his snipped fangs as he strode toward the car.

She followed quickly, her heels sinking into the grass. "I thought that's what the cargos were."

"Not that kind of hunting." Licking his lips, he glanced over at her. "You like?"

With the roll of her eyes, she folded herself delicately into the car. The drive was silent, slightly awkward. She organized the files on her lap, placing her identification squarely on top as she side-eyed her driver. Hunting clothes, indeed.

He could pass for twenty-two in his current get up, the deep brown of the contacts an odd complement to his blond strands. The shirt he wore was fraying at the hem, a hem which rode just slightly above the band of his jeans when he moved.

As they pulled into view of the police station, he began looking for a secluded parking spot. "One kiss."

Smoothing her jack down, she glanced over. "Excuse me?"

"When I spent the night with DeChamplain's Tender. It was one regretted kiss and a whole lot of bitching on my end." He killed the engine and spun the keys on his finger. "I'm coming in."

"No point," she stated, not ready to deal with his admission. "They won't let you down into the cells."

"I want to hear what's going on upstairs when the detective leaves you in there," he explained. "Especially with everything going down in Beijing."

She stared at him, unsettled by the round, brown irises. Then, with a slow blink, she relented. "Fine. But I'm in charge. Got it?"

He grinned, flashing a set of perfectly even teeth. Unnaturally even.

She wondered briefly when she had begun to accept fangs as her new normal.

The pair walked into the station, greeting Clarice at the front desk. The elderly woman wore a bright butterfly headband, its jeweled wings shimmering in the florescent lights. She smiled warmly at Audra before turning an appraising eye on Mickey.

"Detective Whitman is in tonight, dear," she said cheerily. "He should be out shortly." Her eyes darted toward the back office. "Good thing I met our handsome inmate yesterday. Leonard is in a foul, foul mood," she added in a hushed whisper. "Say hello to Mr. Othario for me."

She chuckled. "I'm sure he'll be pleased. I won't be long tonight. My friend will wait for me, if that's okay."

Mick sat his long body on the sofa, his legs hitched up as he tried to find a comfortable position. He looked up at Clarice with his strange brown eyes and gave the woman a wink. Clarice tittered, returning to her computer with mutterings about lookers and their noticeable absence during her youth.

"Send Abernathy in," Whitman's voice yelled,

cutting through the quiet of the station.

She gave Mick a pointed look upon hearing a low growl begin, turning down the hall once the sound halted.

She schooled her face as she entered Detective Whitman's office. "You rang?"

Whitman glared at her, his phone pressed tight to his ear while he finished a tight-lipped conversation. "You provided false information."

Her eyes narrowed, but she remained silent.

"My guy in the feds is lighting up my phone. Seems your intel led his men into an ambush."

"Really." She had mentally prepared for the accusation on the drive. "So after days of casing the place, the feds, with all their surveillance, were unprepared to face a vampire haunt?"

Whitman slammed his hands on his desk. "You said there were dozens there. My guy is saying hundreds poured out of that place."

"You asked for a haunt, I gave you the location of one of the largest in the world. What your buddy did with that information is not my problem. Nor my client's. Release him."

The detective laughed coldly. "No fucking way, princess. You led dozens of men to their deaths. Your boy stays until he gives up his haunt, not some random one on another continent."

"That wasn't the deal," she snarled back.

Whitman laughed darkly. "Deal? Why would that animal be so willing to give up the location of another haunt? He had no link to it, did he?"

Silence.

"You played me," the detective growled low.

She stood in place, hands gripping her files as her mind ran through various options.

Whitman was a vicious, petty man. Jagger would likely pay for his embarrassment if left behind another night. "Mick," she breathed, her lips immobile and voice almost inaudible to even her own ears. "Cough if you hear me."

Whitman sat back in his chair, arms crossed. A strange strangled bark came from the reception area.

Subtle.

"I need the guards out of commission in ten," she breathed, hoping Mick could hear her.

The detective stayed oblivious to her murmurings. "You can have twenty minutes tonight," he stated. "Then we need to renegotiate our terms. I want that creature's resting place in my sights by dawn."

She nodded tersely. "I won't need more than a few minutes," she said, her voice angry and tight.

He led her down the stairs, bellowing at the guards to take a break as they passed through the security door. Ignoring Jagg completely, he locked her inside the cell. "I'll be back in five."

She listened for the heave of the security door closing, launching herself at Jagger once it did. "Everyone calls you a ghost," she whispered frantically. "Can you do it tonight? Here?"

Jagger eyed her warily. "No. I haven't fed on enough fresh blood."

Her wrist was before his fangs before the sentence ended. "Now."

A brow rose. "Demanding little thing, aren't you." His fangs descended without question while his eyes insisted on an explanation.

"Things went a little south tonight," she whispered, gritting her teeth as the sensitive skin of her wrist was punctured. "Whitman won't release you. So we'll do it ourselves. Once you're done here, I need you to rough me up." Jagger stilled. "Pretend rough." He relaxed, pulling a few more mouthfuls into his body. "Take your cues from me and get the hell out when that cell opens. Mick is upstairs, distracting the guards. Or eating them. I don't really care."

With a huff, she realized she truly didn't care about the fates of the guards. She filed the thought away.

Jagger released her wrist, leaving the puncture wounds open. He rubbed her blood onto his fingers, smearing it in her hair and along her face before collecting more and doing the same to himself. "Yes?"

"I probably look like a six-year-old with a nosebleed." She loosened her bun, pulling long strands out and messing her perfectly coiffed hair. "Rip my clothes a bit. Make it look real."

The tear of the fabric was unnaturally loud in the cell, the hard walls amplifying the sound. Pleased with her outfit, she hitched forward, purposely skinning her knees on the cement. "Shit," she gasped. "I forgot how much that hurts. Now try to look scary."

As Jagger bared his fangs, she threw her head back and let out a piercing scream.

****

Jagg locked his arms around Audra, pushing her head back toward the cell door and burying his nose in her neck, his watchful eyes obscured from sight by her hair. The scent of her blood hung in his nostrils, its light taste pleasantly coating his tongue. Another pint would have been beneficial, but she would have been left lightheaded and defenseless. The vibrations of her throat told him that Audra was continuing to scream for the detective to assist her.

When she began to struggle in his grasp, he knew the man was descending the stairwell. He made a production of his attack, piercing his own forearm to cover his fangs with fresh blood. When the detective tore through the security door, keys swinging in his hand, he howled and sank his face into her delicate neck.

Armed with one of those damnable flashlights, the pale man scanned the cell. Jagger turned Audra toward the light, knowing it would cause her no harm as he advanced toward the bars, his pretty shield putting up a convincing fight. The detective cocked his gun, searching for a clear shot of him behind Audra's flailing body.

The man's attention was diverted between the cell and quick glances toward the stairs, looking for the guards who would not be arriving. His mouth moved quickly, barking unheard orders and threats until Jagger felt Audra's arm move awkwardly. In the commotion, he saw the impeccable files she carried drop to the floor, their contents splaying just under the cell bars.

The detective saw them as well, his eyes flashing with desire.

Rearing back, he let loose a roar of fury and hoisted Audra into the air. He slowed his movements slightly and exaggerated each motion enough to emphasize his intense distraction. The detective took advantage of the moment, diving toward the files and grasping their precious information in his white knuckles.

And then Jagger took advantage of his own moment.

****

Audra heard the whispered apology before her legs crumpled beneath her on the cold cement. Detective Whitman was frantic, his movements jerking and reactive, his target gone. The security door inched closed, sealing with a click as the tinny sound of jangling keys hung in the air. She stood slowly, the seconds ticking by as she crept toward the open cell door. Whitman yelled for backup over and over, his voice coarse and face contorted with anger.

As she squeezed through the cell door, she focused her attention on the armed detective, warily moving closer to him. His raving gaze passed over her as he searched the ceilings for Jagger before he finally registered her presence, repugnance pulsing from him. He muttered derisive comments about her under his breath and continued to scan the room, peering into the empty cell.

"Where is he, blood whore?" Whitman hollered, his gun swinging dangerously. Audra's files lay scattered at his feet, their false leads begging for attention.

"Long gone," she stated, eying the weapon trained on her body.

Whitman stepped toward her. "Into the cell," he barked. "Until that fucker is recaptured, you stay."

She held her ground. "My firm knows I'm here."

With a mirthless laugh, Whitman advanced again. "You're no fucking lawyer. You're one of their little groupie sluts, aren't you? Betraying your own kind for the chance to get under one of those things? Fucking disgusting," he spat. "Now where is he?"

"Behind you," Jagg's voice purred. Audra and Whitman looked toward the security door. Jagger and Clarice stood in the entrance, Jagg holding a large link of keys and Clarice assuming a strangely protective stance beside the old vampire.

"Put that gun down now, Leonard," she ordered, her matronly voice full of venom.

Whitman's mouth narrowed into a hard line. "Move, Clarice. That vampire's going down."

"Going…those lights aren't regular lights, are they, Leonard?" Clarice asked, stepping down one more stair to align her height with the detective's. "The hoods. The noise machines. The bullets in that damn gun aren't standard issue either, are they?"

Whitman's hand shook, his eyes darting between his target and the elderly female.

"I've known for a while that you've been toeing the line between intolerant and downright hateful," Clarice said sharply. "You tortured this poor boy."

Audra scurried toward Jagger, ignoring her pride to crawl swiftly between his legs. Jagger stooped his head toward the elderly woman, murmuring into her ear as the first mercury bullet pierced his side. He stumbled back slightly, drawing a scream from Audra as Jagg spun and lunged, the door opening and slamming shut in a blink, the jingling of keys echoing in the cement stairwell.

Blocking the security door window with his body, Jagg held position as the pop of gunshots echoed, one hand covering his ribs while he motioned for the women to head topside.

Moments dragged out before Jagger appeared

behind them, his movements halting. He approached Clarice without a glance toward Audra, placing Whitman's keys into her palm. "Thank you. Give him an hour to calm and then release him. Make sure the other officer is here when you do. The guards are out back, temporarily unavailable. I recommend they find another line of work." A quick kiss on her cheek, and Jagger limped out, leaving Clarice in her chair, her eyes glazed and tired.

Mickey sprinted ahead, bringing the car up to the curb and assisting her into the front seat as Jagg reclined across the back. They drove in silence, Mick texting the others as they wound through the back roads. She sat back, allowing herself to bask in the numbness of the night's surreal developments until the sight of Jagger's scorched leg caught her attention.

"Who?"

"Clarice," Jagg grinned, carefully readjusting his position. "She was hiding in the back room when I found her. She got me good before she saw the damage it caused."

Her brow furrowed as she circled the burn with her fingers. "You poor boy."

Swatting her hand away, Jagger grumbled under his breath too quietly for her to catch.

Mick, however, had apparently heard every word and responded with a snort.

****

Nichol met the trio at the door, his arms crossed as he glared at Audra. "A little warning before you shatter my eardrums would be nice," he bit out, ignoring his rescued brother. Jagger acknowledged his hauntmate with a brief nod, passing through the entrance and

251

disappearing alongside the unnaturally stoic Mick. She cleared her throat and met Nichol toe to toe.

"You could have said something to welcome him back," she chastised.

"And bring attention to his actions that have resulted in human deaths and a declaration of war among our kind? That seems rather cruel."

She tilted her head. "Fair enough. Any leads on Chen's whereabouts?"

Nichol motioned for her to take the lead down to the office. "We've been scanning surveillance from the past three days and have seen no evidence Chen left prior to the explosives. While we'll remain on alert until we have confirmation, we're currently working under the theory that Chen was an intended victim of the ambush. Perhaps our mystery vampire was a turncoat."

She nodded slowly. "Jagg's injured. Gunshots. I don't think Mick is, but…"

"I'll send a couple DeChamplain Tenders to them immediately," Nichol responded, leading her down the stairs to the office.

"Did you see Jagger's tattoos?" she asked quietly.

Nichol hesitated. "Burmese," he replied. "It means 'cursed'."

Chapter Twenty-Seven

Jagger's first shower in over two weeks had been a relief, the heat of the water blasting Audra's dried blood from his body. The water took with it the female scent that had been tantalizing his senses, despite his lack of sexual interest in the woman. The memory of her taking control of his captivity stung his ego and left him feeling more hostile toward her than he was comfortable experiencing. The hot water assisted in washing away the humiliation of relying on a human to extract both his body and mind from confinement.

He toweled off quickly, tossing on the fresh clothes Boy had passed him on his way in, grateful for the steam from the shower obscuring his reflection. His markings.

As he walked down the hall, he trailed a finger along the symbols, pulling his hood a little farther down over his face before he entered the room and sat against the wall, his hood securely over his damp hair and his feet planted on safe ground. His hauntmates had ignored his return in favor of throwing him head on into their surveillance assessments, allowing him to rebuild his dignity and begin redeeming himself. He welcomed the opportunity, his mind focused on his task instead of reliving his errors in judgement. There would be time for that once daylight hit.

Nichol was planning their return to the haunt,

meticulously packing unneeded equipment and texting his contacts along the journey. Louis lay on his side, his sharp eyes monitoring movements across two screens as Dahlia read a book at his feet. Boy held a phone in his hand, providing the illusion he was examining the footage as he surreptitiously monitored Audra and, more telling, Mickey.

There was a palpable tension emanating from Mick, one that had been present since Jagger first ghosted out of the police station holding cell. Mickey had been standing over the two unconscious guards, a look of ennui on his face. Upon seeing Jagg through the glass door, his expression had hardened, giving him a glimpse of Mick's clipped fangs before he tightened his features into the unreadable mask he was currently wearing.

He studied his second youngest brother intently.

Mickey had been the youngest hauntmate for over two centuries, his empathic abilities manifesting more formidably than Kaius could monitor safely in the presence of the other hauntmates. Kai had stalked Mikhail for months prior to bringing him into the haunt, assessing the tall human's speed, strength, and agility of mind as he served Fyodor Ushakov under the command of Catherine the Great.

Kaius had been inordinately fascinated by the ambitious woman, channeling that enchantment into the embracing of another child. Mikhail had proven himself an intuitive combatant, observing his enemy's most subtle of tells during battle and acting on his commander's unspoken instructions before obeying those that were verbalized.

Mikhail was the perfect addition, untethered by

family or obligation and serving throughout a war where casualties were many. Kai took Mick swiftly one night, the screams of dying men veiling the transition howls of their comrade. He was one of the few empathic vampires in existence, most having been driven mad within their first years from the constant bombardment of their hauntmates. The few that survived longer did so through complete isolation, the hermits of the vampire community.

Mickey's continued existence was a testament to the strength of his will and his bloodline.

The guarded expression he wore now was eerily similar to the one he had donned after Kaius had assisted the empathic male with his control and impulses.

Hardened dissociation.

The arrival of DeChamplain in the small office room yanked Jagger from his musings. He stood, catching the quick look of surprise on Audra's face as she visually assessed the old vampire. He bit back a grin, remembering her question about vampire appearances in the Vansburg cell.

No, all vampires were not as visually appealing as the Kaius line.

DeChamplain was a short, stout man turned in his late forties. The jowled male had been considered old during his human years and his age rings placed him slightly younger than Nichol. He was rarely seen outside the security of his own haunt, the two children who resided with him taking care of any vampire business DeChamplain required. A team of dedicated servants and Tenders ran the household, allowing the artistic male to pour centuries of knowledge and visions onto canvases that never saw the light of day.

He liked the peculiar vampire.

"You're welcome to stay longer, should you require it," DeChamplain offered, acknowledging Jagger with a brief nod. His eyes scanned the room, settling on Audra. "You have strange features."

Mick's shoulders tensed slightly, relaxing as Audra chuckled. "So I've been told. Audra Verdi," she said good-naturedly, offering her hand.

DeChamplain looked at the appendage, accepting it for study between his bulky fingers. When his hold did not loosen, Audra shifted her weight.

"We must leave at dusk," Nichol stated, bringing DeChamplain's attention away from her. "Although a studious set of eyes like your own would be much appreciated as we review the footage we have."

DeChamplain released Audra, his attention riveted on the remaining laptop screen. "I have time to oblige," he mumbled, accepting the chair Nichol offered.

Mickey's gaze remained locked on Audra's hand, even as she turned her attention to wrapping cords for Nichol. DeChamplain was, for lack of a better term, socially inept. Jagger had the urge to reassure Mick no harm would have come to Audra. Her hands would likely become part of a vault of artwork secured in the depths of the haunt, never to be seen again.

"Where are they going?" DeChamplain murmured, his finger dancing across the monitor.

Nichol rewound the scene, his eyes glowering as he took in the top corner of the image. "Those are vampire heat signatures," he snarled. He pulled up the drone footage, comparing the angles. "Does this match up?"

The hauntmates joined DeChamplain around the

computer. Two figures, mere blips on the video, tore from the Chen haunt during the fourth blast. They disappeared from the screen within moments, their existence overshadowed by the rampaging Deviants.

"Chen won't be happy," DeChamplain frowned. "He's never moved. Very peculiar vampire."

"Never?" Rhys asked over the speaker.

DeChamplain rose, his dark eyes beginning to glaze with boredom. "He defends from his fortress. It is his ancestral land."

The hauntmates exchanged a glance as DeChamplain moved toward the exit. "I do not dislike your eyes, Ms. Verdi. I will paint them one night. And your hands. I can do without the rest of you, though."

****

"Not a chance in hell."

Dominic remained firm, his arms crossed over his chest and dark hair falling into his eyes. Mickey could feel the protectiveness surging despite their distance. Nichol had managed to isolate the brief recording of the two vampires exiting the Chen haunt, enlarging them as much as he could before the distortion made the images useless.

"Put the decision in her court," Audra countered. "Moll has as much a right to this information as any of us do. And if she can help, it'll put another nail in his coffin. Pardon the expression."

Dominic's jaw twitched. Mick remained out of sight of the camera, giving her a terse nod.

"It's a shift in the balance of power," she continued, encouraged by Mick's assessment of Dominic's feelings on the matter. "If it is Dovidas, she's the only one who could potentially identify him from this footage."

Within ten minutes, Molly was perched on Dom's lap, her neon shirt a distraction on the screen. Nichol launched the video feed, his eyes locked on Molly's expressions as the film ran over and over. Audra watched him adjust the speed slower and slower until Molly recognized the gait of the shorter runner.

"That's him," she gasped, subconsciously accepting Dominic's arms tightening around her. "Longer steps than when he walks, but that's it. See the flat-footed clomp?"

Nichol sat back in triumph as Audra pushed forward. "You're positive?"

"Yes. His knees turn out just like that when he walks. It used to bother me."

She smiled. "Step one, identify the fucker. You can cross that one off your list. We'll be back in a few days. Dominic, Molly, text me if you need anything."

Molly gave her a grateful smile.

She stood, stretching her arms over her head. She caught Mick's intense stare at her midriff and dropped her arms quickly, tugging her shirt down. "Nichol, I'll be up in a few hours to help. I'm off to shower and then off to bed. Me and my weird eyes are exhausted."

****

Mick waited, his back to the door as Audra and Boy slipped away. Louis and Dahlia followed, Dahlia's obvious eagerness for the early morning activities far surpassing the mild interest channeling from Louis. Rhys and Dominic remained onscreen, Molly having disappeared shortly after her revelation.

Rhys sat back in his chair, his bare feet on the table. "Been a long time since it was just us, brothers."

He and Jagg crouched beside Nichol and he stretched out, basking in the contentment trickling from each of the hauntmates. Instead of funneling the emotions down the usual tracks, he allowed them to loop and intertwine in his head, increasing the strength until every other uninvited feeling was drowned out.

"That's cool," Dominic said, a fanged smile on his face. "I can feel that, Mick."

He grinned, flicking his tongue over his clipped teeth. "Well, when you all aren't acting like fucking Neanderthals, I have a chance to try a few things out."

Jagger leaned back on his hands. "So what do we think about Dovidas and the unknown? Same guy as Memphis?"

Rhys nodded. "I'd say so. Same M.O. as well. I'm putting my money on Chen's death. Those Deviants were ready long before the first explosion. No way he was unaware they were being moved into position. Four hundred rabid animals aren't going to corral easily."

"Even a Subduer would be aware of their locations," Nichol added. "We can assume Chen himself had them ready."

"Any chance we can get a sample of the explosives?" Dominic asked. "Maybe in a few weeks, once the site is cleared? A good recon team would be able to confirm Chen's death, as well. Might be good to eliminate one potential issue for sure."

Nichol scribbled a quick note and shoved it in his pocket. "I'll contact a few haunts about that once we get home."

Rhys reached out to Dominic, messing his hair. "You're so smart, Dommie."

Dom swatted at the older vampire. "Seriously guys.

Where is Dovidas heading now? Any chance he'll be back in the States?"

The males grew thoughtful. "I can try to run a face recognition program through airport security, but it might not be effective without a clearer picture," Nichol said. "Or put the word out to all haunts to inform me if Dovidas turns up anywhere. But without knowing for sure who our unknown is or what links either have, we could be advertising a weakness to Dovidas unwittingly."

"How about we get you guys home, contact a team to confirm Chen's demise, and we can go from there?" Rhys submitted. "I have a new Tender that needs a few months of group lessons before I can sell her. You're holding up the line."

****

"We could have gone back to the yard and hot-wired the other car," Audra muttered, cursing Jagger for not remembering the vehicle he had been traveling in a few weeks earlier.

"Perfect excuse to buy a replacement when we return home," Nichol muttered.

The SUV was significantly more cramped with the addition of one more long-limbed male. She adjusted her hips, trying unsuccessfully to give Jagg as much room as he needed beside her.

Nichol's fastidious packing had been thwarted by the DeChamplain Tenders emerging with arms full of food and several bags of blood to tide the humans and vampires over until they reached their final destination.

She bit her lip as Nichol's eyes flicked to the precariously balanced packages atop his electronics. He had gone no more than five minutes between checks, the slight ovaling of his irises indicating his annoyance every time.

Jagg was silent, his ice eyes closed as they rushed through the darkness. Nichol had assured her that Jagger had indeed fed off a DeChamplain Tender before they departed, the mercury bullets of the night before stored in one of Nichol's bags for examination. Every so often, Jagg would arch his back slightly, readjusting his ribs as he healed. It was both unnerving and reassuring.

Mick was as talkative as the others, staring blankly out the window. He was back in his customary uniform, a small jolt of satisfaction zipping through her with the knowledge his youthful 'hunting gear' was stored away in a bag at the bottom of the pile. His eyes had flickered rapidly as the group organized their supplies, switching gears too fast for her to identify which of the males was influencing Mickey the most as they climbed into the vehicle.

Their phones remained silent, with the shimmer of the sports car's lights behind them the only assurance that Louis, Dahlia, and Boy were safe at their heels, despite Louis's cautious driving. The fuel stop had been as eerily uneventful, with only the drivers getting out to hastily top up the gas tanks. It was the final stretch of the successful mission, and everyone was balancing between relief and anticipation.

An hour before dawn, lights appeared on the horizon. She watched the highway signs as they approached the city. "I don't remember going through Indianapolis," she said, breaking the hours of quietude.

"We never travel the same route twice," Nichol explained. "If I wasn't so anxious to get back, we'd be taking an even less direct route. There's a safe commune here."

Mickey snorted, his jaw flexing with tension. "Safe. Safe for vampires. You and Dahlia will be tethered to us at all times."

"Commune is a loose term," Jagger offered. "Think of it more like a hunting lodge."

Chapter Twenty-Eight

Audra fixed Nichol with a harsh stare and Mick was impressed with the male's ability not to flinch away from the accusing look.

"You'll be fine," Nichol stated. "You'll remain with me or Boy at all times. Our visit there serves two purposes. Shelter, and communication. The owners are traditionalists with strong ties to Europe and the East. If Dovidas appears anywhere, they're our best bet for information."

"And how long are we there?" Audra demanded. "Dahlia will be protected, right."

"No more than two nights," Nichol replied, averting his gaze and pretending to watch intently for the turn-off. "And yes. Louis will ensure she remains at his side at all times."

He and Jagger avoided looking at Audra directly. The Stojanovski commune differed notably from the usual vampire haunt. The large grounds were surrounded by miles of electrified barbed fence, the only access a heavily-monitored walking pass-through.

While a few of the Stojanovski line intermittently remained on site, the majority of the vampires within the sprawling grounds were defectors from other haunts, males who sought a more primitive existence within a secure space.

Humans were released on the grounds every night,

with gifts and luxuries lavished on those who were uncaught by dawn. It made the prey adept at hiding, their knowledge of the grounds encouraged and fostered. Killing was technically prohibited on site, so the significant human bait pool had little turnover.

Audra was not going to be pleased.

Each of the Kaius hauntmates had spent some time in the commune over the years, the Stojanovski crew being a well-informed branch of their intel. One large building served as the reception hall, human accommodations, and meeting rooms, while each visiting vampire was provided a secluded bomb shelter on the premises, an underground suite consisting of bare necessities. The single access in and out of the shelters left him on edge, his training to always have another escape route rearing itself whenever he descended into the dim bunker.

He didn't care much for the setup of the place.

"How many bunkers do we have?" he asked, remembering the tight quarters of his previous visits.

"Jackson opened up two grand suites a few years back," Nichol muttered, slouching slightly as Audra's glare continued to burn into his skull. "We secured one for the next two nights."

Jackson was the most business-minded of the Stojanovski clan. He was also intensely vampiric. The small yearly turnover of hunted humans on site was almost exclusively due to Jackson's reputed appetite for rough sex and bloodletting. Though since he didn't technically kill the humans during the hunting hours, he continued to pepper the commune with "No Killing on Premises" signs.

Vampires and their loopholes.

The commune road came into view, massive trees lining the tight pathway. Nichol maneuvered the vehicle skillfully along the narrow passage, following the route by memory as offshoots branched out to deter unwelcome guests. He parked in a small turnout, waiting for Louis to catch up.

"We leave everything but a bag each behind," he ordered. "Security is as tight along the perimeter as it is inside the wire."

The group collected their bags, Louis hefting one of Dahlia's large suitcases into his arm as Mick slung Audra's small bag over his shoulder. Nichol pocketed a few electronics before leading them to the gate. A few quick words were exchanged over the intercom system, and they proceeded into the compound.

Jagger pointed silently at a few of the remaining humans on the land, daybreak less than an hour away. Audra, obviously miffed, walked behind Nichol, but kept her steps just quick enough to avoid falling beside Mick. Her head turned toward snapped branches, jerking to the side when a feminine shriek pierced the air. Dahlia was less aware of her surroundings, her feet scampering at Louis's side while she whispered promises of what dawn would bring him.

He was on edge. As they neared the solo building, Jagger and Nichol began transmitting wariness as well. Jackson stood outside the door, leaning nonchalantly against the wall, his head cocked as he listened to the howls of conquest coming from his guests.

"Nichol Kaius," Stojanovski drawled, meeting the group on the landing to maintain a height advantage. It was a common practice for human males, one that clung centuries after a vampire's humanity had disappeared. "Cutting it close to dawn, I see. Follow me." His dark eyes lingered on Jagger's tattoos, a hint of revulsion in his gaze.

Mickey stepped up to Audra's side, subtly brushing his arm against hers. Any visitors caught up as the nightly hunt concluded could mistake her for prey. As Jackson came to stop, opening the door of a tiny house situated atop a bunker, his eyes fell on Dahlia and Audra. "Will they be partaking in tomorrow's festivities?" he inquired, blatantly appraising both women's physiques. "The addition of Tenders often spurs quite the frenzy for both owners and others."

Audra wisely stayed silent, averting her gaze. Dahlia, however, emitted a giggle.

Nichol's unwavering stare answered Jackson with more clarity than words could convey. With a bow and a wink at Dahlia, Stojanovski left the Kaius hauntmates to file into the house and descend into the shelter. Louis dropped in first, scenting the air and heading toward the farthest room to begin a sweep. Jagger followed, assisting Dahlia. Jagg and Boy joined Louis, heading in opposite directions to flush any intruders. Mick hesitated, torn between sending Audra down before the sweep was completed and leaving her above ground where any number of vamps could burst in and take her.

Audra made the decision for him, pushing past his large form and disappearing down the ladder, not once making eye contact with him or Nichol.

"She is displeased with our location," Nichol observed, motioning for him to head down.

"She's not the only one," he grumbled, landing smoothly on his feet and making way for Nichol to secure the lock and set the code.

"Boy and I will take turns on shift today," Nichol instructed as the hauntmates reassembled in the main room. "There are two bedrooms. Figure it out and get some rest."

Audra moved toward Dahlia briefly, halting in defeat as Dahlia turned to Louis in expectation. Louis flashed an apologetic look toward her before following Dahlia into the first room. Audra fastened her gaze on each of the remaining males, daring them to join her in the second bedroom. Jagger was first to react, holding his hands up in surrender before placing his backpack against the wall of the main room and lying down on it.

"Boy and I will be resting out here," Nichol stated, a slight discomfort echoing in his voice.

Mick stared her down, knowing he damn well wanted to join her, but too stubborn and cowardly to follow the infuriated woman into an enclosed space. He backed up, locking his gaze on her defiant cat eyes while he lowered his bag beside Jagg and held out her own out as a peace offering. With a deep exhale, Audra snatched the bag and stormed into the room.

"I don't know how Rhys deals with these creatures day in and day out," Jagger whispered. "That woman is terrifying."

Nichol hummed in agreement, fidgeting with a small receptor.

"Will Jackson expect us to participate tomorrow night? He looked way too interested in the women," Mick growled.

"Fucking Dahlia," Nichol sneered. "If we have to barter to assure the Stojanovski cooperation, she's the goods. Fucking sheltered Tenders. At least Audra has the bloodslave experience to silence her hot tongue when necessary."

****

Audra slept the sleep of the hunted, her eyes flickering open at every inconsequential sound. By the late afternoon, she had given up hopes of a good rest. She slumped her tired body into the bathroom, smiling briefly at Boy as he stood guard.

In the bloodslave quarters, Boy was feared. He was the Grim Reaper of the compound, the god-like scientist who decided when and how the human rats were fed, and which rats were selected for experimentation. During any given night, Boy's arrival at the cell could mean fresh water or it could mean another hour attached to syringes and tubes.

Although his mute, unblinking presence remained unchanged, Boy's predatory skulk and unwavering gaze was now more likely to save her life than eliminate it.

It was a disturbingly comforting thought.

It was also a welcomed distraction from thinking about another blond vampire who currently did not deserve to be thought about.

She scrubbed herself down quickly in the lukewarm water, unwilling to be caught unawares in this strange place. A basic makeup application, boot tying, and ponytail later, and she was ready to make peace with her empty stomach. She moved stealthily through the bunker, locating the small cooler Boy had hauled down and selecting an array of sandwiches and fruit the DeChamplain Tenders had sent along.

"Should be garlic bread," she mumbled, thinking back to the lecherous look the commune owner had given her. "Garlic and onion."

"It's not much of a deterrent if the packaging is appealing," Mick's voice offered quietly.

She huffed, chewing slowly. "What festivities was that creep talking about?" she asked.

Mickey glanced at his resting brothers, pointing to her room. She piled her food up and followed him.

"A hunt," he responded once the door closed. "One you won't be partaking in."

"One Dahl and I won't be partaking in."

Mick crossed his arms. "You, we will actively resist bartering away. Dahlia laid her cards on the table when she reacted favorably. However, if she participates, we'll send Boy onto the grounds. The likelihood of him tracking her is higher than the rest of us."

She set her food down on the bed. "Tell me this is a joke."

Silence.

"Mick. Tell me you're kidding. You are not going to trade a human being for political favors." She stepped into Mickey's space, her finger digging into his chest.

"Given the choice between you and her, we're all in agreement with the decision."

Her lips tightened. "And if he wants us both?"

"You're the hunting priority."

She turned away, sitting on the bed with her head in her hands. Being pragmatic had served her well for years, her rationalizations soundly defending her actions. A former bloodslave aligning herself with vampires was merely a matter of survival, the recognition that she needed value among the males to continue existing. She could block the emotional connections she had formed with the hauntmates, could separate herself from her decisions with the precision of a surgeon.

But this tore her.

"We're commodities," she breathed. "Nothing more than commodities. All of us. It's an integral part of your social and economic systems. If that vampire decides he won't help you unless he gets us both, Dahl and I will be on our asses in the forest before we can blink."

Mick's eyes darkened. "If that happens, I promise you I will locate you. No one dies in the hunt."

"Really." She looked up at Mick, tired. "What do the victors do with the spoils, then?"

A low growl rumbled from the tall male.

"That's what I thought. I'll be the top priority because I have use to you guys. Dahlia will be an afterthought, because she is inherently flawed through her status. Close the door on your way out, please."

****

Jackson Stojanovski was classically vampiric, tall and lithe with an angular jaw and piercing onyx eyes. His vision raked over Audra as he pretended to contemplate the request for information Nichol presented while Mickey moved with Boy to flank her.

Their action left Dahlia a step behind, an inadvertent indication of Audra's value among the Kaius males, and Mick felt a blast of frustration from Nichol for their pronounced display of possession.

Stojanovski was quick to notice their faux pas, his blackened irises elongating.

"Kaspars Dovidas is a scourge," Jackson mused. "But he pays well. Rumors of your involvement in the destruction of his Memphis haunt have been slithering their way through the continents."

They each maintained a blank expression, neither confirming nor denying the speculation as Stojanovski crossed his arms. "What are you offering in exchange for open ears and a closed mouth?"

"Fifty thousand, to be transferred into the account of your choosing immediately," Nichol stated, opening the barter at a price just attractive enough to avoid insult.

Stojanovski pursed his lips, his eyes straying to Audra's legs. "A low offer for a potential wealth of information."

Mickey adjusted his stance, placing himself between Audra and the interested male. "You have a price in mind."

A hint of fang flashed. "Fifty thousand, one Rhys-trained Tender, and a sporting chance on the field this evening with both of your females."

"One hundred and one Tender," Nichol countered.

As Audra stepped forward to protest, Mick's hand shot out, staying her advance.

Stojanovski's attention focused entirely on her. "This Tender will do," he declared, reaching toward her chin.

"She's no Tender," he growled, standing to his full height as he firmly guided the offending hand away.

The gleam in Jackson's eye intensified. "An unconnected human without Tender status protection? She runs at midnight. The rest of the deal stands." Stojanovski signaled to a pair of large men standing guard at the entrance to the human quarters. "Make sure these two are properly briefed on protocol while I entertain the guests. I'm sure our newest arrivals will be anxious to hear the recent rule changes."

He fought the urge to rip Jackson's head from his body as blasts of caution emanated from Nichol. The tension in the room skyrocketed as the human men advanced on the women. Instinctively, he and Boy assumed defensive positions, corralling the females.

"Stand down," Nichol instructed quietly and Mick forced his body to still despite the compulsion pounding in his mind.

Audra followed Dahlia and the men from the reception room, her head held high as she avoided looking at the vampires who had used her as a bartering tool. He preserved his stoic expression while he watched the doors shut her from his sight.

And his protection.

"I'm sure you'll want to prepare for tonight's hunt," Jackson said flippantly, dismissing them from the room with the flick of a wrist. "The games begin at midnight."

The group descended down to their bunker silently, taking hostile stances around the common room as Mickey secured the latch and changed the entrance code.

Nichol kept his back to the room, the hated leader of a motley crew. When he finally turned, he scanned them over and enunciated slowly. "You're wiser than this, more schooled in the dynamics of diplomacy and protocol. Your attempts to protect Audra jeopardized our negotiation, handed Stojanovski more ammunition to his game. 'Rule changes' is an evolving term up until they're spoken aloud, and Jackson is now adjusting them in his mind." Nic stared him down.

"Until we hear the new rules, we'll be flying blind with only our endgame cemented. We have one hour to decide on a flexible strategy, account for variables, and establish our limits. Tonight is one branch of a larger goal. We require the information the Stojanovski's are adept at collecting in order to deal with the larger threat of Dovidas, his accomplices, and his plans.

"This was not an executive decision. Each one of you knows how this works. You have accepted terms more adverse than these to gain intel in the past. If you cannot adhere to the decisions made over the next sixty minutes, take the car and meet the rest of us back at the haunt in two nights."

Mick took a minute to digest his words, knowing how Audra's involvement was impacting all of their decisions.

Tenders had been bartered by the males for centuries, traded and sold for money, secrets, and power. They were more valuable than diamonds in the vampire world, with Rhys's females being the fairest of all. Audra's connection to the Kaius males made her an appealing target, a complication he hadn't fully anticipated prior to their arrival. Without the designation of Tender, she was at a heightened risk, her companion status raising interest without holding the protection of an official designation.

Jagg eventually spoke up. "Endgame is Audra's capture. By one of us."

He and the others nodded in agreement with Jagger. There had been no question about the only acceptable outcome to the night's events. Nichol looked toward Louis. "Dahlia is secondary, despite what Audra will insist. Are you accepting of this?"

Louis leaned back against the wall, crossing his arms. "I am. She's a willing participant in this farce," he spat. "I place Audra's predicament on Dahlia's shoulders. Her reaction last night sealed both their fates."

When Nichol looked his way, he nodded tersely in confirmation. Louis was a realist, a lone survivor with few concessions for those that lacked self-preservation. It made him as pragmatic as Nichol, a trait the old vampire highly respected.

"Dahlia is relegated to low priority," Nichol amended, pulling out his phone and amplifying the receiver device. "I'll inform Rhys immediately, but I expect no argument. What are the known variables we face?"

"Terrain."

"Audra's ability to hide."

"The other guests."

"Bloodlust."

He squatted on the floor, using his finger to trace a large outline of the property from past experience. "The humans are released from this door," he said, pointing to the middle. "We'll fan out from the center once the horn sounds. Place your direction." The hauntmates crouched beside him, marking their paths to space the hunt equally among them. "We hunt clockwise, covering each wedge until it meets the next. Yes?"

As a chorus of confirmation rose from the others and Mick nodded, his throat tight.

"I have little concern regarding Audra's abilities," Nichol continued. "She's physically fit, strong, and intelligent. She's as much a strategist as you, Mick, though significantly more stubborn. If Dahlia is found before her, we can use the Tender as bait to draw Audra into the open, provided no other vampire has a bead on her as well. We don't want to draw her out into another's fangs.

"Boy, you have a blood link to her. We'll follow your direction once the game begins if you can lock on to her. However," Nichol frowned and stared at the floor, "Stojanovski has been known to have a Subduer on site to make the hunt more equal. We should expect that to be part of tonight's entertainment, and not rely solely on Boy's links to Audra and Dahlia."

Boy lowered his head in acceptance and Mick wished for a fleeting moment that the mute male would update the group on Audra's status. Reassure him she was okay. Pissed off and safe.

"The grounds are usually filled with a mix of young and old," Nichol went on. "I anticipate Boy and I will be at the oldest end of the spectrum, but there's no guarantee an ancient or two isn't lurking. The young ones are easily surpassed in speed and agility, but their numbers could be an issue if the commune is at full capacity. I'll remain alert to Louis and Jagger. Boy, you focus on Mick. If any of you are up against an older vamp, yell. Pride aside, this is necessary."

As the males muttered their acceptance of the edict, Mickey spoke quietly. "The bloodlust will be an issue. For others as well as ourselves. The hunt's a well-coordinated return to our primal state. And I may have difficulty channeling those urges if I become overwhelmed."

The room went still at the open admission of weakness, his hauntmates processing it in silence.

Jagger spoke first.

"Our control deficiencies aren't your failings," Jagg stated, brokering no argument.

He bowed his head, averting his eyes from the group and refocusing his mind on the task at hand.

"Does Stojanovski still insist the captured humans be brought to the reception room for counting and tracking prior to claiming? His brethren were quite strict with that rule," Louis commented.

"I assume so," Nichol answered. "We can also anticipate Jackson's participation in the games tonight. His interest in Audra is obvious. Whoever is closest to his exit must keep one eye on him to ensure he doesn't capture her before we do."

Mick stood, bolting to the bedroom Audra had occupied hours prior. He returned quickly, dumping her belongings into a pile in the middle of the room. "Get the scent of everything she owns into your minds," he said, his voice balancing between an order and a plea. Nichol watched him intently and he tried to force a calm facade while he scattered Audra's belongings across the floor. "Every combination of lotions, soap, shampoos, lip gloss…retain it all."

Chapter Twenty-Nine

"I hate humans."

Audra kept her back to the wall, her eyes continually scanning the expanse of the room as she monitored Dahlia's whereabouts. The cheery Tender was in her element, gossiping and preening alongside the commune's house humans.

She kept a running total in her head, twenty-nine women and eleven males. The cliques formed and dispersed as it drew closer to midnight, the anticipation as palpable as the intense intermingling perfumes.

Some of the humans stretched their muscles in the outskirts, their defined forms flexing and lengthening under the florescent lights. Others adjusted impractical skirts and corsets while balancing precariously on stilettos.

She crunched her toes in her heavy combat boots, grateful for the traction they would provide once the horn went. Dahlia stood among a small cloister of women, her kitten heels and tight denim contrasting starkly with Audra's singlet and cargo pants.

The rules of the hunt were simple. Run, hide, get caught, get counted, feed, and fuck. Staking a vampire with would result in a long, torturous death at the hands of Stojanovski himself. Revealing the position of another was punishable by imprisonment, as was revealing oneself for preferred vampires.

Though this edict didn't stop the more ambitious humans from dousing themselves in signature scents to draw the attention of their desired captors.

Humans.

She shook her head quickly to refocus. When had she begun referring to men and women as humans? More importantly, when had she stopped identifying with her own species enough to not consider herself human? She studied the expressions and body language of the room, assessing their hopeful eyes and overtly sexual posturing with disdain. This was a hunt, and she wasn't going to be caught unless she wanted to be.

The windows of the upstairs room provided a fair view of the grounds she would be running into within the hour. She had examined the varied terrains with a critical eye. The thick forested area would provide ample coverage and the benefit of height if she managed to climb the trees.

The grassland was dense, allowing for a body to sink into the foliage and disappear from sight providing one didn't have to move. A rocky hill, crafted to supply caves and crevices in which to crouch, was tempting with its shadowed slopes and darkened crannies.

But it was the swampland that appealed most to her. The brush wasn't tall, but the water would mask her scent while providing visual coverage among the clumps of cattails and rushes.

She assumed most of the others would avoid the area, given the guaranteed filth and smell. And that meant most of the vampires would avoid the swamp as well. She could move through the water slowly without detection, its far banks extending past the barbed fence.

Back to the wall, she thought wryly.

A lesson well-rehearsed in the bloodslave quarters.

The head vampire appeared in the doorway, causing the humans to fall into a reverent hush. His eyes sought her out, tongue darting across the tips of his elongated fangs when he spotted his target.

"Into the hall, my lovely quarry," he called to the group, keeping his gaze on her. "Tonight, I'll be joining the others. I look forward to your best efforts."

His announcement was met with a buzz of excitement, the men flexing in anticipation, the women primping on their way through the door. Her sights on Dahlia, she brought up the rear of the group, ever aware of the interested stare of the vampire who joined her.

"Your companions are a protective bunch," he conversed. "For you, at least." His eyes tracked her gaze to the back of Dahlia's pixie cut. "The willing don't spur the blood. There's little satisfaction in charging down a wounded gazelle, and a predator requires the thrill almost more than the spoils."

She kept her gaze straight ahead, refusing to acknowledge the dangerous male at her side.

"Vampires weren't meant to be bottle-fed," he said softly. "Sometimes we need an escape from the cultured practices we've cultivated over time. A reminder of our roots, the awakening of our instincts."

He left her, striding through the group to welcome his guests.

As the humans clamored to the four exits doors, she held back. She was acutely aware of her vampires in her peripheral, their hardened expressions void of emotion.

The Kaius haunt vampires, she corrected mentally.

"Quarry!" the head vampire bellowed over the din.

"There have been two changes to our usual event."

The humans stilled, turning to listen attentively.

"For tonight's festivities, we have forty humans for sixty vampires, myself included. This will require you to be more creative in your techniques, as competition tends to bring out the animal in us." He chuckled, numerous guests joining in the merriment. In the corner of her eye, she saw the Kaius hauntmates spread out among the other patrons.

"We have two special guests among our prey tonight. The Kaius haunt has brought with them a Rhys-trained Tender and a...companion female." She remained still to avoid drawing more attention as Dahlia waved her arm above the throng of humans. Stojanovski met her glare and continued. "The second change will greet the quarry as they exit. Ten-minute head start."

The humans became more heightened in their expectancy, their bodies thrumming with the thrill of the chase. She kept one eye on Dahlia as she surveyed the vampires. Tall, short, young, old. Their physical appearances gave her no clues as to their strength or age. The fangs of some elongated in anticipation, their irises ovaling. The humans began the ten second countdown, their voices growing louder with each number.

Five.

Dahlia was squeezing through the masses and toward the door.

Four.

Audra looked behind her, uncomfortable with her back exposed to the enemy.

Three.

Nichol watching her intently.

Two.

Boy's long blond hair was tied back.

One.

Mick's jaw twitched.

The blaring horn echoed in the room and the exits flung open for the swarm of humans to escape, a red spray dousing the first bodies through the doors.

Blood.

The first wave screeched in surprise before tearing past the mist and into the darkness. The others followed, hiding their eyes and shielding their mouths from the droplets. Audra tore after Dahlia, the last out of the room as the ten-minute countdown for the vampires began.

The surging spray pelted her skin, covering her in a viscous, sticky mess. She scanned the escapees, hunting for the short Tender. Acquiring a bead on the woman, she raced after her, gaining ground quickly as her booted feet held traction.

"Dahl," she hissed, grabbing the woman's arm. "Come."

Dahlia spun, her eyes glittering with the frenzy. "We're all heading this way!" she exclaimed, breathless from the short exertion. "The vampires favor the treed areas."

"Which is why we don't want to be there," she said.

Dahlia sighed. "No, Audra. You don't want to be there. These are the games a fun master plays, the thrills he provides between cleaning and baking and fucking. This," she gestured toward the scattering bodies in the darkness, "is the excitement I've been craving since

Rhys turned me out into the haunt. It's not for you, Audra." Glancing over her shoulder, she shook her head. "Go. And good luck."

Audra stayed rooted where she stood and she watched Dahlia follow the pack, her small stature disappearing into the woods with the others.

****

The seconds clicked by robotically, leisurely and unyielding to the weight of the tension infused in Mickey's body. The scent of blood filled the air, a mixture of A, B, and O swirling and permeating the senses of every vampire in the room. The younger males were beginning to show signs of a rising bloodlust, their decreased control amplified by a heightened sense of anticipation.

He monitored his hauntmates, gratified to find them in full domination of their impulses. His eyes scanned the closed exit where Audra had run, willing himself to see through the wood and into the darkness. The doors had slammed shut as Audra's heels left the frame, the shower of blood no longer raining down and seeping under the cracks.

He was almost completely detached from the emotions of his hauntmates, confirming the earlier suspicion that a Subduer was among the guests. The Subduer was weaker than Dovidas, as Mick could still feel a muted resolve echoing from the rest of the Kaius hauntmates. He scanned the other vampires for any indication another had noticed the dampening.

Nothing.

The addition of blood to the hunt was multi-purposed. The overpowering odors drowned out those of the humans, their cheap perfumes and bottled sprays no match for the vampire infatuation with their life supply. The competitiveness among the guests had ratcheted up upon hearing the ratio of humans to vampires, and the blood-soaked grounds only served to ramp it up higher. Bloodlust was a very real threat to every human on the premises, the young vampires easily consumed and the old ones willingly so.

Nichol's determination and confidence held his head above water whenever he thought about the potential outcomes of the night's events. The eldest brother's stance was primed, his muscled form taut, ready, and focused. Jagger was at Mick's back, with Louis at his side. The two males would hunt together, an unspoken agreement to combine Jagg's age and strength with Louis's hearing.

Boy appeared completely unaffected by the stimulus surrounding him. Spending his nights in the bloodslave quarters had steeled his senses and numbed his reaction to blood and fear. His blue eyes held a hint of anger, a far reach from the deadness that traditionally inhabited his expressions.

The seconds counted down, revving the males up into a frenzy. The Kaius hauntmates jostled into position, their size and reputation opening the throngs of vampires as the final ticks of the clock echoed. Unlike Audra, the hauntmates were determined to be second out of the gate. If Stojanovski had any more surprises, the first out would be caught unawares, paving the way for the second wave to enter the night unimpeded.

Two.

He flexed his thigh muscles, preparing to launch himself over the young vampire in front of him.

One.

The thrill of the hunt echoed across the brothers, centering their goal.

The buzzer signaling the start of the hunt pierced the ears of the vampires, a slightly disorienting experience for the young, eager males at the front. They clumsily pushed the doors open and were casually tossed aside by the stronger vampires when the possibility of another unexpected event was eliminated.

He propelled over the weaker vampires and tore into the night, the clean air clearing away some of the blood haze that had snuck into his senses.

The further he ran from the central building, the better he could observe the whereabouts of his hauntmates. Nichol slowed, assessing the forested terrain with the prowl of a lion, his smooth gait moving toward the outer rim of the trees.

Louis and Jagg had been quick to scan the grassland, their cohesive turn away from the flat region indicating they had eliminated it as a potential hunting ground. Boy stayed his path, his long body scaling the rocky peak with an unnatural gracefulness and speed.

His boots slopped through the marshy swamp, the cold dampness inching into the cuffs of his socks as his weight brought him deeper into the mud. Several males were at his heels, their postures bent while they scented the cattails for specks of drying blood. Shrieks of delight and fear punctured the night as a few vampires found their conquests. Mickey counted them off. Four. Five. Two more. The majority had come from the forested area.

Nichol approached the swampland from the left as Jagger and Louis closed in on the right. The four of them covered the breadth of the land, fanning out and communicating through quick hand signals. Boy stood atop the rocky hill, his ancient eyes scanning the perimeter.

Fourteen.

Fifteen.

As the first hour passed, unsuccessful vampires became more predatory, their formerly cultured movements now hunching and stalking as they roamed the landscape. He continued his trek through the swamp, stopping for stretches to scent the air, the rushes, the mud. He was centered, completely engulfed in his mission and entirely detached from his prey.

Nichol had sent Jagger back to the central building, with implicit instructions to report if Audra was captured. Nichol rejoined Louis, and the three males scoured the land under Boy's watchful stare.

The second hour came and went, and the amount of game left on the premises dwindled further. With thirty-two caught, there remained eight humans for twenty-eight covetous vampires.

The swamp was a difficult hunt, the increasing foot traffic displacing the mud and turning over scents. Many of the younger vamps had become less stealthy in their rising hunger, their ovaled eyes almost glowing in the darkness.

"Mikhail."

He froze, cocking his head toward Nichol's voice.

"Eyes on Boy."

Turning toward the rocky hill, he saw Boy descending slowly, methodically, his blue eyes trained on someone.

Stojanovski.

Along the far wires of the slough, Jackson was advancing silently across the deep water. Mick, Nichol, and Louis approached the marsh, their cargo pants weighed down with the heaviness of the water drenching them to their thighs. Other males noticed the swarm, following in an almost desperate hope of success. He scanned the area for the thousandth time, searching for a hint of ebony hair or angry cat eyes.

Whatever Stojanovski saw, it was hidden well from him.

Thirty-six.

Thirty-seven.

At this point, he was hoping Audra would appear at the compound on the arm of a young vampire, one Jagger could easily take down or bargain with. Boy was still too far off to assist the males in their hunt, but his impending presence was somewhat reassuring as he dropped silently from the rocks.

Louis was moving closer to Stojanovski, his body already emerged up to his chest. Nichol followed suit, a slight flash of disgust crossing his features as he sank deep into the sludge.

Thirty-eight.

Jackson didn't acknowledge the Kaius vampires as they closed in on his position. His attention was drawn to a thick clump of cattails, their sturdy stems unwavering despite the increased ripples in the water. Mickey was farther from the target, his speed increasing as he drew nearer.

Thirty-nine screams.

Stojanovski stilled, his muscles tensing as he focused intensely on the rushes. Mickey's mind calculated the distance from his own position instantaneously. Neither male was close enough to reach the cattails in a single launch.

He slipped silently under the sludge.

****

The silt continued to harden, tightening her skin and becoming increasingly uncomfortable as Audra's boots sank a fraction more into the base of the swamp. The caked mud on her lashes obscured her vision while the muck in her ears muted her hearing.

A sitting duck.

Her position ignored for much of the hunt, she could now make out a swarm of hungry males closing in on her. The varied depth of the marsh affected her ability to judge the massive heights of the Kaius vampires against those of the others, leaving her unsure whether the closest of the predators was friend or foe. She focused on keeping still, her tongue wedged between her teeth to prevent her teeth from clenching on the grit in her mouth.

The advance of the vampires halted. She kept her eyes squinted, the whites hidden behind her muddy lashes. The figure in front of her froze in place, taking a deep breath before sliding into the dark water.

In her peripheral a male launched himself at her, his elongated fangs glimmering in the faint moonlight. She steeled herself for the attack, refusing to scream as the others had when they were taken down. Her leg instinctively stepped to the side to better steady herself.

A strong grasp on her calf.

A burning pain scouring her neck as she was pulled under.

She fought frantically against the grip on her leg, kicking like a roped bull until a second hand seized her other thigh. The hands continued to grapple up her body until they grasped her face. Having not had time to prepare for the underwater assault with full lungs, she was beginning to panic.

A second pair of hands plunged into the water above her, fingers finding and digging into her shoulders, yanking her back as the first pair adjusted their hold, bringing her flush with a hard body. The hands at her shoulders released, their scrambling movements tangling in her ponytail. She could feel her rational mind vanishing as survival mode took over and she fought with everything she had, a rabid animal in a box.

Her legs beat against the water, arms pushing against her captor's chest while he fought to cocoon her in the murky sludge. His mouth sealed over hers, fangs piercing her lower lip to force her mouth open.

Air.

****

Breathe in, stubborn woman, Mick snarled in his mind while he grappled to remove Stojanovski's fingers from Audra's hair. As her chest expanded against him, he unhooked his fangs from her lip, released the seal around her mouth, and pushed away from Stojanovski, turning to place Audra beneath him as he kicked toward the shallower water. She had stopped fighting him, her body wrapped around his while he found ground beneath his feet.

He broke out of the swamp with a roar, staking his claim against the other predators swarming him. Audra gasped at his shoulder, her lungs struggling to inhale. Stojanovski stood across the deeper water, his blackened eyes moving between the hauntmates as though calculating his chances of swimming across the swamp before he was taken down by one of the Kaius males.

Nichol remained at Stojanovski's back, a vicious reminder of the strength behind his younger hauntmate. Louis and Boy flanked Mick on either side, their low growls a warning to the others to keep their distance. A dozen vampires encircled the group, young males torn between intelligence and impulse. They watched Stojanovski, awaiting his reaction to the loss of the final game of the hunt.

He clung to Audra, supporting her weight as she regained control over her body. A jolt of calm surged through his mind. Looking up, he saw Nichol staring him down. The older vampire flashed his fangs, tilting his head toward the central building.

"Don't fight," he whispered into Audra's ear before he picked her up and flung her over his shoulder. She tensed at the sudden movement before going limp in his hold. Secured with the hauntmates behind him, he turned and began his trek out of the swamp, his prize dangling down his back while he strode past the unsuccessful vampires, meeting each eye as he passed them. Most were younger than himself, mere pups in the vampire world. The few older males bared their fangs, their feet rooted to the ground as Boy and Louis joined the procession.

The cleared land around the reception hall appeared miles away as he trudged through the swamp. Jagger stood at the cusp of the land, falling into step with the others once they reached him. Audra remained still, her steady breathing a reassurance. He forced himself to remain centered, his goal not yet achieved as he still needed to claim the night's prize among the commune guests in the hall.

The males crossed the plain and through the threshold, the room silencing as the final prey was carried unceremoniously to the center of the floor. Jagg and Boy flanked Mickey, their hard eyes scouring the area for danger. Nichol was noticeably absent, along with Louis.

Whatever revelry had overtaken the group earlier dissipated as the crowd awaited the arrival of their host. Very few of the unsuccessful hunters entered the room, their egos forcing them to retreat underground for the remainder of the night. Those who did enter joined their older hauntmates, hopeful their successful brethren would share their conquests.

A low growl rumbled through his chest as he eyed his own hauntmates, undeterred in his warning when he was met with eye rolls and a smirk. Stojanovski finally graced the room, Nichol and Louis at his back. Despite his foul swamp odor and waterlogged appearance, Stojanovski took command of the room as he crossed it slowly, eyes locked on the filthy woman hanging on Mick's shoulder.

He motioned for him to lower Audra, Nichol's quick nod putting Mick at ease enough to place her feet on the ground, his arm holding tight to steady her. Despite the layers of mud and grime, Audra squared her shoulders, her head straight and eyes narrowed in defiance.

"Our victor," Stojanovski called out, his voice lacking the bravado of earlier. A man appeared from the entryway to the human quarters, a small box in hand. Jackson took the package without acknowledgement, placing it within Audra's reach. "Your reward. Personally selected for you by me."

Audra's eyes shot to Boy for guidance, her hands closing around the edges with the silent bow of his head.

Mick ignored the slight.

Nimble fingers lifted the lid just enough for Audra to see its contents before she closed it tight, a grim look overtaking her features.

"We're in agreement?" Nichol queried, moving toe-to-toe with Stojanovski.

"We are."

Nichol motioned the hauntmates toward the exit, waiting until the others strode out before following.

Chapter Thirty

"We'll make Peoria before dawn," Nichol said quietly, maneuvering the SUV smoothly onto the highway and meeting Mickey's eyes. The sports car followed course, its headlights bouncing off the mirrors as they aligned onto the road. "There's a bolt hole on the outskirts that Kaius has kept for decades. It's fully functional, though likely a little dusty."

Audra hadn't moved since Mick had escorted her from the commune and into the passenger seat. She didn't scream. Or cry. Or argue. Merely held her prize in her lap and blinked intermittently.

He would have preferred any reaction over her sullen silence.

Boy was immobile in the back seat, his long legs spread awkwardly with the limited room.

"You did well," Nichol stated, breaking the stony silence. "Better than any of us anticipated, to be frank. It reflects well on your self-preservation skills. Most humans would not have been as thorough in their attempts to cover their trail and their scent. Despite your objections to the hunt, your ability to hide as long as you did while unfamiliar with the territory was impressive. As was your disguise, even if it is slowly cracking off onto the floor."

Mick fought the urge to touch her, to reassure himself she was okay. "There's a strong shower in the bolt hole."

"You'll have first access, since you probably aren't comfortable in your current state," Nichol chimed in. "I'll instruct the others to give you the time you need in there."

"Nichol. Mickey." Audra finally acknowledged them, her gaze changing from blank to exasperated. "Your babbling is really pissing me off."

He ducked his slight smirk out of sight, straightening his expression. "I'm distracting myself from the putrid odor of your clothing."

Audra huffed and remained silent for the rest of the drive, her annoyance an improvement from her apathy.

The bolt hole land was spacious, an unkempt treed lot that stretched back from the highway. The long gravel road led to a tiny shotgun shack, an abandoned room sitting atop a significantly larger underground bunker. While Nichol collected the most important tech bags, Mick lifted the floorboards to enter the lair, the small hinges unnoticeable to the human eye among the uneven knots and grains of the wood.

The hauntmates descended into the darkness, their backs loaded with bags and gear. Audra was last to enter, her strong footsteps slowed by the obvious physical discomfort she was experiencing. He started the generator, flicking the switch to heat the water in the large tank Kai insisted upon in every hidden compound he had. Audra wandered around the quarters, orienting herself and flaking mud around the rooms until she found the bathroom.

"Why is there a toilet in here?" she called out.

"Tender transfers pass through here," he responded. "We can take it out, if you'd prefer."

A snort. The rush of shower water.

The males busied themselves removing their boots, their muddied feet leaving large tracks on the floor as they stood around patiently, none anxious to sit on Kaius's clean furnishings.

He was keenly aware of Nichol's monitoring of him, hazel eyes tracking his every movement as Mick paced the floor, attention on the locked bathroom door.

"Why don't we head topside and work off some of this energy?" Jagger suddenly suggested, rocking on his heels to the monotonous song he had been humming. "I'm hungry, tired, and really fucking wound."

Louis was first to head back up. "I'm in. I could use a good ass-kicking."

The hauntmates clamored above, leaving Audra in peace.

"Boy and I will square off," Nichol stated. "Mick and Louis can work on Jagger. We can switch it up in a bit. No weapons. No long-term injuries."

****

Audra pulled on the one clean outfit she had left, the baggy sweatpants and singlet feeling as luxurious as silk after sitting for hours in the damp synthetic fabric of her cargo pants. The silence from the bunker had her cracking the door as she quickly ran a brush through her hair, leaving it long and wet down her back as she glanced into the hall for movement.

Hefting her bag over her shoulder, she wandered through the small underground loft before selecting a bed and tossing her things on it.

"Nichol?" she queried into the silence. When no answer came, she climbed the ladder to the escape hatch, pushing it up with a grunt.

Blood. Growls. Fangs.

She jumped from the bunker, her senses going into overdrive. The movements around the shack were lightning quick, her eyes catching only glimpses of the violence encircling the small house. She scrambled back into the bunker, rifling through Nichol's bags for the knives she knew he stashed everywhere. Her fingers encircled a serrated blade and she scrambled back up the ladder onto the open plain, prepared to join the fight.

Ascertaining the enemy was impossible, her human eyes unable to make out details in the dim moonlight, incapable of focusing on the preternatural speed of the predators in full battle. Her heart thumped in her ears as her body prepared to fight or run.

"Nichol!" she yelled, her voice weak against the expanse of the terrain. Nichol stopped. His form became crystal clear as he lifted a hand in acknowledgement, only to be knocked to the ground by his attacker. She jumped forward, her mind and body centered on the defense of Nichol as she launched herself on to the back of the assailant and drove the blade deep into his broad shoulders.

The attacker reared up with a roar and spun, catching her mid-fall and cradling the back of her head as they dropped. Her wrists were restrained instantly while her body formed to the ground beneath her, a head lodging between her neck and shoulder. She thrashed and snarled, refusing to allow herself to be used as fast food.

Her blood was hers, goddamnit.

A soft licking along her jugular.

She froze her movements, remembering the tear

caused by Nichol mere weeks ago. The licking continued, a contented growl coming from her attacker.

"She got you good, man."

Nichol's voice came from behind her as the licking continued. She arched her head back in confusion as Jagger's arm came into view, pulling the serrated blade from her licker's shoulder blade.

He turned the knife over and whistled. "That's going to sting for a bit."

The large male on top of Audra finally lifted from her, his arctic blue eyes smiling, even if his lips weren't. "Sorry," Mick said, rising off her and offering a hand. "Instinct and all."

Her heart was still hammering, her hands clammy. "I...what the fuck?"

Nichol collected the blade from Jagger, turning it over a few times before wiping the blood onto the grass. "We were just letting off a little steam in a friendly match. Friendly. No weapons."

She looked at the males, taking in their filthy clothes, bare feet, and relaxed postures. Running her hands through her hair, she took a deep breath before pummeling Mick with her fists. "Your instinct does not tell you to lick someone who stabbed you!" she yelled, her hits getting faster. The sheepish smile on Mickey's face only frustrated her more. She pushed against his chest, a hint of satisfaction when he stepped back.

"We didn't mean to freak you out," he said softly, not making a move to stop her ineffectual fists.

"No? Well, fight back," she growled, adjusting her stance to withstand a hit. "You all get to beat the ever-loving hell out of each other. Fight. Back."

Mick put his hands in his pockets, and she saw red.

All the fear and tension of the past two weeks was wiped so easily from their faces, while her own was still fraught with images of Jagger's burnt skin, Mickey's convulsing form, and Dahlia's words.

"Fight me!" she screamed, turning to the others. "You owe me. I have no equal. No sidekick." She turned back to Mick, egging him on with her finger pointing squarely into his chest. "How am I supposed to burn off the last few days? Vacuum? Bake a cake? What?"

Mickey's arm swung up, blocking her accusing finger. She recovered quickly, landing a punch to his abs before he swooped her legs out from under her and she landed on the hard earth with a thud, flinging her leg across his ankles.

She continued to kick at him as he drew nearer, her feet and calves bruising against the iron stance and sending just enough pain through her body to feel it, to feel animated and alive. She scrambled to her feet and ran full tilt into Mick, her shoulder knocking him slightly off balance as her fists resumed their assault on his torso.

****

The beating couldn't last long enough for Mickey. Audra's small fists hammered at him, striking him over and over as she expelled her anger and fear onto his chest. Every so often, he would block a hit, moving smoothly enough to cause no damage to the little hellion, but with enough force to give her something to fight against.

It was reminiscent of Dominic's early training sessions.

Jagger, Louis, and Boy had disappeared

underground, likely battling in the bunker over who got to shower first. Nichol stood guard, one eye on the horizon as the night drew to a close.

Audra cursed, her voice growing hoarse from the screaming profanities she unleashed as she pounded on him. A quick gesture from Nichol and Mick stilled Audra's fists.

"The sun's rising. We can continue this downstairs," he offered, his voice calm.

She glanced at the sky, her eyes wild and hair more so. A deep breath heaved her shoulders as she steadied her temper and centered herself. "No. I'm good. I...I'm good."

He offered her his arm, pleased when she took it and allowed him to guide her back to shack. "You're a tough little thing," he mused, rolling out his shoulders. The sting of the stab wound was abating already, the muscles and skin knitting together.

She grunted inelegantly.

"She doesn't find you threatening," Nichol spoke behind them as they lifted the floorboards to crawl down the ladder. "You were too messed up to remember, but Audra was very complimentary about your fangs during our first days in Vansburg. Something about her being grateful they were so much smaller than Jagger's."

His eyes narrowed at the not so subtle jab to his masculinity, digging his 'small' fangs into his lower lip to maintain an angered expression when Audra looked positively abashed. "Nothing about me is small," he growled out, hiding his amusement at the blush coloring Audra's face while she descended down the ladder.

He and Nichol followed suit, joining their significantly cleaner hauntmates in the main room. Nichol strode to the bathroom to shower, leaving Mick and Audra dirty and standing still to avoid tracking the mess throughout the bunker.

"So where will we be tomorrow night?" Audra asked as the shower whirred to life, all fight gone from her voice.

"Lincoln," Nichol's voice shouted from the bathroom. "Former Tender's house."

Audra looked up to him, sending a small chill down his spine. "There are Former Tenders?"

"They're a rare official designation," he answered. "Usually occurs when the vampire dies a few decades into the Tender's service and the Tender has been taken on in a marriage-like arrangement. Rhys is charged with assessing whether the female can survive independently without revealing anything to her human counterparts. Most want reassignment, but the odd one lives out the rest of her life as part of the underground."

"Couldn't be any worse than that commune," Audra muttered.

Louis stretched along the sofa. "It wasn't so bad." Audra shot him a glare. Louis raised his hands in surrender. "Just saying. I hypnotized my first vampire. It was kind of cool."

Mick grinned broadly at his friend. "You're the reason Stojanovski was so amenable to releasing us without a fight?"

"Of course. Nichol isn't that good a negotiator."

"Shut it before I rip your throat out," Nichol barked over the racing water.

Louis flipped his finger toward the closed door of

299

the bathroom, a gesture Mick knew he wouldn't be brave enough to do to Nichol's face. "It won't hold long," Louis warned. "But there are enough witnesses to the release and the acceptance of our agreement. Getting both of those was more important at the moment than the longevity of the compulsion."

Audra crossed her arms, her face going thoughtful. "That's a bit of a risk," she said slowly. "I assume vampire hypnosis is not something widely approved, especially when it involves negotiations. Do you anticipate blowback?"

The rapid shifts from aggressive spitfire to blushing female to astute strategist was affecting him far more than he was willing to admit.

The shower turned off, Nichol's voice carrying through the bunker smoothly. "Stojanovski is a smart player. He was bested on his own turf, in more ways than one. He won't tell anyone his mind was weak enough to be compelled by a vampire as young as Louis. Though he'll likely refuse to deal with our haunt face-to-face for a stretch. He did, however, manage to secure a Rhys-trained Tender in exchange for his cooperation, so he can't be too bent out of shape. And lucky for us, Dahlia was more than happy to remain at his side. Mick, you shower next. Water's cold, but I think you need it."

Chapter Thirty-One

Mickey stood at the door to the bedroom, his arms folded over his chest. Audra had been sleeping for hours, the afternoon sun hidden by several feet of earth and concrete. He monitored her steady breathing and even heartbeat, searching for the slightest glitch or stutter.

"She's fine," Nichol said quietly from his position in the main room. "She's strong."

"Yep."

"You aren't connected," Nichol ventured.

"Nope." He could feel Nichol's unblinking gaze on him, assessing him. He knew the calm facade engulfing him since the Stojanovski commune was not his own. It was a concerted effort on behalf of all his brothers to keep him cocooned until they returned to the haunt where they no longer had to be watching their backs at all times. "I can read you," he muttered quietly.

Nichol grunted. "We've been well aware of that for over two centuries."

"No, I mean deeper. I can delve a lot deeper than the strongest one or two emotions you guys emit." He refused to turn toward Nichol. "Fuck, it feels like years ago," he huffed. "Back in the hotel. The first night. I was so fucking jealous of you, knowing she was in your room. And you were giving off so many weird signals." He ran a hand through his long hair.

"I try to avoid reading any of you. Anything you send off that's strong is one thing, but those quieter ones aren't any of my business. They belong only to you, so I keep my distance. But that night I didn't. And I'm sorry, man. It was never my place to dig that deep. Especially intentionally for my own dumbass reasons."

He steadied his stance, ready to take whatever beating Nichol decided to lay on him. Jagger's quiet hum was the only sound in the bunker, a soft lull indicating he was deep at rest.

"What did you discover?" Nichol queried, not moving from his position by the exit.

He chuckled humorously. "You like her. As a hauntmate. An equal. You willingly accept her into our group."

"She's not as annoying as Dominic," Nichol stated. "Nor as emotional as you. Quieter than Jagger. More reliable than Kaius and less crass than Rhys. I would say I prefer her to the five of you." He went silent for a moment before Mick caught sight of a flash of fang. "We're BFFs. I believe she's threatened to purchase us matching necklaces."

Of all the reactions he had anticipated with his revelation, humor was not one of them.

Nichol wasn't funny.

"You aren't pissed," he noted, refusing to probe his brother's emotions for confirmation.

"I'm not. It makes sense that over time your ability to read and anticipate would grow. The capacity to delve further, to assess and filter, is something we can perhaps work with when we return home. If you can securely hold on to those more placid threads, we may be able to limit the impact of our larger, more intense emotions during situations such as the ones we've faced recently."

He nodded slowly. "Basically, create smaller bubbles within each of your rivers. Similar to the one Louis has most of the time."

"Exactly," Nichol concurred. "Your ability to read Louis is interesting. You mentioned long ago that vampires not of our bloodline only give off an echo that is barely readable."

With a grunt, he hooked his thumbs in his belt loops. "We had an unintentional blood-mixing caused by stupid injuries from stupid dares. He came online, and never fucking left."

A companionable silence resumed in the bunker. He maintained his vigil, unsure about what he was watching for, but refusing to stop. Audra slept peacefully, completely encased by the blanket. Every so often she would change positions, but not once did she awaken. Nichol eventually switched places with Boy, urging him to take a few hours rest as well.

Although he refused to verbalize it, he was far more rejuvenated watching the sleeping woman than any amount of rest could provide.

****

The closer to Lincoln the small convoy got, the more relaxed they became. Music began filtering through speakers, banter became more playful, and insults were traded freely between the hauntmates. Audra had awoken shortly before dusk, refreshed and demanding and making Mickey question whether he was developing a fetish for commanding women.

The males were set to work immediately, tiding the muddy messes left throughout the bunker as Audra made subtle jabs about their inability to properly wield a broom or cloth.

Dominic's car followed slowly, Louis at the wheel. Nichol commandeered the SUV, pushing the speed limits on the empty highway and falling back with a grumble when Louis didn't keep up.

Mick relaxed back and listened as the vehicle occupants maintained an open phone connection, allowing all the hauntmates to interact with each other as often and as loudly as they wanted. Louis automatically repeated everything the SUV passengers said, keeping Jagger fully engulfed in the conversation.

On Nichol's sly commentary, Mickey was being harassed about his 'small fangs', with Jagg preening loudly over the speakers and Audra aggressively protesting the interpretation of her words from the Vansburg cell.

"Hold," Nichol said quickly, noticing Rhys's number coming up on his smartphone. "I'll three-way Rhys."

The males grew more rambunctious as they chatted with Rhys, talking louder and louder to overtake each other. After a rather definitive round of good-natured insults, Rhys called out for Audra.

"Here," she replied, her cheeks flushed with laughter.

"I'm texting Mickey a link right away," Rhys said, his voice crackling slightly as the convoy hit a valley. "You, Mick, and Jagger are fugitives from the law, sweetheart. Well, technically Meredith Abernathy is."

His phone buzzed. Audra leaned over the seat to read the police report. "Holy damn, you're right!" she exclaimed, peering at her likeness of the screen. "I look good."

"You're a hot fugitive," he grinned. "So am I. Jagger looks like a serial killer."

After Louis repeated the statement, Jagger barked back, demanding the link as well.

"Just keep in mind that we'll need to retire Ms. Abernathy for any future missions," Rhys said.

"I'll wipe her existence from the internet," Nichol stated. "I saved the link to every page Meredith Abernathy appeared on in anticipation of this."

"Of course you did," Audra crooned. "You're my little genius with bite."

A chorus of ooohhs and aaahhhs followed the endearment. Nichol rolled his eyes and flashed his fangs in the rearview mirror. "All right, Rhys. We're pulling into Lincoln now. I'll text you before dawn."

The Holst residence was on a quiet cul-de-sac in the southern outskirts of Lincoln. Mickey instructed the drivers, his memory of the area fighting to keep up with the new construction since his last visit. Urban sprawl had overtaken the once segregated community, engulfing it into the larger city.

He had been initially hesitant about stopping at the Former Tender's house now that it was surrounded by winding side streets and cramped housing, but Rhys had assured him the neighborhood was safe, its inhabitants reclusive during darkness.

"It'll be good to see Bee again," he said as they slowed in front of the Victorian-style house. "I think the last time I laid eyes on her was seven or eight years ago. Wonder how she aged."

The vehicles backed into the long driveway, primed to vacate if necessary. The males loaded their backs with bags and cases, Audra carrying her small knapsack over her shoulder. As they approached the entrance, the door opened to reveal the tiny blonde hostess, her bright blue eyes smiling at the motley crew.

****

Mediocre.

Inferior.

Third wheel.

Audra adjusted the force of her smile, toning down the crazy and amping up the interest as her hauntmates ignored her in favor of Bianca Holst.

Her hauntmates, not Bianca's.

With the exception of Boy, who stood behind Audra's chair, the others were enamored with the woman, vying for her big blue eyes to turn to them attentively. The petite hostess sat perched in a large armchair, her white mini dress riding up on her tanned thighs and her long blonde hair being flicked back demurely every few minutes. She looked like she had just stepped off a 1960's magazine cover.

Between Bianca Holst and Brigette Bardot, she would struggle to decide who was more perfect.

The males lounged on the sofas, their legs and arms encompassing as much space as possible. Years of work with alpha males in the corporate world had taught her a lot about body language. Watching the guys slip so easily into a competition to dominate the room, and by extension the stunning hostess, left her feeling slightly off balance. Never one to submit to jealousy, she found herself assessing the female as a rival might, measuring her own attributes against the witty, intelligent woman.

Bianca was everything she had witnessed in Rhys's

Tenders, but more. More enticing. More confident. More intellectual. More inviting. Her enunciation was impeccable. And she was the sweetest, most inviting hostess she had encountered in her life. A tray of dainties sat on the coffee table, along with a variety of wines and heated carafes of assorted blood types.

Bianca had repeatedly drawn a reluctant Audra into the conversation, inquiring about her life, her experiences, and attempting to bond over a feigned perplexity regarding the male mind. She had returned the social niceties on autopilot, her attention more drawn to Mick's stupid grin at Bianca than the woman's responses.

Her fingers felt gritty against the delicate fabric of the high-backed chair, her nails still rugged from her ordeal in the swamp. Rhys's sweatpants, so comfortable in the car, were intensely out of place amid the elegant furniture and expensive decor. In her usual attire, her armor, she would have been more capable of holding her own with the cultured Former Tender. In her current state, however, she was channeling more beast than beauty.

"Audra," the soft voice called to her, "May I impose upon you to help me carry a few things to the kitchen while the guys haul their things downstairs? I fear dawn is arriving far sooner than I would like."

She rose, cognizant of her bare feet as she collected the carafes and followed the delicate woman.

"You must be exhausted," Bianca said with a light laugh. "Having to navigate all that testosterone. I swear the Kaius males are the most intense, endearingly brutish haunt in North America."

She gave the woman a tight smile, setting the

dishes near the sink. "They can be pretty overwhelming at times, but they keep me occupied."

"I'm sure they do," Bianca replied with a wink. "Good to see they haven't lost their Casanova edge after all this time. Those boys are legendary," the petite woman sighed. "They are good to have in your court."

Mick wandered in, his hands in his back pockets. "Towels, Bee?"

"Back hall, middle shelf, honey. You take as many as you need. And leave your laundry on the top stair. I'll throw a few loads in during the day," Bianca offered with a smile.

Audra squeezed past Mickey awkwardly, attempting to pass through the small doorway without touching him. "Good to meet you, Bianca," she said by rote. "I better shower up and get to bed."

Bianca waved cheerily at her before turning her attention to the tall blond in her sights.

****

Audra tossed and turned, the luxury of the bed lost to the musings and laments of her mind. Mickey had remained upstairs with Bianca long after the sun had risen. The back rooms held no windows, allowing him to stay topside into the early afternoon. After drifting in and out of a restless sleep for hours, she rose and showered, glaring at the neatly folded clothing on the sink.

She spent more time on her makeup and hair than she had since she posed as Meredith Abernathy, though the effect was lost when she donned her faded cargo pants and black singlet. Sighing at her reflection, she tiptoed upstairs to grab a quick snack.

"Rise and shine!" Bianca's voice called to her from

the front sitting room. "Come, honey. I have some fruit and muffins waiting for you."

In the light of day, the ornate decor of the house was even more impressive. She couldn't resist looking around as she sat, admiring the opulent chandeliers and tapestries.

"It is a bit much, isn't it," Bianca laughed, pouring a cup of hot coffee and passing it over. "Johan was such a collector. Most items are original, though I admit a few have met their accidental demise during cleaning."

"Stunning," she commented honestly, her eyes moving from one outstanding piece to the next. "There's so much history in this room."

Bianca nudged a silver platter of muffins toward her. "It's a way to pass the years, I think," she said, smiling wistfully. "Some vampires collect art, some collect properties, some collect memories. I feel they need something to cement them to life's evolution until they find a mate."

"Were you and Johan connected?" Audra asked. "I realize it's a personal question, but…"

"Heavens, no!" Bianca gasped. "No, never. Gratefully not. Having a male that obsessed? No, no, no." She shook her head, blonde locks bouncing as she did. "We were mates. No different than any human married couple, I suppose. He was my soul mate, and I hope I was his, even if the connection never occurred. Why do you ask? Are you concerned about Mikhail's devotion?"

She swallowed quickly. "No. No, of course not. Not Mickey. I was merely curious for a friend back home."

Bianca folder her legs underneath her backside, her

sheath dress fanning across the chair. "I was just going to say that while Mikhail isn't connected, he's most definitely infatuated. Poor boy," she chuckled softly. "He is really lost when it comes to you. I can see why. You're quite intimidating."

She frowned.

"May I give you a little advice from a woman who's been around these boys for a few decades?" Bianca asked, leaning forward. "The Kaius males are a beautiful lot. They're strong, intelligent, skilled, and dangerous. And they're phenomenal lovers."

She glared at the half-eaten muffin in her hand.

Bianca grinned. "But they're emotionally stunted as a whole, and prone to act like high school boys when they are truly attracted to a woman. Given how encompassing the trait is among them, I believe it must be in the Kaius genetics." She paused a moment, topping up Audra's coffee and reaching for a strawberry.

"Mickey's quite enamored with you. Even if he hadn't said anything to me this morning, I knew. He watches you much like my Johan used to watch me, observing us for no other reason than to experience us."

She was quiet for a moment. "We aren't really suitable for each other. We argue. A lot."

"Oh, honey," Bianca smiled. "Try to remember that aside from their youngest, the Kaius males have spent centuries in the company of Tenders.

"I know Rhys is very insistent on rotating the women through the haunt on a frequent basis, but in doing so he's made it almost impossible for his brothers to learn how to interact with women after the initial honeymoon phase is over. While fresh blood is exciting, there's a connection that comes on its own with decades of the same lover."

As Audra sat back, crossing her arms, Bianca cocked her head.

"Mikhail said you were a former bloodslave, with no Tender training. It can be daunting for a vampire to interact with a woman who's not focused on his every whim after centuries of females trained to court him. Daunting and exhilarating. Johan was quite taken aback the first time I held my ground against him. He threatened to return me. But we both knew he wouldn't. It got him so revved up…"

Bianca's voice trailed off as her eyes fell on a small marble statue.

"How long were you together?" she asked, her curiosity piqued.

"Sixty-three years," Bianca replied, standing to show off her hourglass figure. "You would never know it to look at me, but I just turned 96." She did a little spin and returned to her seat. "Mickey is struggling with the idea he can be attached to a woman without being connected. I think he came to me this morning for reassurance that it is indeed possible for a male to latch onto a woman without any freaky chemical force. Now, the sun will be setting soon, and those boys rise pretty quickly. Let's heat up a few carafes and pack a few snacks for your trip home."

Chapter Thirty-Two

Home.

After a flurry of activity, packing and goodbyes and hugs, the Kaius hauntmates were on their way, hours from their familiar compound and brethren. Mickey lounged in the back of the SUV, content to listen to Nichol explain the extensive underground the Kaius males had cultivated over the centuries to a rapt Audra. He stretch his legs to the side, his foot coming into contact with a box.

"Hey Audra," he interrupted. "What is this anyways?" He held up the reward Stojanovski had given her.

"Check for yourself."

He opened the lid, growling when he saw the contents. "Chosen just for you, right?"

Audra rolled her eyes. "I'm extra special, I guess."

He lifted the pewter collar from the box, examining the craftsmanship of the jewel placement. "These are real," he muttered, poking at the rubies adorning the offensive object. "Asshole."

Audra laughed. "My thoughts exactly. Who does that? Who gives a strange woman a collar?"

"Vampires," Nichol answered seriously. "It's actually a symbol of hierarchy among the Tenders of old vampires. The more expensive the collar, the more adored and coveted the Tender."

Audra scoffed. "Good. Give it to a Tender, then."

He turned the collar over in his hands. "Stojanovski obviously saw something in you he wanted badly. Smarmy fucker."

"We could give it to Rhys. He should be able to sell it or piece it off. Or we could buy you a trophy case and put it on display," Nichol suggested, radiating a tinge of humor when she agreed without argument.

Audra cocked her head to better see Mick. "Did Bianca have one when Johan was alive?"

"No," he said slowly, thinking back a few decades. "She's a lot like you. Not quite the kind of woman you leash. God, Nichol. Could you imagine Bee's reaction if Johan had tried this shit? He'd have been staked by the balls and left on the lawn for the sun."

Nichol grimaced, his fangs on full display. "I once witnessed a fight between them. Johan lost all control, yelling and breaking everything he could get his hands on while she just crossed her arms and stared at him until he felt foolish enough to end the destruction." He paused, looking over at Audra. "They were disagreeing over what color to paint a hallway. Once he settled, he explained that when she cocked her brow, it sent him over the edge."

"A woman who sends a perfectly rational, calm male into an uncontrolled rage with a single look?" Mick gasped in feigned surprise. "I've never heard of such a thing." He gently booted Audra's seat.

"Not my fault you guys have the emotional control of a band of toddlers," Audra said haughtily, sitting a little straighter.

He grinned and settled back in his seat, reaching out to assess his brothers. Anticipation of their arrival home echoed across each of them, their spirits up as the highway moved swiftly behind them. He wrapped himself in the high, allowing his mind to drift to Bee's advice.

He knew he had been caught watching Audra's descent into the basement suite when Bianca smiled like a Cheshire cat. He strode down the hall to grab towels, ignoring the squeaks of giddiness coming from the Former Tender.

"You like her," came a singsong voice tinged with surprise. "Does she know?"

He did his best to ignore Bee, lowering his head so his hair would drop into his eyes as he tried to maneuver past her to the stairs.

"I didn't think so. Mickey. Honey. Come sit."

He took a moment to consider bolting away before deciding a woman's advice might not be completely terrible at this point. Placing the towels at the top of the stairs for his hauntmates, he joined Bianca at the small dinette. They talked for hours, just as they used to almost eight decades earlier.

Of course, they were clothed and upright this time. That was a different experience.

The Former Tender was bouncing in her seat, alternating between thoughtful reflections and teasing him for having what she defined as a 'crush'. When he explained some of his less-controlled interactions with Audra, Bianca sat back and crossed her arms, the subtle lift of a brow letting him know just how little she thought of his actions. As he detailed the hunt and subsequent capture at the Stojanovski commune, she feigned a swoon. His descriptions of Audra's disagreements with Rhys brought about laughter and head shaking.

"So maybe once things calm down, I'll, I don't know, present my case," he finally threw out. "Maybe see if she's on the same page?"

Bee's bright blue eyes stared at him, unimpressed. "Sure, Mikhail. Nothing woos a woman quite like a rehearsed soliloquy of umms, maybes, and point-form arguments with charts and graphs. The rumor mills are churning, sweetie. There's no calming down in the immediate future. So you either man up now, or accept that if you wait, it may be too late."

He rolled his eyes. "It's not like she has a lot of options."

"She has Boy, Mickey. And he watches her just as much as you do. You guys always did underestimate him. It would be a big mistake for you to do so now."

He glanced back at the lights of the car behind them. In the hectic departing of dusk, he had kept one eye on the old vampire, noting Bianca was completely correct. Boy anticipated Audra's every need, his silent movements going unnoticed by the others as he collected the shirt she dropped, reloaded a small cooler of food to ensure her favorites were on top, and kicked away small stones from her path to the vehicle.

And she had had his blood, providing him with a link to her emotions.

When Audra's hand reached into the back seat and patted his knee, he realized he had been growling low in his chest. The warmth of the hand stilled his rising ire while simultaneously pulling him into the moment. He placed his own hand on hers, trailing along her fingers, exploring the impossible softness of her palms before inspecting the rugged nails.

Audra flinched and attempted to jerk her hand from him, sighing in exasperation when he tightened his hold and resumed his examination. After a while, her arm muscles began to twitch in protest, the angle no longer agreeing with her. He reluctantly moved her hand back to her own lap.

Decidedly unhappy about the lack of contact, he adjusted his position in the back seat, placing himself directly behind her. He reached up to her shoulders, feeling the heat of her body through the rough fabric of her clothes as he entertained himself. Lightly tracking the seams of her shirt with his fingers, he filed the places that drew almost imperceptible shudders into his mind for another night.

The sensitive skin along the inside of her arms brought a slight hitch in her breathing.

Nichol glared at him through the rearview mirror. "Stop that."

Audra shifted in her seat, moving closer to his hands. "Yeah. Stop that."

Emboldened by her subtle movement and disregarding Nichol's annoyed barking, he brought his fingertips to the nape of her neck, watching in fascination as goosebumps rose on her skin. Her shoulders rolled, her head dipping marginally forward to encourage him. Both hands ghosted the accessible vertebrae before spreading across the back of her head, winding through the aqua and black strands and grazing the shells of her ears.

His grip grew firmer as he rolled his fingers across her scalp and down to her shoulders. The knots in her muscles relaxed as he began massaging her slowly. The speed of the SUV increased, Nichol muttering quiet curses toward him.

The Kaius haunt breached the horizon too quickly for his liking, his hands tingling from the heat of her skin as he worked her muscles and tangled into her hair. For the better part of two hours, she remained still and silent, the only notable changes being her increased heart rate and deeper breathing.

Had he still been human, he would have been sweating with the effort to maintain a relaxed facade.

Nichol sped into the garage, the rising door barely missing the roof of the vehicle as he braked hard. "You two get out," he barked. "I'll unpack."

Audra rolled her eyes, unbuckling her seatbelt and folding her long legs out of the car. She disappeared into the haunt without a look back. Mick stayed in place, willing his obvious excitement to reduce before he got out. He turned his focus on to his brother, wincing at what he found.

"Sorry, man," he grumbled to Nichol, whose tension had skyrocketed over the last leg of the drive. "I wasn't paying attention."

Nic fixed a look on him. "I won't hold it against you. But you're detailing the vehicle tomorrow night. The scent of...her scent is overpowering."

He was well aware of how irresistible Audra's scent of arousal was. He had stopped inhaling ages ago, realizing it was dangerously close to triggering less gentlemanly actions. "I will," he assured Nichol. "I'm heading...yeah...I'll head to the com room in a bit."

"Sure you will," Nichol grumbled, unloading the first round of bags.

By the time he reached the bunkers, the sound of Audra's shower was filtering down the hall. He slowed at her door, contemplating how much of a creep he was when he instinctively tried the locked knob and momentarily debated picking the lock. He ran a hand through his hair, deciding to take the civilized route and listen for her from his own bunk.

Because standing at his door with an ear pressed to the wood wasn't pathetic.

By the time the shower was turned off, he was far too turned on for his own good. Visions of her reaching up to rinse the shampoo from her hair played in his mind over and over like a bad porno. As the minutes ticked by, he could envision her brushing out her long locks, carefully applying her lipstick, zipping up one of those tight skirts she favored. By the time her lock clicked, he was too amped up to open his own door.

"Mick?"

Assuming a slouch to hide the evidence of his thoughts, he opened the door to a meticulously groomed Audra, her black pencil skirt and heels worn as naturally as she had donned cargos and steel toe boots.

"Is everyone meeting in the com room?" she asked, completely avoiding his eyes.

"Yeah, soon."

She nodded, averting her gaze down the hall nervously.

Fuck.

Now she was skittish around him. Nervous. She shifted her weight before stepping up flush against his body, one hand reaching up over his shoulders to grip the nape of his neck as her soft lips met his.

By the time his mind figured out precisely what was happening, it was over. Audra's eyes narrowed as she examined his. He licked his lips, his gaze drifting to her mouth. "Eyes up," Audra commanded, sending a bolt of lust straight to his dick.

He obeyed immediately so she could resume the intense assessment. "Ah. There you are," she murmured, having found whatever she was searching for. "I figured if I waited for you to make the first move, I'd be seventy by the time you got around to it. Let's go. Nichol's expecting us."

Yes, ma'am.

****

Rhys sprawled out in his chair, the tension of the past few weeks gone from his body. Simone knelt at his side, her deft fingers circling his calves as his brethren filtered into the room. Jagger spun his chair backwards, straddling it and quietly appraising the new Tender at Rhys's side.

The ruckus of Dominic and Molly's entrance was tempered with a harsh glare from Nichol, the oldest male having been in a heightened state since his arrival home an hour earlier. Justine eventually wandered in, followed immediately by Louis.

Interesting.

"Before we hunker down for the day, I want a quick review of what the next few weeks will be focusing on," Nichol began, his computer screen flaring to life.

"Shouldn't we wait for Mick and Audra?" he asked, absently toying with Simone's curls.

Nichol scowled. "No. I have a recon team near Beijing ready to move in and collect samples once the FBI moves out. If it isn't cleared within the next three weeks, they'll send in their best guys and we'll use whatever they can find. Agreed?"

The hauntmates muttered affirmations as Boy snuck into the room, his normally empty eyes tinged with anger. Rhys adjusted his position to keep an eye on the male. "I have a few things I want to interject, before we get into the heavy stuff," he said quickly, recognizing Nichol's excessive impatience. "I…I'll hold off a moment. Audra's almost here."

The clicking of her heels grew louder, with the loud thump of boots keeping time with her quick steps. Mickey and Audra strode through the door, Audra taking a seat and Mick standing behind her, a smirk on his face.

Interesting.

"As I was saying," he continued, "there are a few changes on the Tender front. Justine is currently in auction and looking to bring in more than enough to cover what we lost with Dahlia."

Justine smiled proudly, sitting a little straighter in her chair.

"Simone will be moved into the Tender quarters and put on regular rotation. I have two Tenders that were partially trained up north arriving tomorrow from a haunt that's combusting with internal drama. They need a little tweaking prior to resale. And I have one being returned for retraining and placement."

"Which one?" Jagger asked, his study of Simone complete.

"Lis. I'm unsure when she'll arrive. Her owner has connected with a random woman and no longer requires a Tender. Could be months from now. He still hasn't secured the female."

Mick grinned. "Lis was awesome."

As Jagger enthusiastically agreed and Louis looked decidedly interested, Audra's right hand rose to tap Mickey's chest.

"Not that awesome," Mick corrected. "Annoying, actually."

Nichol grunted. "Audra, I've ordered a trophy case for you. It should be here within five days. Once it arrives, we can display Stojanovski's collar."

She chuckled, nodding.

"Can we put Dovidas's in there, too?" Molly asked, expectantly.

He had wondered what she had done with the vile object, keeping one eye on the garbage can in her room for signs of it. Neither of them had spoken about it since the night he'd cut it from her throat, officially freeing her from Dovidas physically, if not mentally.

Audra smiled at her. "Proudly."

He watched Dominic nuzzle Molly's neck, lightly kissing the spot the metal collar had burnt her pale skin. He turned back to Nichol. "Anything else we need to know tonight?"

Nichol pulled up his inventory spreadsheets on the computer. "Tomorrow we make a list of what we have, what we need, and what's on order. Jagger, your Deepfryer arrived and will require assembling. Louis, I want you to help Dominic assess the vehicles tomorrow and start researching new purchases.

"Everyone needs their own wheels. Compile an acceptable list and the others can choose from there. Mick, you'll be my lead contact with Beijing, effective at dusk tomorrow. Audra, see Rhys for whatever help he needs with the new recruits and keep that snark off your face. Have a good day. Get out of my office."

He patted Simone's ass as she walked off with Justine, eager to begin her foray into the rest of the hauntmate beds. Audra stomped out of the room, her displeasure with her assigned duties evident. "She seems tense," he purred. "Someone should help her with that."

If a vampire could scramble, Mickey definitely did.

****

"Absolutely incredible," Audra was muttering under her breath as Mick caught up with her. "I cannot believe how patriarchal this is."

He walked along side, wisely keeping silent as Audra fumed.

Fuck, she was hot when she was angry, her cheeks flushed and eyes flashing.

She ignored his subtle nudging toward the bunkers, instead walking to the common room while she grumbled her discontent. After a few false tries, she got the television on and flopped onto the large recliner to scan through the channels.

He stood at the entrance, his thumbs hooked in his belt loops as he waited for her ire to simmer down, checking in quickly with the others and content that the status quo had been achieved once again.

Louis's empty bubble was tinged with mild interest. Nichol was frustrated and annoyed. Rhys was horny and regretful, likely over the loss of his private blood supply. Jagger was close to Louis, his melancholy mood lifted slightly by desire. Dominic was hungry but happy.

"It really is fascinating to observe," Audra whispered, breaking his concentration.

He glanced over to the television, unsure what she

was referencing until she walked over to him and cupped his face in her hands.

"It's taken a while to figure out which one is you, but I think I have it now," she said softly. "Right now, you're channeling Jagger more than the others. Empty it?"

He focused on draining Jagg's lust, making room for another to move into the forefront.

"That's Nichol. Try again."

One by one, he rotated through his brothers, slowly emptying their emotions from his mind as much as he could while Audra watched him intensely. He knew he had reached success when her lips rose to his again. This time, he kept up with what was happening, completely engulfed in the sensation of her mouth as it moved slowly against his.

Her tongue swept across his lips, leading him into the deeper kiss he had craved earlier. She tasted like mint and chocolate as she gently pushed him against the wall, her lips travelling down his neck, her tongue flicking against his collar bone. When his hands gripped her hips, she captured them in hers and placed them behind his back, continuing to pepper kisses over his throat.

Apparently satisfied with his position, Audra began exploring him with her hands, running them across his chest, over his abs, down his arms. She took her time, fingers alternating between ghosting his skin and pressing against his muscles. When she moved her attention to his thighs, he let loose a low growl.

A single brow raised.

He dug his fangs into his lip, drawing blood to focus his control while she resumed her trek, kneeling to touch every inch of his calves and pulling up the hem of his pants to trace the rings on his ankles.

"What do these symbolize?" she asked, sitting back on her heels.

"Age rings," he muttered, pushing his palms against the wall. "Your eyes can pick up the decades."

Leaning closer, she scraped her fingernail along his calf muscle. "You're two hundred and forty?"

"Yeah, but I have it on good authority I don't act my age." he replied closing his eyes, the sight of her on her knees before him testing his ability to stay motionless against the wall.

"Open them."

His eyes flashed open, irises elongating as he narrowed in on his prey. His gorgeous, leggy prey in stilettos and a blouse that bowed open just enough for a glimpse of cleavage. His arms released from behind him, reaching to pull her to him.

"Arms. Back."

With a snarl, he placed his arms behind him again, going against every urge his body had. She ran her fingers up the insides of his thighs, mapping the outline of his erection without touching it before she rose to her feet, pulling the hem of his shirt up.

"Arms up," she instructed as she brought the fabric higher. He obliged, allowing her to remove the shirt slowly. He reluctantly latched his hands behind him again, keeping his eyes locked on her every movement. Delicate fingers undid the buttons of her blouse, unwrapping her body for him at a painfully unhurried pace.

The clothing dropped to the floor, revealing a white lace bra encasing the breasts he'd been fantasizing about for weeks. The bra joined the shirt on the floor, exposing the rose pink of her nipples.

"Audra," he growled hoarsely. "I…"

Her body pressed against him, her skin searing his as her lips connected with his again, tongues warring. He wrapped one long arm around her, holding her tight to him as he ground his hard-on against her and slid his other hand between them, hiking her skirt up roughly in his desperation to feel the heat of her core. As his hand cupped her panty-clad sex, she rocked against his palm, a quiet whimper escaping her. Slipping his fingers under the damp lace, he sought out her nub with his thumb as he pushed two fingers inside her. Her head fell back, her eyes closing at the sensation.

"Open them," he whispered as he bowed his head into her long neck.

The scent of her arousal was driving him further from his control, its sweet vanilla coating his fingers while he worked her. Her nails dug into his shoulders and her forehead dropped to his chest.

"Holy fuck, Mick," she gasped, her hips grinding against his hand. "I'm…oh god…I'm…I…"

The more she tried to talk, the faster he moved his thumb over her nub, snarling when her body tightened on his fingers and she moaned his name. When the first flutters of her orgasm hit, he captured her cries with his mouth, losing himself in the sensation of her walls clenching on his hand. Her hold on him tightened, her complete surrender almost breaking him as her whimpers subsided, her grip on his shoulders relaxing as he held her flush to him.

Audra's cat eyes gradually came into focus, blinking slowly. Her lips pursed into a smirk and she brought her hand between them to cup his erection.

"Audra," he warned quietly, his vision trained entirely on the woman currently palming him, his lust ratcheting up into dangerous territory. "I am really, really close to snapping."

She stepped back, removing the warmth he desperately craved.

Another step, fingers adjusting her skirt.

And another.

Audra stalked backwards until her spine made contact with the other wall, her eyes locked on his. She lifted her arms over her head, holding her own wrist.

Tilted her chin to the side.

He was on her instantaneously, one hand securing her arms while the other found purchase on her breast. He flicked and rolled the hardened peak as his tongue and lips ravished her neck, moving down her body in desperation. His tongue found her other nipple, drawing it into his mouth.

His mind began to shut down as he released her wrists, dropped to his knees, and hiked her leg over his shoulder, his instincts warred between tasting her and filling her. Her low moan when his tongue ran between her folds ended the war, her aroma making his dick harden painfully. He licked her hard and fast, groaning as her thighs trembled.

"Mick," she panted. "Please."

He slid two fingers back inside her, stretching her as his tongue vibrated against her nub.

"Nooooo," she moaned. "Mick…please…you…" Her hands tangled into his hair, gently tugging his head up. "Stand."

He rose to his feet hesitantly, the recesses of his

mind still cognizant enough to pull away from her even if his core was barreling ahead. When her hands began skillfully undoing his cargos, he held back a howl. She wrapped her fingers around his sensitive shaft as he pushed her skirt up and gripped her lace panties with both hands, tearing them at the seams and tossing the destroyed fabric to the side.

He removed her hand from his erection and lifted her against the wall, lowering her slowly on to him and burying his head into her neck as he slid inside her tight heat. Fully encased in her sheath, he stilled, memorizing every shudder and tremor her body teased him with. She rocked her hips, the friction sending jolts through to his fangs.

"Killing me," he muttered into her skin.

"Then fuck me already," she panted, her arms tight around him.

Instinct took over. His hips slammed into her, sliding her firm ass up and down the wall as she whimpered and begged for god, for him, for more. The tightness of her channel, the movement of her breasts, the moans, the taste of her arousal still on his tongue, the aroma of desire.

His senses were completely engulfed in the moment. His balls tightened, signaling his impending release as he reached between them and continued to pound her into the wall. Her body tensed, spurring him on.

"Mickey!" she moaned as she came, loud enough for his hauntmates to hear. With his name on her lips and her heat gripping him painfully, his orgasm tore through him with a snarl as his fangs descended on her throat. When her blood hit his tongue, he thickened inside her again, releasing immediately as her body continued to clench around him.

His senses slowly came back online, his tongue gently laving at the puncture wounds while he rocked inside her. He adjusted his grip, holding her thighs tight to him as her breathing regulated and her heart rate evened out. Her tangled black and turquoise hair obscured her face, her head still collapsed on his shoulder. As he moved to lower her to her feet, she whimpered her protest.

"Noooooo," she murmured, her lips skimming his skin. "Can't we just stay like this a little longer?"

Checking her hold on him, he moved them to the sofa, awkwardly grasping for a blanket folded across the armrest before reclining onto the seat, Audra securely wrapped around him. He arranged the cover over her, for both her modesty and his own growing sense of possession.

"Mick?"

"Hmmm?"

"Who's Lis?"

He grinned into her hair. "Lis who?"

Chapter Thirty-Three

Audra's hands held tight to her hips, well aware the effectiveness of her anger was defeated by her sexed-up hair and half destroyed bra. "You didn't have to be so rude."

Mickey lay back on his bed, completely comfortable with being utterly naked during a disagreement. "I wasn't rude. I was forceful. He shouldn't be lurking around here anyways."

Huffing as she crossed her arms, she glared at the hot male and his stupid enticing body. "He lives here. He has every right to be around. Telling him to 'fuck the hell off' was completely unnecessary."

"Your moans are for my ears only. Next time, Boy won't hang out in the hall to wait for you. He'll go to the com room like he should," Mick stated, his eyes raking lasciviously over her breasts. He adjusted his hips, drawing her attention from his arctic blue eyes down to his painfully large erection.

She narrowed her gaze and turned purposely away. "I have to get out there, anyways. I'm late enough as it is."

As she reached for the doorknob, he pounced. His arousal pushed against her ass as his fingers dove under her skirt and slipped beneath her panties. "You are so fucking wet," he growled, his tongue trailing the shell of her ear. She released the doorknob, her hands flying instinctively to his long blond hair.

"I don't care," she argued, her breath hitching as he worked her. "I have work to do."

He bent down, nuzzling her neck and trailing his fingers lightly over the inside of her arm. "Once more, and I'll leave you alone until dawn."

Arching against him, she continued to protest. "You've promised that every night this week."

Done with talking, he threw her over his shoulder and set her on the bed, his head buried between her legs before she could form another sentence. She writhed under him, tangling her fingers into his hair and whimpering when he moaned, sending the vibrations through her body. As she began chanting his name, she could feel him grin against her skin in victory.

****

"I'm telling you, one of these nights I'm going to stake that bastard," Mick called over his shoulder to Nichol. "Every fucking day, Nichol. He seeks her out every fucking day."

Nichol grunted, the tiny screwdriver in his hand looking absurd. "Be patient. Once she has your blood, you'll override him, and you can skip off into the sunrise and burn for all I care."

He scanned through the haunt emails, deleting the remarkable number of spam messages. "I'll patiently insert a boot in his ass if he doesn't cut it out," he grumbled. "We've only been doing this for what, two weeks? Not exactly enough time to get to that step. Besides, I'm not sure I need Audra coming online, too. You bastards are hard enough to monitor before adding in a female."

Nichol paused thoughtfully. "Two weeks, yes, but

you've been dancing around each other for months. Has she asked for your blood?"

He shook his head. "Flat out refuses to talk about it. Like, at all. She's all fine for giving hers up when we're…well, yeah. But when we're not…you know…she's all squirrely and weird. Like she worries she'll offend me or something."

"Have you offered?"

"Well, no. I don't want her to think she has to."

Nichol looked him dead in the eye. "So you're confused as to why a former bloodslave doesn't treat your blood as a commodity she can demand on a whim?"

He lolled his head back. "When you put it that way, I feel like a total ass for taking hers."

"It's easier to take what's offered than to risk requesting and being denied."

Running a hand through his hair, he huffed. "Point taken. Maybe I should just drop the idea for now."

Standing to tighten a screw on top of the hard drive, Nichol gave him a hard look. "You don't want to know she's not as invested in you as you are in her."

"That, too," he muttered. "Any more info from Kai?" He wasn't in the mood to continue the highly personal conversation Nichol was instigating.

"All he's said is Dovidas has not shown up anywhere near where he is."

"And where is he?"

Nichol glowered. "He hasn't said."

"That's fucking helpful."

The males worked the rest of the evening in silence, Nichol tweaking the hardware and Mickey watching the phones and messages for any communication from Beijing. Shortly before dawn, the others filtered into the room for their nightly debriefing.

Nichol had instituted dusk and dawn check-ins to ensure every member of the haunt was on the same page before the day hit. Audra was last to arrive, Boy predictably behind her. She walked straight over to Mick and ran a hand through his hair before taking her seat.

Rhys's boots hit the table, earning a glare from Nichol. "Little problem. I'll be delivering Justine in eight days. It will likely take a week there and back, so count me absent during that time. My new trainees are adapting quickly, but one of you will need to take over while I'm gone."

Jagger leaned forward, his eyes watching Rhys's lips carefully. "I can go in your place," he offered. "A week or two won't set me back. The Deepfryer is completely assembled, but I'm waiting on a few wiring mechanisms to arrive before I can get it functional."

"Works for me," Rhys grinned, his fangs on full display. "I hate Minnesota in February."

Nichol entered the agreement into his calendar. "You'll ensure all weaponry is prepared before you leave, yes?"

Jagger nodded, humming a lilting tune. "Dominic can process and inventory any orders that arrive during my absence."

"Mick, you're up next. Tell the others what movement has occurred in Beijing," Nichol instructed.

He leaned forward, placing a hand on Audra's knee and regretting it when his attention was pulled to the heat of her skin. "The, uh, recon team has been unable to connect the explosives to others used in the area over the past decade, meaning whoever set them is likely not local." Audra's fingers intertwined with his. "However, they were able to identify fresh scents from the Chen line in the surrounding area. It's believed Chen is holing up somewhere close, recovering with the assistance of whatever children survived the blasts."

"Are we talking Deviants or vampires?" Rhys queried.

"Different scent, possibly an ally. The scent of Deviants always vary from their creator, so whether or not those hauntmates were in the explosion themselves is unknown. The team is monitoring the situation, but remaining on the outskirts for now," he concluded, his hand traveling higher up Audra's thigh until she stayed his progress.

Nichol looked to Audra, who glanced at Boy before talking. "We've had some good results with the cell mate adjustments this week," Audra began. "By keeping humans of similar strength together and isolating the strongest, we've had fewer altercations during meals. The most aggressive are being given supervised jobs, mostly cleaning and dishes. It isn't ideal, but it is an improvement."

She scanned her notes. "Nichol, I've put through a large nutritional order that contains quite a few new items. Vitamins, fresh produce, and iron-rich quality meats along with three stoves. Better food will improve the health and blood of the bloodslaves and should reduce illness significantly."

With a nod, Nichol moved on to Louis and Dominic. "Vehicles have been ordered and are ready for pickup," Dom said. "Louis and I will convoy over the next few nights to bring them in. Once we have them on site, you can get your hands on them."

Nichol cracked a small smirk. "I'll load those bastards up with all the newest gadgets. No one drives them until I've fabricated the insurance and plates and altered any online information regarding their state of sale. Audra, did you and Molly managed to assemble the trophy case?"

Molly grinned. "We finished it yesterday and moved it into the common room. It looks good, but it's big."

"I'm sure you two will fill it with the spoils of victory over time," Mick stated, giving Audra's leg a quick squeeze. "We done here?"

Nichol nodded. "Last thing, Kai has been in touch, as has Stojanovski. Neither have heard any rumors about Dovidas's whereabouts as of yet, but it does take time for news to travel. Kaius should be returning within the month. Stojanovski requested I tell Audra 'hello' from him."

Audra cocked a brow. He snarled.

"Don't stress it, Mick," Rhys interjected. "Stojanovski considers himself a major player in vamp politics. He's just trying to rile us. I've refused his requests for a Tender for decades. Now that he has Dahlia, he's poking the beast."

Audra frowned. "Why did you refuse him? Will Dahlia be safe in with him?"

Rhys sat back. "She'll be fine. The regular humans that run in his hunt have a greater chance of problems with him. But Dahlia will be paraded around as a prize, brought out as a symbol of status. She'll be living the good life for a long time, since Stojanovski is too cheap to invest in another one. Stingy bastard."

****

Molly and Audra peeked through the locked door to the training room.

"What's with the plates?" Audra whispered, completely confounded by the items Rhys was arranging on the coffee table.

Molly squinted. "Those are the expensive ones," she said authoritatively. "The new Tenders must be very good. I had the cheap ones because they kept falling off my head. I may have thrown a few, too."

She rolled her eyes. "He seriously trains them to walk?"

"And talk. And sit. It's very thorough. I overheard Rhys telling Dom that one of them is a nurse and the other is a skilled violinist," Molly said, awe in her voice. "Whoever trained them was good, but Rhys said they're still rough around the edges. That's probably why he's doing the basics with them again. Their skill sets are already established, as well as their sexual education, so he has to work on those little touches that set Rhys Tenders apart from the rest."

"I still find it barbaric," she grumbled as the two women emerged from their quarters, their hair curled and makeup impeccable. Both stood before Rhys with their hands clasped behind their backs and their heads tilted slightly to the side. "I mean, look at that. It would be a cold day in hell before I stood like that awaiting instruction from Rhys, of all vampires. Stupid humans."

Molly giggle. "Do you even hear yourself? You sound so much like Nichol sometimes. It's eerie."

She jabbed Molly in the ribs and dragged her away from the show. "All right," she laughed, "You've distracted me long enough. Now how's it going with

Dom?"

"Oh no no no no," Molly grinned, wagging a finger at her. "You know damn well he and I are solid. Now it's my turn to ask you. How's it going with Mickey? Aside from the sex. Because we can all hear you. Every time."

Her jaw dropped for a moment before she collected herself. "Good. We're good."

"Everyone can hear that," Molly snorted. "But has he linked to you?"

Linked.

The idea scared her, the thought of her emotions being added to the web Mickey untangled night and day. Fearing hers would be the ones to overwhelm the precarious balance he kept in his head, she'd been terrified of the night he would bring it up.

Shifting her weight, she straightened her shoulders. "Come on. We promised Simone we'd meet her in the common room ten minutes ago. We should swing by before we load Jagg."

Molly slowed her steps. "What do you think of her?"

With a sigh, she reduced her pace. "She's sexy, new, ambitious, and hitting on my guy every night while wearing red lingerie. I adore her."

Molly barked a laugh. "I'm with you on that. Seriously, no one bends at the waist to pick anything up. Or has to stretch her neck that often. Or adjust her boobs."

Hushing Molly with a snicker, she led her in to the common room, determined to stifle her opinions of the provocative woman. "Hey, Simone," she greeted. "Why don't you join us down in the bloodslave quarters? We have to stock Jagger up before he goes."

Simone rose from the sofa, her long legs on full display beneath a sheer red dress. She strode alongside the others, Audra in her business suit, Molly in her faded jeans and rainbow t-shirt. As they rounded the corner toward the bloodslave quarters, the women ran into Mick, his arms loaded with electronic gadgets.

"Hey, honey," he said, his fangy smile flashing in the dim lighting. He dipped his head to kiss the top of her head as he passed, ignoring the other women and nodding toward the common room. "A minute?"

She gestured for the others to go on without her and followed Mick. "What's up?"

Mickey adjusted the load in his arms and hesitated, staring at the floor as if formulating his words. When he finally looked up at her, she watched in fascination as his eye color morphed for a few seconds before settling on the arctic blue she had come to know were Mick's and Mick's alone.

"I want you to have my blood. Tonight," he stated.

She crossed her arms and narrowed her eyes. "No."

His fangs elongated as his calm expression morphed into irritation. "Why not?"

"The better question is why," she countered, stepping closer to him to better monitor his eye color. "What's the rush? And why is it such a thing for you guys?"

Adjusting the load in his arms, his lips drew tight. "You'll live longer. And I'll be able to keep track of your moods and sense you if you're in trouble. It's not 'such a thing'," he snarked. "It's just what we do."

She cocked a brow. "So it's expected."

"I...no, it's not fucking expected," he barked in

frustration.

"Well maybe I don't want you to keep track of my moods," she bit back, her mind flashing to his convulsing body on the floor of a motel bathroom. "Maybe that's a part of me I get to keep to myself. And you don't need any more bombardment than you already receive."

He turned away, storming across the room and dropping the pile of electronics on the sofa. "Why are you being so fucking difficult about this?"

"Why are you making such a big deal out of it?"

She knew she was goading him but couldn't stop herself. The mere thought of him offering out of some ridiculous sense of obligation irked her, that he would be so careless about his own safety.

He prowled across the floor, the muscles across his back rippling with tension. "Forget it," he growled. "Doesn't fucking matter that I have to smell Boy in your veins every time you walk by, every time I kiss you. I'll deal. Just forget it."

She recoiled slightly. "So this is a jealousy thing."

"No," he groaned, running a hand through his hair. "I totally screwed this up." He looked up at the ceiling for a moment before returning his attention to her and scooping her hand in his. "Audra, just...my blood's yours," he said, his blue eyes pleading. "Tonight, next month, next year. Hell, I'll wait until the next decade for you. But I love you and it's yours, and whenever you're ready for that step, I'm already there. I've been there for a while, and you need to know that. No strings, no bargains. Yours and yours alone."

She studied him for a moment. He shifted his weight under her stare, his jaw flexing, viper fangs grazing his lips.

God, he was beautiful.

She stepped close to him. "What if I'm the one to push you over the edge? If letting me in is the thing that overdoses you for good?"

"What if you're the one to keep me from drowning?" he countered, releasing her hand. "Like you did when Jagger dragged me under? Because all I remember from those nights was pain, confusion, and you. You talked to me. Fed me. Sat with me. I heard you. Felt you. And as long as I did, I had something to grab. I trusted you to keep me from going under."

With a deep breath, she closed her eyes. "Promise me I wouldn't kill you."

"I can't. Linking won't kill me, but I do and say a lot of dumbass things and someday, yeah, you may kill me. With good reason."

She rose up on her toes to kiss him. He remained still, his hands shoved deep into his pockets as she trailed her lips down his neck toward his collarbone. "So you love me, do you?" she murmured into his skin, snaking her hand under his shirt to feel the taut muscles underneath.

"Fuck yes," he grunted as his hands gripped her hips.

She leaned away from him, reaching between them to unzip his cargos. "It's a good thing you do, because I happen love your stubborn, hard-headed ass, too," she whispered before nuzzling his jugular.

"That wasn't as terrifying as I thought it would be to say," he groaned, arching his neck to give her access. "And I'm not...I'm really, really not complaining, but what are you doing?" he panted, glancing toward the door and inching her skirt up her thighs.

"It's called 'make-up sex,' " she purred, grazing her teeth across his throat. "Now shut up. You said anytime, anywhere, and we've got twenty uninterrupted minutes to link before Nichol comes looking for us."

A word about the author...

Katja Desjarlais is a music teacher by day and a paranormal romance writer by moonlight. She is an unapologetic music addict and has an obsession for bad Bach puns despite her irrational aversion to Baroque. Her favorite words include "plethora" and "dapper," and she is physically repulsed by the word "moist." Katja's interest in the paranormal can be traced to her early childhood film choices and to the revolving book collection on her phone.

Desjarlais lives in the Okanagan Valley with her husband, three children, and two black cats. She loves traipsing through the United States with her family during the summer months and attending heavy metal concerts any time she can.